Saving Gideon

# AMY LILLARD

*Saving Gideon*

B&H
PUBLISHING GROUP

Nashville, Tennessee

978-1-4336-7752-6


Published by B&H Publishing Group
Nashville, Tennessee


Dewey Decimal Classification: F
Subject Heading: AMISH—FICTION \ LOVE STORIES \
SELF-ESTEEM—FICTION

Publishers Note:
The characters and events in this book are fictional, and any
resemblance to actual persons or events is coincidental.

1 2 3 4 5 6 7 8 • 16 15 14 13 12

To my mama, Pat Essary, an eight-year (and counting!)
breast cancer survivor. God is good.

# Acknowledgments

A book is not written by the author alone. So much goes into the creative process. There are almost too many people to name, but I'm gonna try.

Thank you, first and foremost, to my agent, Mary Sue Seymour, for truly without your guidance (and twisting my arm behind my back) this story would have never come to be.

Thanks to my editors, the Julies, for their tireless work and seeing Gideon's potential even through my love of passive voice.

Kudos to my family for listening to my endless story ideas without pleading a migraine, even though I know most times you wanted to. I love you guys!

And to my husband and son for eating pizza, hamburgers, and whatever was in the cabinet when "Mommy has a book due." You are the best!

I must give a shout-out to my "writer friends": AJ Nuest, Sarah Grimm, Arial Burnz, Karen Crane, and Laura Marie Altom, for the endless support and choruses of "You can do this!" Y'all mean the world to me.

And the biggest thank-you of all to God, for giving me this story, the focus to get it on paper, and the means to see it through. This book is proof positive that with God all things are possible.

# *Prologue*

The rain turned slowly into snow. The change happened so gradually that Avery Ann Hamilton hardly noticed until the slushy drops had built up on the blades of her windshield wipers.

Great. *Just great.*

As if being in this backwoods part of Oklahoma weren't enough. First the rain . . . and now she had to deal with snow.

And slick roads.

And . . . heartbreak.

She should have stayed in Dallas, but no. Instead, she had wanted to surprise her fiancé by showing up in the Sooner State where he was scoping out land for on-location shoots. She would surprise him and tell him that he had won. She'd caved. He had begged her to elope to Vegas with him, but she had been holding out for the big wedding: long, white dress; horse-drawn carriage; and doves released at sunset.

But in the middle of a fund-raiser she was attending with her father, it hit her: *What was she waiting for?* A year was a long time. She loved Jack, and he loved her. There was no reason to wait. If he wanted to get married in Vegas, then that's what they would do. Now. Tonight. No carriage, no doves.

Without stopping to change clothes, she hopped on the last flight between Dallas and Tulsa, rented the first car she could get, and drove to neighboring Clover Ridge. The town boasted only four hotels, so she had no problem spotting her own Mercedes—loaned to Jack for this trip—sitting off to one side.

She parked next to it, stepped up to the unlocked motel room door, pulled it open, and saw . . .

Enough.

Enough to know that Jack had used her. Enough to know that he had never really loved her, and enough to know that he—like everyone else—had used her for her father's money.

Poor, little rich girl.

Avery turned the heater up a notch and dashed back her tears. At least she had her car back. Not that it mattered. But Jack had taken so much from her; he wasn't about to get that too. No sense feeling sorry for herself. What was done was done, and she was beginning to accept the hardest part of all: She would never find true love, someone who'd love *her*—not her father's money.

She had thought Jack was that person. Dashing Jack with his Hollywood good looks and writer's intelligence. He had swept into her life, made her laugh, told her she was beautiful—he'd done everything right.

Right down to conning her.

She could see it clearly now. She had been played by a master, an actor who wanted to make it big, who needed funding for his movie. A man who needed her father's money but never really needed her.

She shouldn't be crying, she told herself as the tears trickled down her face. She should be used to this kind of treatment by now.

A low-pitched whine came from the passenger seat. Avery glanced over. As if sensing her distress, Louie V., her sweet little Yorkie, cried out his own despair. Avery smiled through her tears and risked stroking sweet little baby's back before returning both hands to the wheel. She loved Louie. Probably more than a sane person should love her dog, but she didn't care. *He* was one male she could always depend on.

The snow was falling harder now, harder than the tears she fought. All she wanted was to get back to Dallas and forget that this weekend—and Jack—had ever happened.

"Turn right," the disembodied voice of her GPS system dryly intoned. "Last exit before road ends, point four miles."

"Now you tell me." Avery peered through her tears and the snow, and into total darkness. No street lights, no billboard signs, just country and snow and black.

"I don't see it. You see anything, Lou-Lou?"

Louie V. let out a yappy staccato of a bark.

"Turn right," the computerized voice said again. "Road ends, point two miles."

Road ends? How could the road just end? And where was her turn?

Orange and white barricades blocked what remained of the roadway. Avery spotted a poorly marked exit and veered right onto the alternate route.

"Going south, southeast. Two hundred and sixty-three miles to destination."

She looked to be on some back country road, miles from anything save a few old farmhouses. That was the thing about a navigational system—a person had to trust it to get where they were going. And that's all she could do at this point—trust it to get her there.

Swirling white flakes relentlessly spiraled toward the ground with a surprising single-mindedness, but maybe further south, the snow would ease up. She could hope.

For now all she wanted was to be home, in her bed, with the covers pulled over her head and the servants on red alert to steer clear. Maybe then she could start the healing and the accepting that she was going to go through life as an old maid. Oh sure, they called it "bachelorette" these days, but it was just a euphemism for "couldn't find a man."

How ironic. Every need fulfilled except for the one she really wanted—to be married and have babies. She wanted to go to school plays and well-baby appointments, to baseball games and driving lessons. And she wanted a husband who shared her dream, a man who would work side by side with her to build a family and a home.

But she would never have that. Her father's money would always get in the way.

It didn't matter. It was a hopelessly old-fashioned fantasy. June Cleaver meets *Little House on the Prairie*. But it was her fantasy. Her dream. And she would tuck it away, tell it to no one, and go about her life of being a "bachelorette."

Avery turned up the wipers, leaned forward, and squinted through the window. The pavement had long ago given away to gravel. If she pulled off the road, who knew what she would pull onto? Or how long she could stay there without causing an accident herself.

"Next turn, sixteen-point-two miles."

She jumped at the sound of the GPS voice, and pulled the wheel to the left. The car slid, hydroplaning in the mud and slush, then tottered to the edge of an incline. She didn't have time to breathe before the car teetered, then rolled, flipping over and over and over again.

A strangled cry escaped her lips as she slammed against the

driver's door. Her seat belt stayed in place, while she lurched in the other direction, the arm rest and gear-shift lever jamming her side. She discovered a million other sharp angles in her car that she had never noticed before.

After an eternity, the car stopped. Surely bruises had begun to form. She was shaken and tired and heartbroken.

And her head hurt. Really, really bad.

She took a deep breath, but the pain had seeped into her very being. Louie whined and cautiously scrambled into her lap. The accident had thrown him, bag and all, to the floorboard, but he looked like he'd managed to come through his wild tumble without injury. He licked Avery's fingers, and she gave him a half-hearted scratch behind his ears. *Could have been worse. Much worse.* She winced as she tried to retrieve his bag, the motion draining the last of her strength. She needed to get out and assess the damage, but right now she couldn't keep her eyes open. She wanted to rest. Just for a minute or two.

She laid her head against the steering wheel, aware for only a brief moment that the action set her horn to blaring through the cold, snowy night.

# 1

The Oklahoma sun spilled golden rays across the pasture. It was a beautiful day, the kind only found in the wild month of May. The sky was impossibly blue, the birds chirped from the tops of trees covered in new foliage. Across the pasture, the newborn lambs called out to their mothers in soft bleating sighs. Everything was perfect.

He surveyed the land and felt a satisfaction he had never felt before. Not a prideful feeling. No, that wasn't proper. But a sense of peace and well-being that he hadn't felt in some time. He stroked his beard and smiled. All was right with the world. He had it all: a beautiful family, a profitable farm, and a God who saw fit to bless them all. It seemed to take him half the day to count his blessings. Even for that he was grateful.

As quickly as those thoughts flitted in and out of his head, the sky turned to an angry gray. Storm rolling in—and Green Country storms were nothing to scoff at. He needed to get the animals to safety before the worst of it hit.

He looked around, that presence of peace escaping him. Where were Jamie and Miriam? He needed them. He needed them to go down to the lower pasture and make sure the lambs were sheltered. Make sure they weren't too close to the raging stream.

He looked up and saw them, his wife and son, struggling with the trunk of a dead tree. What were they doing? Didn't they know the tree was dead? The animals needed their help.

Then it hit him.

He'd been here before.

This was his chance. A second chance. He needed to stop them. Before it was too late. This time it wasn't about saving the sheep, but saving them . . . his family.

He ran across the pasture toward them, his words ripped from his throat by the swirling wind. *Go back! Leave it alone! You're too close to the edge!* But he couldn't run fast enough. He couldn't scream over a whisper. His throat tightened, and he watched in horror, anguish washing over him as he saw them fall toward the rushing waters.

Gideon Fisher bolted upright. His body trembled. Sweat poured off him.

He'd had the dream again. How many times in the last eleven months had he had that dream? More than he could count. More than he wanted to count.

Even with his eyes open, he saw them still. Every night he dreamed he could save them. Every night he failed.

He pushed himself out of bed, wincing as his bare feet hit the chilly floor. The fire must have gone out.

A cold front had moved in, bringing with it a howling wind and swirling snow. It was unusual, but not unheard of, to have such a storm early in April. Even in Oklahoma. It would spell bad news for the farmers. The delicate shoots of hay and alfalfa would be burned by the cold. The tender peach trees just now budding and flowering in promise of fruit would be ruined. A snow this late in the year would mean no pecans, few apples, and even fewer strawberries.

Not that he had anything planted.

He shuffled into the kitchen and stoked the fire. The bright orange embers spat in feeble protest before they sparked back to life. Gideon threw another log on top of the pile of glowing ash, then cocked his head.

A far-off wail captured his attention. The constant drone reminded him of the tornado siren tests the city ran every Wednesday to make sure the equipment worked properly. But they never ran the tests in the dead of night. And it wasn't Wednesday.

It sounded like . . . well, it sounded like a car horn.

He shook his head. His nearest *Englisch* neighbor was a two-mile walk through the pasture. They were good neighbors. They never gave him strange looks or tried to take his picture. And they never blew their car horn at this time of night.

Someone was in trouble. Gideon pulled on his coat and the rubber boots he used to wear when he fed the pigs, then he grabbed up the battery-operated lantern he kept on the porch for emergencies. No one made a racket like that in the middle of the night without there being something wrong.

As he stepped from under the shelter of the front porch, the snow swirled around him on fretful gusts. The wind was stronger now. The wet, fat flakes piled where they landed, built up by their weight and number. It was a doozy of a storm and not the best night to be in trouble.

He headed off toward the road. It would be quicker to cut across the pasture, but far more hazardous. His lantern only illuminated three yards directly ahead of him, so Gideon kept his head down and his feet pointed north until he reached the slated fence that lined his property. Turning east would take him to the

Bradleys' house, his *Englisch* neighbor, but something told him to turn west. Through the dancing swirls of snow, he could just make out a set of red lights about a quarter of a mile down the road, off to the side and in a field where nothing was planted.

*Probably some irresponsible* Englisch *teenager with more money than sense.* Most likely took the corner too fast for the weather and veered off the road. Or someone's teenager in *rumspringa* . . .

It wasn't right to make assumptions, to pass judgment, but sometimes it was so hard not to. All he had wanted when he moved out here was peace and quiet. He wanted to get away from family and friends and the soothing talk and the well-wishers. It wasn't the Amish way, but he couldn't do it anymore. He just couldn't do it.

Gideon shook aside those thoughts as he drew nearer to the car. The clear light from the lantern flashed off of shiny silver paint—and even shinier chrome of a crumpled-up fender.

He was no expert on *Englisch* automobiles, but he could tell this one was very costly and very damaged. The windows were tinted black as pitch, and he couldn't make out any of what was inside, just the constant bleat of the horn and the hiss of the engine.

With gloveless fingers he tapped on the window. "Hello?" he called, rapping a bit harder. "Hello?"

No answer.

Not wanting to waste another minute, Gideon grabbed the door handle and pulled. Stuck. He pulled again. The door let out a mournful groan, but creaked open about half an inch. Placing one foot against the front panel of the car, Gideon braced himself and pulled again. The door screeched and popped as it opened, the dome ceiling light illuminating the interior.

He wasn't sure what he would find, but it surely wasn't this wisp of a woman slumped over the steering wheel, her forehead pressed against the horn.

He exhaled, not realizing until that moment that he'd been holding his breath. He should move her, but . . . what if her neck was damaged? Or broken? What if she had internal bleeding and by moving her he caused it to be worse, or even fatal?

What if she froze to death while he stood in the snow and mulled over all the "what ifs"?

As gently as he could, he cupped her shoulders and pulled her away from the steering wheel. Then he eased her head back against the seat rest. Blessedly, the horn stopped, but was immediately replaced by the irritating *yap, yap, yap* of a tiny pooch.

The woman's skin was as pale as buttermilk, and he thought for a moment she might already be dead. Then he noted the shallow rise and fall of her chest and the foggy tufts of her breath. Just under the feathery cut of her bangs, a nasty-looking bruise had started to form. A thin cut bisected her left eyebrow, and blood trickled down her cheek.

"Missus?" He knew she wouldn't respond. She was alive, but unconscious. With a goose egg like the one she had, it was no wonder.

He hesitantly reached out a hand and pushed back her hair. It was as dark as a raven's wing and twice as shiny. Soft as down—and thick with blood.

A low growl issued from the passenger's seat. Gideon momentarily turned his attention from the woman to her dog—if one was feeling generous enough to actually call him that. The whelp couldn't have weighed more than five pounds, but Gideon had the feeling that if pressed the dog would defend his mistress with sharp teeth and all the bite he could muster.

He extended a hand and let the tiny canine smell him. The silky-looking demi-beast whined, then licked Gideon to show his approval. Then he sat back on his haunches and cocked his silvery-tan head to one side as if waiting for what to do next.

"That makes two of us," Gideon muttered.

One thing was certain—he had to get the woman out of this weather before she froze to death. She wore only a scrap of a dress. A spangled little thing of green and silver that looked as if it had been made of dragonfly wings and stardust. In it she seemed like some sort of pixie princess, but it couldn't be very warm. Her shoes weren't much better—tiny straps of silver and sparkly stones—hardly enough to call shoes and certainly not made for walking through unexpected snowstorms. Not that she would be walking anywhere.

Gideon calculated the time it would take to get to the Bradleys' with her carried over his shoulder in a fireman's hold. The mental picture included her head lolling around as he struggled over the treacherous distance covered in snow. Then he considered the journey without her, and then back, and how long it would take to get her into town and . . .

The numbers were not promising.

He didn't want to hurt her worse. And as much as he didn't want her at his house, he couldn't leave her here. If he had been a praying man, he would have asked God for guidance, to help him, to help *her*. But Gideon hadn't prayed in a long, long time.

He set his lantern on the crumpled top of her car, then stripped off his coat and covered her with it. As gently as he could, he scooped her into his arms, and cradled her to him like a child. He was careful not to let her head fall too far forward or too far back as he reached once again for his light.

Her dog growled. Gideon sighed. He couldn't leave the beast in the cold any more than he could his mistress. His mutts could stand the weather, but he had a feeling this little dog was as pampered as they come.

"And what should I do with you?" he muttered as snow fell

around him, landing on her eyelashes, and the pale, smooth curve of her cheek.

As if sensing it was time to go, the dog crawled into the gigantic brown handbag overturned in the passenger's seat. Then he poked his head out as if to say, *What's taking you so long?*

Still holding her, Gideon wedged himself into the driver's seat, his feet planted on the snow-covered ground. He snaked one arm through the light-colored handles of the bag, took a deep breath, and stood, managing to keep both woman and dog safe in his grasp.

The walk back to his house seemed longer than any he had ever taken. Bitter cold nipped his face and hands. The handbag containing the woman's dog banged against his right leg. With every step he took, the lantern slapped against the other. The dead weight of the woman—even one as tiny as she—became a burden after the first hundred yards. Or maybe the burden was carrying her so gently. It was hard not to jostle her as he picked his way over the frozen ground. He was painfully aware of the steps he took, how jarring they were, how cold the wind blew, and how pale she was. With every step his boots, heavy with caked-up snow, were nearly sucked from his feet. By his constant whine, the dog seemed none too happy about the bouncy ride and relentless snow. But Gideon trudged on, the way lit only by the lantern dangling off his arm.

He could only hope she wasn't hurt internally, and that by moving her he hadn't sealed her death. He couldn't stand another life on his conscience.

Slowly he made his way back up the road and down the unpaved driveway that led to his house. He'd left the oil lamp burning in the front room. Golden light shone through the window, beckoning him like a sailor to a lighthouse. *Just a few more yards.* His breath puffed out in bursts of cloudy vapor. The snow continued to fall, but it had lost its urgency and now the flakes, still as large and wet, drifted lazily toward the waiting ground.

Getting the door open was no easy feat, but no one locked up out here and with a little cautious shuffling, Gideon managed to get his injured pixie out of the storm.

The temperature inside the house was marginally better than outside. With no one to tend it, the fire had fizzled out once again, and though the coals still burned brilliant orange under their blanket of ash, they gave off very little heat.

He laid the woman gently on the couch. She moaned as he moved his arms from beneath her. He considered that a good sign. Maybe she wouldn't be out much longer. Maybe she would wake up and tell him who she was and what she was doing driving around on a night like this.

He removed her shoes and placed them next to the big brown handbag he'd deposited on the floor, then he covered her with his coat.

The tiny pooch stuck his nose out and sniffed around. He looked longingly up at the sofa, seeming to measure the distance, and then thought better of it. He whined, and Gideon wondered if the dog had ever been allowed to jump before. The little thing leapt into the air and scrambled onto the woman's belly, settling himself down on top of Gideon's coat.

Gideon stirred the glowing coals, added a couple of logs to the grate, and in a few short minutes the fire roared once again. The wood glowed, the light casting golden orange shadows onto her face.

*Pixie.* The word sprang to mind once again. During his *rum-springa* he'd read a book about a faraway, made-up land filled with magical creatures—fairies, gnomes, and pixies. His houseguest seemed to be the embodiment of the latter. She had a heart-shaped face with a pointed little chin and dark eyebrows to match short,

inky curls. She looked beautiful in an other-worldly kind of way—
beautiful, privileged, and as pampered as her dog.

But if he remembered the story correctly, the pixies caused all
the trouble and the eventual downfall of the fairy kingdom.

Gideon shook himself free of the spell that seemed to surround
them. He shouldn't be standing there, staring at her and thinking
about long-ago books, he should be—it took him a minute to collect his thoughts—he should be cleaning her wound, gathering
more blankets, and seeing if he could rouse her.

*Think about it!* He shook his head. *If she didn't wake up after the
way you carried her, she ain't gonna wake up anytime soon.*

The terrible thought occurred to him that she might not wake
up at all . . . ever.

He pushed it away, trying to remember what the doctor had
told his brother Gabriel when his oldest boy had fallen out of an
apple tree and conked his head.

*Let them sleep, but try to wake them up every hour or so. If they don't
respond, you have trouble.*

Gideon peered out the window where the snow had piled upon
the ledge. *Ach*, would he have trouble. Enough of it that he wasn't
about to borrow any. He'd just take it one step at a time.

He added another log to the fire, then made his way to the
linen closet to get some quilts. She would be more comfortable in
the bed, but the living room would be warmer. He scooped up the
whining, growling whelp of a dog, retrieved his coat, then covered
the woman with the quilts before depositing the dog back into his
original position. He fetched a washrag to clean the nasty-looking
gash on her forehead, wetting it in the washstand basin before
warming it by the fire.

He tried to be gentle as he pushed back her hair once again
and touched the rag to the gash, but his fingers felt big and clumsy
against her skin. He dabbed at the dried blood and winced at the

depth of the cut. It probably needed stitches, but the hospital was a long way away.

He dabbed it a few more times, and satisfied the bleeding had stopped, went to the kitchen and found the next best thing—a small tube of Super Glue. Returning to her side, he took a deep breath before applying the glue and pressing the sides of the wound together.

Her eyes fluttered open, big and unfocused. They settled on him, and in a split second, it occurred to him that they were the exact same color of the grape-flavored gumdrops Mr. Anderson kept over at the general store. It had to be a trick of the lighting. He couldn't be sure because as quickly as they opened, they closed again.

Surely the plunge of his stomach was nothing more than relief that she had awakened at all.

"Are you all right?" he asked, hoping she hadn't fallen back into unconsciousness.

"Head hurts," she murmured.

Not a lot, but a start. Gideon smiled despite himself. "I bet it does."

"What happened?"

"You had a wreck," he said, using the words he'd heard from the *Englischers* in town.

"My whole life is a wreck." Her defeated tone tugged at his heart.

"An automobile wreck."

"Where am I?"

"My house."

"Oh," she said. "You rescued me."

"No—"

"Thank you . . ." She turned her face away and once again drifted into oblivion.

Gideon stood motionless in the fire's flickering shadows, but he wouldn't let himself think too much about what she had said. It wasn't true. He hadn't rescued her. Heroism wasn't his strong suit. He didn't have it in him.

⚜

Gideon stayed up all through the night, stoking the fire and rousing his little pixie every hour. She didn't seem to mind, even asking him his name, though he doubted in the morning she would be able to remember waking much less anything they had talked about.

She dozed while he kept watch, sitting up in the hard-backed rocking chair. At the first light of dawn, he allowed himself a nap. And this time, thankfully, he didn't dream of Miriam and Jamie and the guilt that haunted him, but of a violet-eyed pixie and the little dog she carried around with her in a purse.

⚜

Blinding white-blue sunlight hit Avery square in the face, but she refused to open her eyes. Her head hurt . . . bad. The light turned red behind her eyelids, making her head pound as the blood throbbed through her veins. She should've had those blackout shades installed no matter what her father—or rather her father's decorator—said about the matter. This was ridiculous.

Unable to take the brutal light a minute longer, she tried to turn over, but every bone and muscle protested. Had she been hit by a bus? Then last night returned—Jack, the motel, the back roads of a small Oklahoma town, her car, and then . . .

Louie inched closer to her side, rose up, and licked her hand. Sweet Louie V., fine and whole despite the tumble he must have taken.

Avery winced as she stroked his silky fur. With much effort she forced her eyes open and took note of her surroundings. She was in a house. A very small house.

There didn't seem to be much more to it than the space where she lay. The room led into an open kitchen with a large rectangular table and sturdy-looking chairs. The fireplace had a thick, wooden mantel, and an odd-looking stove squatted in one corner. There was something strange about the house, but she couldn't figure out what. Maybe because there were no pictures on the walls or trinkets sitting about, just a china hutch full of dishes and a large box containing wood for the fire. Or maybe it was the lack of care. The furniture would have been beautiful if not covered with a thick layer of dust and neglect.

How did she get here? She squinted, straining to remember. Then it came back to her—the snow, losing control of her car, and then a warm fire and gentle hands washing her face. A man had awakened her several times during the night.

Avery turned her chin, and there he was, head resting at an odd angle, propped up in the rocking chair near her. His hair, dark like rich morning coffee, had just enough curl to make it interesting. It was cut close to his face, almost as if someone had plopped a bowl on his head and trimmed all that stuck out underneath. His skin held the first hint of a tan, a golden glow with just the slightest trace of pink high on his cheeks accented by the vague shadow of morning beard growth.

She had wispy memories of him waking her up in the night, asking if she knew the date, the year, the president's name, and how many fingers he held up. As if sensing her gaze upon him, he opened his eyes. They were a smoky moss green, clouded and troubled. Once he realized she was awake, his expression changed, his eyes turning hooded and guarded. It happened so quickly she wondered if she had imagined that vulnerable expression at all.

"You're awake." His voice sounded rusty.

"So are you," she said in return, but her crack at humor made her head pound anew. She reached up a hand to find a tender knot near her eyebrow.

"Does it hurt?"

"A little." She attempted a smile. "A lot."

"That's a nasty bump. I don't have anything but Tylenol. Or I can give you some of the tea Clara Beachy brews up when, well, it's said to be good for pains."

If she wasn't mistaken, he blushed at his own words. And tea? What in the world did tea have to do with pain?

"I'll get it for you." He stood and Avery noticed his commanding size. He was tall and broad and yet his shirt hung on him as if it had been made for someone else. Thinking about it made her head throb, so she quit and lay back on the pillows, closing her eyes. She just wanted to rest. To lie here on this lumpy old sofa and just continue to lie there until she felt better. Or died. Whichever came first.

She listened to him putter around the kitchen. At her father's house the kitchen was off-limits, off the main foyer and practically in a different county, so the sounds were foreign to her. A clunk here, a swoosh there, and then the whistle of the tea kettle. The splash of water, the clink of a spoon, and sure and steady footsteps across the wooden floor.

His body blocked the sun, casting her into shadows. "Here." He held out a brown earthenware mug filled to the brim with steaming hot tea. "I added honey," he said, "to cut the bitter, but I can still get you that Tylenol if'n you want."

Gingerly, she pushed herself up to take the mug from him. "This is fine." She blew across the top then took a tentative sip. It tasted like burnt grass and cloves.

Somehow she managed to drink all of the . . . tea. Mostly because he stood over her and made sure she downed every last drop.

She forced a smile and handed him the mug, then eased back against the pillows and pulled the covers to her chin. It wasn't modesty, but heat she needed. Despite the warmth the tea had infused to her system, the tiny little house was cold, and her tiny little dress was, well, tiny.

The big man walked to the fireplace and stirred the ashes, adding more wood from the box. In no time, the orange blaze roared, warming Avery from all the way across the room.

She so desperately wanted to just lie there and forget the world, enjoy the warmth rolling off the flames, but she couldn't. Not yet anyway.

"My car," she asked after he turned around.

"Well," he drawled as if choosing his words very carefully, "I'm no expert, but it looked purty bad to me. Course'n it was dark last night. And snowin'."

Avery wanted to nod, but she managed only a single dip of her head before the simple movement sent waves of dizziness crashing all around her.

"Steady now." He moved to her side.

"Yes," Avery murmured. She closed her eyes against the spinning, but that only seemed to make it worse, so she opened them again.

"Maybe in a day or two we can head out and take a look at the damage, but—"

"A day or two?" She dared not raise her voice much over a whisper.

"The snow will be gone this afternoon, maybe tomorrow. As soon as the ground dries up a little, we should be able to get over there."

"Oh."

"Course'n we'll go on foot. It'll be at least three or four days before I can get the buggy out. Molly and Kate do not like so much havin' mud on their feet."

"Molly and Kate?"

"My horses."

Then it clicked into place. The simple way he dressed, the lack of modern appliances, the beautiful handmade quilts that made up her bed. "You're Amish?"

"*Jah*." He nodded. "I am Plain."

Tall and handsome, with slashing dimples and those haunting green eyes, the man was anything but *plain*. His answer charmed her, but she hid her smile not wanting him to think she was laughing at him.

Oh, the irony. Jack had come here to find the Amish, but instead he found . . . a new lover. She had come out here to find Jack and had instead found the Amish.

"I am thinkin' you should rest now," he said.

"Yes." She snuggled down under the beautiful handmade quilts, their colors exquisite, each stitch perfect, and she wondered about the woman who had made them. Maybe his mother or sister? Or wife.

She peeked at him again. Didn't Amish men have beards?

"Thank you for saving me," she said, her eyelids growing heavy despite the fact she had just woken up. Being cheated on and then knocked in the head could do that to a person. Or maybe there was something to that tea after all . . .

He stared at her blankly. "You already thanked me."

Avery closed her eyes. "Mmm-hmm. Tell me your name again."

"Gideon," he replied. "Gideon Fisher."

Biblical . . . suited him. "Avery," she murmured in return. "Avery Ann Hamilton."

Then she drifted off to sleep.

When Avery woke again, it was late afternoon, and she was alone. Through the window, the blue bowl of a sky had turned a pale shade of lavender that would deepen to purple and eventually black. From somewhere outside came an unfamiliar *whack*, *whack*, *whack* that had both rhythm and unpredictability. It was a soothing sound.

The tea must have done the trick. Not only did her head feel significantly better, *she* felt significantly better.

Louie V. lay sprawled on a bed of scraps in front of the hearth looking all the more like the spoiled and catered-to canine that he was. The crackling fire cast flickering shadows over his black and tan fur, making Avery realize Gideon hadn't been out of the room for long. The fire still licked at the logs in long, orange strokes, sending smoke up the chimney, but not the sweet scent of burning wood.

Surprisingly enough, Avery found the odor pleasing. Each of the six fireplaces in her father's home had its own set of gas logs that flickered and put on a grand show, but never actually burned. This, she decided, was so much better.

She eased herself into a sitting position, a spring poking her in the backside. She shifted her weight and got another poke—this time from a different spring.

When she stood, her bare feet sank into the soft wool of the rug that lay in front of the couch. The air was warm but not enough so, and she shifted the quilt to drape across her shoulders. She was sore, but it wasn't unbearable. Thankfully nothing was broken—not even her heart. She'd gotten away lucky.

At the creak of the couch, Louie lifted his head. When he caught sight of her, awake and standing, he wagged his little stump of a tail, then laid his head back down on his front paws. With a shuddering doggie sigh, he was asleep once again.

"Good to see you so worried about me," Avery said.

"I was very worried." The deep, masculine voice came from the doorway. Gideon stood there, a load of wood in his arms, black round-brimmed hat on his head.

Two things registered in her mind: The whacking she had heard earlier had been Gideon chopping wood, and she stood in his living room wearing practically nothing.

She wasn't exactly indecent, but she did feel exposed standing there in a dress small enough to fit into a cereal bowl. The quilt hung over her shoulders but offered her no real modesty. She had worn dresses like this her entire adult life, but now all of a sudden, it felt less than appropriate.

Avery wrapped the ends of the quilt across her, folding her arms at her middle and covering herself as nonchalantly and as best she could. Gideon turned away, removing his hat to hang it on the peg just inside the door. Crossing the room, he placed the wood in the box close to the fireplace, not looking at her even when he had finished his task.

"You're up." He glanced around at everything but her—the floor, the ceiling, the fire, out the window.

"So are you," Avery said, hoping her flippancy hid her embarrassment. What must he think of her, a man so devoted to God that he had none of the creature comforts the rest of the world enjoyed? No electricity, no car, no running water.

Surely he had running water. He'd made tea earlier, but she hadn't looked to see where he'd gotten the water.

Avery let out a pent-up breath. She came from a world of the wealthy and privileged. Some of her friends drank from the time they got up in the afternoon till they dropped into bed in the wee hours of the morning. Some gambled, raced cars, jetted all over the world for the tiniest flight of fancy. But that had never really been her style. She had always wanted a home, a husband, and a yard full of kids. The few friends she had confessed this dream to had laughed and called her hokey. But standing there in Gideon's house, she felt no different than the jet-set crowd that called her friend.

She pulled the edges of the quilt tighter around her, protection from her thoughts and not from the cold.

"Is there . . . I mean, where's the bathroom?" She hoped there was one, and that it was inside the house. She knew the Amish held an aversion to electricity; she just didn't know how they felt about indoor plumbing.

"Down the hall on the left." He pointed the way.

Avery padded across the so-cold floor in the direction Gideon had indicated. Thankfully the bathroom wasn't much different than a regular one, except it had a newer feel than the rest of the house. The walls weren't marked up where things had been knocked against them over the years. The ceiling looked recently painted. There was a sink and a toilet and a deep claw-footed bath-tub. There were—of course—no lights. But the window over the tub let in enough of the waning sunshine that Avery could finish her business without difficulty.

She washed her hands in the sink, the water as cold as melted icebergs, and studied her reflection in the mirror above the lava-tory. If she hadn't known it before, it was certainly evident now—the Amish were not a vain people. Or at least not Gideon Fisher. The mirror over the sink was actually a hand mirror held up with a nail through the hole at the end of its faded pink handle. Avery could make out only parts of her reflection, but that was probably a good thing. Her hair was in bad need of a washing, matted and squashed to one side where she had slept on it. Day-old mascara added dark smudges beneath her eyes. An angry-looking bruise added unwanted color to her forehead just over one eye and adjacent to a cut that looked as if it had been glued together. She shuddered as a vague memory of her Amish rescuer tending her wound in the night flitted across her mind's eye. All in all, she looked a mess. No wonder he stared at her like she had crawled out from under a rock.

With a small sigh at her disastrous reflection, she turned and made her way back to the living area. Gideon stood right where she left him, staring into the fire as if it held all the answers.

"Are you hungry?" he asked as she approached, his gaze still riveted on the dancing flames.

Surprisingly she was. Or maybe not so surprisingly. She had eaten nothing but some rumaki and a handful of crab puffs in the last twenty-four hours.

As Avery warmed her hands in front of the fireplace, Gideon seemed to pull himself from his thoughts, and headed toward the kitchen. He opened a strange-looking upright box—some kind of refrigerator, maybe?—and started pulling out containers.

His motions were quick and capable as if he had been taking care of himself for quite a while. He pulled a large knife from one of the drawers and bread out of a wooden box, slicing it with efficient precision. In minutes, he had plates on the table, silverware crossways on top instead of next to them, glasses of milk poured and waiting, and platters of meat and bread sitting in the center.

"Come," he said with a jerk of his hand.

The wooden planks of the floor were cold against her feet as she made her way to the table. She scooched sideways into the chair, keeping the quilt around her as best she could for both warmth and covering. As she slid into place, Gideon sat a big bowl of potato salad on the table.

Her mouth started watering as he took his place and started dishing out generous helpings of the food onto his own plate.

He nodded toward her. "Help yourself." All the people she had met from Oklahoma sounded like a perfect cross between the country twang of western Arkansas and the elongated drawl of East Texas. He had the accent of his German ancestors.

Avery did as he bade, helping herself to the thick slabs of rye bread, stacking them together with slices of cold roast beef and a side of the potato salad.

She was surprised when Gideon picked up his fork without praying.

"Aren't you going to say grace?" The words slipped from her mouth before she could stop them.

He paused for a split-second before dishing up the bite to his mouth and chewing thoughtfully. He took his time swallowing before he answered. "Plain people do not pray out loud at the supper table." Then he scooped up another bite and shoveled it into his mouth. Though Avery hadn't seen him bow his head and give even a silent thanks for their food, she had the feeling the subject was closed.

The food was delicious. Cold, but filling. And Avery felt better than she had in a long time. Warm and content, very close to happy. Only one thing put a damper on her mood.

"Gideon," she started, sitting her fork down beside her empty plate and watching him finish off the last of his own meal. For such a big man, he didn't eat much. "Do you have a phone? For emergencies, you know?" Her cell phone was still in her car, but it might just as well have been on another planet.

He wiped his mouth and stared at her for a second or two, but it seemed like an eternity. With that one innocent question, she felt like she had insulted his entire way of life.

"No."

"I . . ." Why was she having such a hard time talking to him? Maybe it was the guarded look that had returned to his eyes. "My father might be worried about me and—"

"As he should be."

Avery stopped. "What's that supposed to mean?"

Gideon leaned back in his chair, tilting his head to one side in a thoughtful pose. "Not many fathers let their daughters traipse around the countryside wearin' next to nothing. Even *Englischer* ones."

"I'm not . . ." She stopped herself. She *was* an *Englischer*, as he said. She *was* traipsing around the countryside, as he said. And she *was* wearing next to nothing—just as he said. Even worse, her make-do covering had slipped.

He looked at her bare shoulder, pointedly.

Avery jerked the quilt back into place. "I left Dallas in sort of a hurry."

Gideon crossed his arms. "Not in so much of a hurry you couldn't manage to bring your mutt along."

"Louie V. is most certainly not a mutt. He's pedigreed, bred from champions and—"

"Punier than a barn cat."

Avery opened her mouth, then shut it, opened it once more and realized yet again she had no comeback to his observation—however true and hurtful. "He was very expensive," she muttered, thankful he made no comment about the cost of her dog.

Instead he pushed himself back from the table. "I'm goin' out to the barn to check on Molly and Kate." Before she could utter a word, he pulled on his mud-caked rubber boots and headed out the door.

༄ﾟ ༄ﾟ

Gideon held the match to the bowl of his pipe and puffed on the end. Fragrant smoke billowed around him, mixing with the smell of wet earth, hay, and horseflesh. He took another puff, eased himself down on a hay bale, and rested his head against a brace post.

He didn't need to tend to the animals. He had done that right before splitting the firewood. No, what he needed was a clear head. And the barn was as good a place as any for that. Still, he'd come out here and given them—Molly, Kate, and Honey, the one milk cow he'd kept—a fresh toss of hay and a few extra strokes with the brush. And now he would have a little smoke.

Maybe when he returned from the barn she'd've . . .

She'd've what? Disappeared?

Regardless of what he had thought the first time he'd seen her, she was not a pixie. She was not magical. And she'd be at the house when he returned.

All the more reason to keep to the barn.

He closed his eyes, but all he could see was the creamy white curve of her shoulder, so he opened them again. He'd had to get out of the house, take refuge lest he give into temptation and reach out a hand to see if her skin felt as smooth and soft as it looked. He hadn't given her *Englisch* dress a second thought in the middle of a snowstorm when he was trying to get her to warmth and safety. But now that she was out of danger, it filled his mind. It had been a long time since he'd thought about touching a woman. A long, long time.

When he'd sold his farm and bought this one, he'd had one purpose in mind—to come out here and wait to die. That was all he deserved. Miriam and Jamie were dead, and it was his fault. Not God's will as the People would like to believe, but the avoidable mistake of a man. A man who wanted his family back. Since he couldn't have that, he was eager to join them.

He knew it was wrong to be prideful and since he couldn't help it, he had always kept those thoughts to himself, but he had been proud of his family. Miriam was everything he could have wanted in a wife—sweet, gentle, and obedient—the quintessential Amish woman. Jamie was the best son a man could ever ask for. He'd been blessed with Gideon's dark hair and Miriam's clear blue eyes. The purtiest child he'd ever seen. Active, inquisitive, and unwavering in his faith and devotion to God and to Gideon.

And he had failed them. Sent them to their deaths. Killed them both.

Gideon shuddered, swallowing down the tears that threatened at the back of his eyes. He wasn't going to cry anymore. He had shed his tears. He had asked God why. He had asked God to take him too. And then he'd asked God why some more. But he hadn't been given an answer. So he stopped asking God for anything.

Now all he could do was wait until the unmerciful God decided to take him and relieve him of the torture he faced here on earth. He'd moved out here, away from the others, to find solace in the days, even if the nights were filled with terrible dreams.

But now what little peace he'd claimed had been shattered.

By Miss Avery Ann Hamilton.

What kind of name was Avery, anyway? Wasn't that the brand of those stickers the Fitch girls used to label their jellies to sell in the market? Who named a woman like that after sticker labels? She should be a Belle or Misty, or Anastasia, some type of otherworldly name that went with her pixie face and big gumdrop eyes. But she wasn't a pixie, a fairy, or otherworldly. She was a woman.

An *Englischer.*

And she didn't belong here.

Four days—at the most—and she would be gone, back to her world where people carried rat-sized dogs around in oversized bags, wore shiny dresses, and drove expensive cars. Not in the world of the Plain people.

Until that time, until the effects of the storm had passed, he was stuck with her. He needed to make the best of it. And that would start with an apology

He stood and tapped out his pipe, then walked over to the feed bins. He opened the middle one, scooped out a cup of dog food, and headed for the house.

*It had seemed like a good idea at the time.* Avery glanced around the disheveled kitchen. Really, it was only fair. He had, after all, prepared their meal. The least she could do was clean up. Not that she had ever been called to "clean up" before. But honestly . . . how hard could it be?

Except she couldn't move around in the kitchen wrapped in a quilt, so she'd shed her covering in favor of convenience. Now she was cold. Even activity didn't help. Her feet felt like popsicles on the ends of her legs. Goose bumps covered every inch of her body and now she was beginning to wonder if she would ever be warm again. Not because it was so cold in the house, but the water! *Brr* . . .

She closed up the containers and placed them back into the refrigerator, and she figured out how to work the sink—mainly because it was no different than a regular one. But no matter which way she turned the handle, and no matter how long she let it run, the water didn't warm up.

She found a bottle of commercial dish soap under the sink, poured some in, and plunged her hands into the icy water.

She wasn't sure why it was so important for her to do this—and to continue past the point of torturous discomfort—but it was.

Maybe because he looked at her like she was useless fluff. She knew that look well, that indulgent, "Isn't she sweet?" look all her father's cronies gave her. From them, she was used to it. She could take it, even. But from Gideon Fisher . . .

Something about him challenged her, made her want to step outside of herself and try things she had never done before. Like washing dishes in icy water!

She had just placed the last glass in the drainer, when Louie V. barked. Avery turned to find Gideon there, one hand on the door knob, the other holding a plastic scoop half-filled with some type of food.

All at once she wished for the quilt back.

Without a word Gideon poured the food in one of the small bowls sitting to the right of the fireplace. Avery hadn't noticed them earlier, but before she could comment, Gideon headed past her toward the back of the house.

Avery stood rooted to the spot as if her feet had somehow become one with the boards of the floor.

Louie wasn't having the same problem. He jumped up from his bed of rags and trotted over to the bowl to eat, his stubby little tail wagging the entire time.

Then Gideon was back.

"Here." He thrust a stack of clothing into her surprised arms.

Avery looked down at the garments. A pale blue shirt, no doubt Gideon's by the size, a pair of black flap-front pants—also Gideon's if the size were any indication—and a pair of socks— warm-looking, hand-knitted socks.

"I . . ." The words escaped her. "Thank you."

"It'll be a couple more days before the roads are clear. You can't . . ." He waved a hand toward her, but didn't finish the sentence.

"Traipse around in next to nothing?" She managed to hide her smile, but the twitch in her lips took the sting from her words.

"*Jah.*" He gave her a solemn nod, then turned to set a fresh bowl of water in front of Louie. When he straightened, he eyed her seriously. "I must apologize for what I said."

"It's okay." Avery shifted from one bare foot to the other, suddenly unable to meet his steady gaze.

"It is not our way to judge. And that's what I have done."

"Really," she started, "it's all right."

He answered with a curt nod of his head.

Avery stuck her hand out from under the stack of clothing. "Truce?"

"*Jah.*" He glanced down at her fingers but turned away without touching her.

# 2

Sunday morning dawned bright and sunny. Avery woke on Gideon's couch to birds singing and impossibly clear sky visible outside the curtain-less windows. It promised to be a beautiful day. Another like this one, and it wouldn't be long until the roads would be dry enough for the horses to travel. Not that she wanted to return to her father's house and all of the inquisitive stares and insensitive questions. But she supposed it had to be done.

She had wasted no time last night changing out of her cocktail dress and into the clothing Gideon had given her. The shirt was gorgeous, the color somewhere between the Oklahoma springtime sky and the bluebonnets that grew like beautiful weeds all over east Texas. Although the garment covered considerably more of her than her dress, she found it a little too intimate to run around in just a man's shirt and fixed on his pants as well. They were miles too big with a flap in the front held together with four buttons across the top. She'd tightened those as best as she could, cinched them around her waist with a scrap of cloth from the basket in the

kitchen and hooked them over her shoulders with the attached suspenders. Then she'd rolled the legs up to just above her ankles to
keep them from dragging on the ground. They were a little worse
for wear—considering she'd slept in them. And she would die a
million deaths if someone actually *saw* her in them, but at least she
was adequately covered. Maybe now Gideon would stop looking at
her like *that*.

The sun was faithful and warm, and the last drifts of snow
on the north side of the barn were finally starting to melt. Avery
stretched and propped her bare feet up on the wooden porch railing and watched the farm go by. At least what there was of it. She'd
thought a farm would be a little busier than Gideon Fisher's seemed
to be. But what did she truly know about farms? Nothing. Big, fat
nada.

Still, Gideon had disappeared in the barn about an hour ago—
her traitorous companion hot on his heels—and neither one of
them had come out again. Didn't he have fields to plow and crops
to harvest and what not? And wasn't he going to church? After all,
it *was* Sunday.

And what did she care?

Except that she had never felt more useless in her life. All she
had done since she'd been here was wash the dishes in unnecessarily cold water—Gideon had showed her that very morning how he
used water heated in a bucket by the fire to wash the dishes—and
sit around. And that didn't seem quite right.

Her father always had a billion things for her to do—appearances to make, volunteer work, benefits to attend. It wasn't hard
work, but it kept her busy.

Gideon had saved her life, clothed her, fed her, shouldn't she
give something in return? She was on a farm. There were no benefits to attend, but shouldn't she do *something*?

She should. And she would start by finding her host and . . . and . . . well, finding her host was something, now wasn't it?

Avery stood and started off the porch, stopping only when she got to the smooth patch of red dirt at the bottom of the stoop. She didn't have on any shoes. She surveyed the uneven ground that separated her from the barn. A few tufts of brown grass lined the well-worn path that was mostly mud with only a few spots packed down since the snow had melted. Her Manolo Blahniks were no match for this type of terrain and that left her only one option.

Despite the rising heat of the day, the path was cool on the soles of her feet, but not unpleasant. In fact, the experience of walking barefoot across a country farmyard was surprisingly pleasant. The sun was on her face, the ground soft beneath her feet, the rolled up pants legs brushing against her ankles as she made her way to the barn.

Three dogs lay in the sunshine just before the cool, shadowy entrance to the barn—a beagle, a black and white border collie, and a spotty dog she guessed to be some sort of heeler. None of them moved anything save a small wag of their tails as she passed them by. Her furry friend was nowhere to be seen.

Avery stopped just inside the door, taking a moment to let her eyes adjust to her new surroundings. It was dim even with the top half of the Dutch doors open on the other end. She could say one thing about the barn: it was neat. Fresh smelling, clean hay scattered across the packed dirt floor and perfumed the air as she trod on it. And it was big, with a trussed roof and expansive loft stretching the length of the barn. And empty . . . except for a lone cow in one stall and a couple of horses housed just to the left and opposite the tack room.

Okay, that was three things, but Avery was so proud of herself for remembering the term "tack room" that she wasn't keeping count. An "uncle" of hers over in Ft. Worth, one of her father's associates, owned a sprawling ranch. Avery had gone out there once, toured the barn and ridden a gentle mare . . . and she'd loved it. It was just so far from Dallas. She often thought of going again, but there never seemed to be enough time. There was always a party to go to, or a ribbon-cutting ceremony, or some sort of event to attend.

He was sitting off to one side in the corner of the wide wooden stairs, so quiet and still that she almost didn't see him at all. Or maybe seeing him sitting there instead of milking a cow or throwing some hay confused her. He seemed to be taking the slower pace of the Amish culture very seriously.

"I—" she started, unsure of what to say now that she had actually found him. "I was looking for you."

"And you found me." Louie V. lay at his feet as if he had found a new master in Gideon Fisher.

"Right." Avery rocked back on her heels, enjoying the prickly feel of the straw beneath her feet. "I came to see if I could help you with anything."

"No." Simple man, simple answer.

"Yeah . . . well . . . okay. I just thought I could do something. I feel okay, you know. Farms are busy places, aren't they? I mean, isn't there always something to do, sun up to sun down and all the time in between?" *Why was she rambling?*

"I s'pose."

"Well, then, what can I do?"

"Nothin'."

"Nothing?"

"It's the Lord's Day. We only do what is required of us on Sundays."

Avery nodded. "Right. I was wondering about that. Church

and all. I mean if you need to leave . . ." She couldn't very well go with him dressed in her clothes or his.

She wasn't sure, but she thought Gideon's eyes hardened just a fraction, hiding that vulnerable light which crept into them when he thought she wasn't looking.

"No."

"You don't have to stay here for me."

"I'm not."

"Okay." Avery didn't believe him. She waited for him to load up another excuse, but he didn't.

After several tense heartbeats, she turned to go. A pile of quilts and a pillow stacked on the landing next to her host captured her attention. She didn't know much about horses or the soft equipment they used, but these surely didn't look like horse blankets. And she had never heard of a horse needing a pillow. For anything.

She turned to face him. "Did you sleep here last night?"

"Here?"

"Here. In the barn."

Gideon crossed his arms over his chest, his nonchalant pose of earlier vanishing in one fluid motion. "And what's it matter to you if'n I did?"

"Well . . ." What truly did it matter to her where he slept? "It seems sort of silly to me that I slept on the couch and you slept in the barn and nobody slept in that big, old bed in there."

"It is not silly." He stood and even with the distance between them, Avery was impressed by his formidable height. "We are not married. We are not chaperoned. The elders will be vexed enough to discover you're here with me, sleepin' in the house." He shrugged. "That is not somethin' else I need on my conscience."

"What isn't something you need on your conscience?" Avery eyed him, her brow furrowed.

"Compromisin' your good standin'."

Was he serious? "Because I'm here with you? Alone?"

Gideon nodded. "*Jah.*"

He *was* serious! And Avery was touched.

"But I'm an Englisher." She uttered the term she'd heard Jack use to refer to non-Amish folk.

"*Jah,*" Gideon agreed. "But you are still a woman."

Gideon's comment rang through Avery's ears for the remainder of the morning. Even after he pulled on his mud-caked rubber boots and loaded her into a wheelbarrow to take her down to look at her car. It was an odd, but fun way to ride down the country lane with the sun on her face and her fanny planted in a piece of farm equipment. She enjoyed it. And there was no way she could have made the quarter-mile trek down the road and back barefooted. She had a few tough spots on her feet from wearing high heels, but she had those regularly tended to keep them to a minimum.

Avery glanced down at her French-tipped pedicure as she stood on Gideon's front porch. What kind of shoes did Amish women wear? She wished she had paid more attention to Jack as he had talked about his movie—the gonna-blow-*Witness*-out-of-the-water film that he had written and wanted her father's funding to produce. She had only half listened as he spoke of his dream because she was too focused on him. Funny how that seemed a lifetime away when it had only been a couple of days.

Her car on the other hand, wasn't going anywhere anytime soon. Not without a tow truck. Avery shuddered at the memory of the crumpled piece of metal that was once an S class Mercedes. From the looks of it, she was lucky to be alive and blessed to be in one piece.

She gripped the porch railing a little tighter, the paint flaking off under her hands as she sent up a silent prayer of thanks to whoever might be listening and to whoever was watching over her.

At least she had gotten a few of her personal items out of the car—her purse, her makeup bag, and her cell phone. There were fourteen missed calls from Jack and one from her father.

She pulled the shiny device from her pocket and studied it as if it had all the answers. But it didn't. Anything it contained would only bring more questions. With a heavy sigh, she punched in the numbers to her voicemail and calmly erased all of the messages from Jack without listening to them. He didn't have anything to say that she was willing to hear. Her father on the other hand . . .

"Avery." His voice was as matter-of-fact and as coolly business-like as ever. "Jack tells me you're having a 'girls' night' in Aruba. I guess this means you won't be back for the Cartwright benefit. I was depending on you to be there. Maris has another engagement and, well, I suppose we'll find a way." He sighed to show his frustration with her and her obviously selfish decision to take a vacation without first notifying him. "I trust you'll be back before the Dunstan Pro-Am. I'll expect you then." No "good-bye." No "talk to you later." No "I love you." Just a click and nothing more.

Avery stared at the phone for several seconds trying to decide what had just happened. Jack had gotten to her father first. He probably already had the money for his movie. She was supposedly off gallivanting in Aruba, and no one was looking for her. She wasn't certain if that was a good thing or not. She sucked in a slow breath, tamping down the anger that threatened her perfect day. Jack had gotten away with sleeping with another woman and still reaped the benefits of his relationship with her. Maybe it served her father right to lose that kind of money if he never once questioned where she was and why she was there.

She turned off the phone and slipped it back into her pocket.

The Dunstan Pro-Am was three weeks away. Three blessed weeks of peace and solitude. She had half a mind to actually fly to Aruba, only she wasn't sure how she would get to the airport from here. Right now, though, "here" was as good a place as any.

Just then, Gideon strode around the side of the house, Louie V. following behind like a lovesick groupie.

"My word," Avery admonished, looking at the mess of her pedigreed dog. "Look at you!"

His paws were caked with dirt and mud, and the silvery bow she'd tied to his topknot was missing. The longer hair around his face hung free, blowing back as he trotted after his new friend.

Gideon stopped, glancing down at himself before shrugging.

"Not you. *Him*." She pointed at Louie. "He's filthy."

"A little dirt never hurt nobody."

"Says you." She admonished him with a quick glare toward his mud-crusted boots.

"It'll be good for him."

"I don't see how." Her beautiful dog was, well, he was disgustingly dirty.

"Because he's a sissy dog." Any sting in Gideon's words faded as he scooped the animal into the crook of one arm and joined her on the porch. "Time for dinner, no?" He opened the door and carried her pedigreed pooch inside as pretty as you please, leaving Avery no choice but to follow.

"No," she said, the screen slamming as she entered the house. Maybe it was her father's voicemail. Maybe it was the physical state of her dog. Or maybe it was the fact that her precious baby abandoned her for their host. Whatever the reason, a spark of annoyance flared inside Avery. "It's not time for dinner. It's time for *lunch*."

Gideon turned to face her. "Around here we call the noon meal dinner. It is noon, so it's time for dinner, *jah*?" Something in his quiet smile or the way he held her dog made her anger melt away as quickly as it had come.

"*Jah.*" Avery smiled, mimicking him.

"Here." He thrust the dog into her arms along with a warm, wet rag. "You clean his feet, and I'll get our *dinner.*"

Avery hid another smile as she gently wiped the mud from Louie V.'s tiny paws, all the while watching Gideon from under the cover of her lowered lashes. She just couldn't figure him out. Gideon, that was. One minute he acted like he would rather she were anywhere but here, and the next he was caring for her dog as if he loved Louie as much as she—which was impossible.

He lived in this house alone. He had evidently been taking care of himself for a while. And he didn't have a beard. That was one thing Avery did remember Jack saying about the Amish. The men grew beards—but not moustaches—after they got married. But Gideon didn't have a beard, so it would stand to reason he didn't have a wife. And that was something which piqued her curiosity. He wasn't *that* moody. In fact, he was a good-looking man, caring and gentle, and hardworking. No, the house wasn't perfect. The inside was dusty and careworn and the outside needed a couple coats of paint, but it wasn't anything that couldn't be corrected. He wasn't a genius or a millionaire, but to a caring, gentle, hardworking young Amish woman, he'd be quite a catch.

Avery finished Louie's feet and sat him down, then chanced another look at her host. Once again he had pulled the container of cold roast beef from the bottled gas-powered refrigerator along with the half-empty bowl of potato salad. Once again he carved thick slices of the dark rye bread, then motioned her over to join him. And once again—and she watched closely this time—he did not bow his head before digging into the meal.

They ate in silence, Gideon making no attempt at conversation. Avery wasn't offended. She wasn't sure if quiet meals were part of the Amish culture, but she had been eating alone for so many years, she didn't think twice about eating her fill without saying a word.

Afterward, they washed the dishes together, and Avery couldn't believe herself—washing dishes not once, but two days in a row. It wasn't so bad, and again the thought of a wife popped into her head. Back home, the houses were always spotless. Her father kept a team of domestics to clean everything from the garage and pool to the attic and kitchen. Surely such an undertaking would be the duty of the wife. After all, she had heard the Amish weren't big supporters of equal rights. So why was Gideon standing beside her rinsing and drying while she washed?

She glanced down at his left hand as he took the last plate from her. No ring, and no sign there had ever been one. But that didn't mean anything. She thought she'd read once that the Amish didn't wear jewelry of any sort—including tokens of their vows.

So he could have a wife and no ring. A wife who had gone to visit family or friends. Or maybe to help someone in need. It would explain why he didn't want to stay in the house alone with her.

"Gideon, are you married?"

He stopped, his fingers white-knuckled as he gripped the plate she'd just handed him. Then he seemed to visibly relax. Until that moment, she hadn't realized how tense he'd been.

"She died," he said quietly. Then he set the plate down with a gentleness that belied the grip he'd had on it just seconds before, and stalked away.

She watched him stride out of the house and tried to tell herself that she *needed* to know what had happened. What if there was something wrong with him? What if he was some sort of crazy, a deviant who went around rescuing women from freak spring snow-storms, feeding them and giving them shelter and wheelbarrow rides and then . . .

Who was she trying to kid? She wanted to know because he

intrigued her. She bit the inside of her lip and stared at the empty doorway. She could have picked a better way to ask though, instead of blurting it out like a teenager.

And hurting him.

She found him in the barn, in the same spot where he'd been that very morning. He sat there in the cool dimness, elbow braced on one knee, twirling a straw of hay between his thumb and forefinger. Like he didn't have a care in the world.

"I believe it's my turn," she said, softly approaching him.

He looked up slowly as if he had known she was there all along, but wasn't going to acknowledge her until she spoke first. Still he said nothing.

"To apologize."

"It's not necessary." He tossed the hay aside, but didn't meet her gaze. She had the feeling that if he did, she would see pain and vulnerability etched there. He must have loved his wife very much.

"It is." She took another step toward him. "I was callous and hurtful and—"

"It's fine." His words grew louder, his jaw clenched.

Avery wasn't sure if he was trying to convince her . . . or himself.

"I'm sorry," she whispered, then turned to go back into the house.

"Tomorrow mornin'." He halted her progress with those two simple words. "I'll take you to town tomorrow mornin'. First thing."

She spun around to face him. "I've been thinking about that."

"You can call your people to come and get you. A fancy tow truck for what's left of your car. I'll stay with you if you like."

"I'd like to stay here with you for a while."

He opened his mouth, but shut it again instead.

"Just for a couple of days. I don't want to be a bother, but I don't want to go home right now."

"I don't—"

"I can pay you."

"I do not need money."

*Good plan, Avery.* Tempt a man with such simple needs with the vulgar offer of cash. "Then I can help out. Paint the house." *How hard could that be?* "Help you with chores." After all, if she could wash dishes in frigid water she could do almost anything.

He opened his mouth once again, she was certain, to tell her no.

She kept her gaze on him, her voice pleading. "Gideon, please." She was unsure why it was so important for her to stay. Maybe because today had been the most peaceful day she'd ever had. She could use a few more before heading back to Dallas and all the questions and sad stares and whispers behind her back that were sure to come.

He cocked his head. "Just a couple of days?"

Avery resisted the urge to smile in triumph. "No one even needs to know I'm here."

# 3

The roads are clear," Gideon said over a cold breakfast the following morning. Avery stared into her bowl of homemade granola cereal and fresh milk, then glanced longingly at her glass of orange juice. If only it were coffee. Gideon seemed not to notice the lack of caffeine to jump-start the day, or perhaps he didn't need it.

But Avery did. Boy, did she.

She wasn't about to tell Gideon, though. She wasn't sure why he had agreed to let her stay, but he had. That was all that mattered. And she wasn't about to upset things now with something as unnecessary—though much loved—as coffee. He had only agreed to a couple of days, but she was confident that when the time came, she could convince him to let her stay awhile longer. Until then, it was peaceful country living. Three wonderful weeks of quiet and solitude—much-needed quiet and solitude.

"Can't leave your fancy car in that field forever."

Of course he couldn't leave her car where it was. He couldn't very well plant around it, now could he? "You don't have to worry about that. I called a wrecker yesterday. I guess there were quite a few accidents the other night." She stole a look at him. "They can't get out here until tomorrow. Is that okay?"

"*Jah.*" He stood and once again Avery was struck with just how *big* he was. "But I have other business in town as well."

Avery drained the last of her juice, then stacked their plates and carried them to the sink. "Are you going to a store? Can you pick me up something while you're there?"

Gideon hesitated for a fraction of a second, then nodded. "Whatever you'd like."

"Strawberry yogurt. The low-fat kind, please. And some Oreo cookies." She smiled her best "pretty-please" smile.

He stared at her as if she had lost her mind.

"Is that all right? Can you do that?"

He nodded, but continued to give her that strange look.

"I'll pay for it. Here." She thrust her credit card into his unsuspecting hands. "That should take care of my stuff and anything else we need. Supplies and such." She shrugged one shoulder.

Gideon turned the thin piece of plastic over in his hands, then gave it back. "No."

"But—"

"We'll square it up later. For now I'm goin' to town. I'll get your yogurt. And your cookies. I'll get some supplies, too, but I'll not be usin' your fancy money."

His voice rang with finality, and Avery knew better than to try and change his mind. Instead, she watched from the living room window as he harnessed his horses, Molly and Kate. A man in a wide-brimmed hat seated in a dark buggy with an orange caution triangle posted on the back and two beautiful, shiny brown horses pulling at the front. They made quite a sight ambling down the country road. Had it not been for the modern safety measure, she would have believed she'd stepped back in time.

Gideon's farm *felt* like another time. A slower time without the stress and modern demands she constantly faced. She could breathe here—breathe and breathe easy.

Avery stepped out onto the porch and inhaled deeply. She hadn't had a Xanax since she found Jack in his hotel room with another woman. Hadn't felt the need, that crushing pressure of anxiety on her chest, the weight of the world on her shoulders. This was the perfect place to hide out, relax, and gather herself before returning to Dallas.

Avery sank into the wooden rocker and propped up her feet on the porch railing. It had quickly become her favorite spot. She could sit on the porch for hours, the wind blowing her hair, the smell of spring on the breeze. The rocker sat in the cool shade, but the tips of the sun's rays touched the ends of her toes.

She should have asked Gideon to bring her some clothes from town, but that seemed like too much of an imposition. She glanced out to the horizon. It really didn't matter what she wore, no one was going to see her anyway and that in itself was liberating.

Louie scratched at the door, whining to be let out. Or maybe he was already missing Gideon.

With a sigh, Avery opened the screen. He trotted down the porch steps and scampered over to where the big boys lay in front of the barn. In addition to Gideon's pack, there were at least three extra dogs gathered in the shade—a big black one, a medium-sized spotted one, and a rusty-yellow dog that was missing one leg. Louie V. flopped down beside them, like he'd always been one of them. They in turn barely acknowledged his presence, like he had been doing it for years.

And like she'd been doing it for years as well, Avery returned to her rocker where she could watch the cars pass by on the country road. Not that there were many. That's exactly why no one would know she was on the farm. It was too far out for anyone to just "drop by."

A flash on the road told her someone was near. Probably an "Englisher"—as Gideon called non-Amish folk—out driving around to catch a glimpse of the Amish going about their daily routine. Avery smiled to herself. They sure would be surprised if they caught sight of her in Plain men's clothing and her modern haircut.

Before Avery could move into the house, a young Amish girl pulled her bicycle to a stop in the yard. Gideon's dogs, the extras, and Louie V. all jumped up and ran to greet her, tails wagging and tongues lolling as they barked out their welcome.

A little on the plump side, her pale blue dress tightened at the waist. She had a round, pleasant face that was both sweet and unassuming. She put down the kickstand and turned toward the house.

Avery wasn't sure which of them was the most surprised.

The girl's cornflower blue eyes widened. "I—" She stammered, then glanced around as if to make sure she was at the right house. "My uncle lives here."

"Yes, I know." Really, what else could she say? "I'm Avery Hamilton, your uncle's . . . guest." So much for no one knowing she was there.

"Is this your dog?" She crouched down and was immediately swallowed up by the prancing legs and swinging tails. Her head popped up above the fray. "Can I hold him?"

"Sure."

When the young girl stood again, she held Louie in her arms while he tried with all his might to lick every bit of her he could reach.

Avery laughed. "I think he likes you."

She cradled him to her face. "I like him too. One day I'd like to . . ." She looked up. "I'm Mary Elizabeth." She waded through the dogs to get to Avery.

"Nice to meet you. One day you'd like to what?"

Mary Elizabeth shook her head. "It's not important. Where's *Onkel*?"

"He's gone to town."

Her eyes got even wider than they had before. "*Town* town?"

"I suppose. He had some errands to run."

"Wow!"

"Is that strange? That he went to town?"

Mary Elizabeth ducked her head. "He doesn't get out much. Not since . . ." She looked away. "I brought roasted chicken." She made her way back through the sea of wagging tails toward her bike. "*Grossmammi* made it. She's my grandmother."

"Gideon's mother?"

Mary Elizabeth nodded, apparently relieved Avery got the whole family relationship thing. "That's right."

She pulled the large Tupperware bowl out of the basket on the front of her bike and handed it to Avery.

She took it, flabbergasted. Who was this new Gideon? Until now, she had thought him a loner with no one save the memories of his wife to keep him company. But now he was a man with a mother and a niece and at least one brother or sister.

Yet he didn't "get out much" and kept to himself. And despite his devout faith, he didn't pray.

"There's bread too. *Grossmammi* always packs him bread."

Avery didn't have to ask to know that Gideon ate by the grace of his mother. Because he didn't know how to cook? Or because he wouldn't eat at all unless someone provided the food to him?

That haunted look she had seen in his eyes had not been a trick of the lighting at all. He was haunted, maybe even heartbroken, over the death of his wife. He must have loved her very much.

Avery sighed. She wanted a love like that. Many times she thought she'd found it. But one thing always stood in her way: her father's money. Jack wasn't the first. There was Max who wanted money to start his own business. Justin had wanted money to fund his research trips to Africa, and Tyler had just wanted money.

She supposed it came with the territory, being born into the Forbes top twenty and all. But she was—had been—just romantic enough to believe that one day she would find that special someone who could see past the dollar signs and the zeros after her name and get to the real person.

She knew now that it would always be about the money.

Avery shook away those thoughts. Louie scampered into the house in front of them as they carried the food inside.

Mary Elizabeth went about putting things away. "I have cookies," she said, as if she harbored some dark and juicy secret. "They're supposed to be for *Onkel*, but I don't think *Grossmammi* would mind if we ate a couple. You can't accept guests without an offering of food. It's bad manners."

"Guests?"

Mary Elizabeth's dimples deepened. "I'm not really sure who's the guest in this particular situation, but," she paused, "I have cookies." Her eyes twinkled as she unwrapped a cloth. She did indeed have cookies. Delicious sugar cookies with just the right amount of orange-flavored icing.

And she knew how to make coffee on the wood-burning stove. Good coffee.

"Can I ask you something?" she asked Avery as they sat across the table from each other eating the last of the cookies they dared to sneak.

Mary Elizabeth chewed on her bottom lip, and Avery wasn't sure if she wanted to answer the question. "Sure."

"Why are you wearing my uncle's clothes?"

Avery let out a soundless sigh of relief. "I came kind of unex-pectedly, and I didn't pack very well." An understatement, but still true. "So your uncle loaned me these clothes until . . ." She really didn't have the rest of that so she waved her hand around a little and let her voice trail off, hoping it would satisfy the inquisitive girl.

"Can I ask you something else?" She leaned forward in her chair, but waited until Avery's nod before continuing. "Did you meet my uncle during his *rumspringa*?"

"I'm going to have to say no, because I don't even know what a rum spring is."

"*Rumspringa*. It's when Amish boys and girls go out and experience the world before they join the church."

"Then definitely, no."

Mary Elizabeth's eyebrows rose, and she sucked in a breath. "That's *your* car in the field! Isn't it!"

"Yes." Couldn't get much past her.

"But why didn't you go to town with *Onkel*?"

"Listen, Mary Elizabeth." Avery sat down her half-empty coffee mug and eyed the young girl. "I'm going to be staying with your uncle for a couple of weeks. I would appreciate it if you didn't tell anyone I'm here."

"But that would be lying."

"Not really. Not if no one *asked* you if your uncle has a visitor."

She seemed to mull that over. "*Dat* would still call that a lie. And you'll need a chaperone."

"We do not need a chaperone."

"Maybe *Dat* would let me come."

"You have school." Avery realized denying the need was not going to get her anywhere. Evidently the Amish had hang-ups—however noble and charming—about appearances. But there would be no need for worry, if Mary Elizabeth would just agree to keep quiet about the whole thing.

Mary Elizabeth pulled a face, typical teenager even in the Amish world. "Oh, I don't go to school anymore."

"You haven't graduated?"

Mary Elizabeth drew herself up to her tallest height as if that could counter her cherub face and innocent eyes. "I am fourteen."

"Oh." Avery didn't know how to respond. "And?"

"And I don't go to school anymore. My job now is to help my *dat* with the boys, and to cook and clean."

"And not go to school."

"I have passed the eighth grade and learned all I need to know."

*If only that were true for us all.*

Mary Elizabeth shook her head, a smile wiping away the tension on her face. "You *Englisch* are so funny. You go to school for years and years, but Amish go to school until the eighth grade. Then they go home and learn how to be Amish husbands and wives."

"And that's where you learn how to . . . ? Avery waved a hand toward the wood-burning stove.

"Make coffee?"

"Light the stove."

Mary Elizabeth nodded. "*Jah. Dat* taught me."

*Dat, dat, dat.* All the young girl ever mentioned was her father. Avery wasn't sure about Mary Elizabeth's mother, but after her blunder with Gideon the night before, she wasn't about to ask.

Avery pointed toward the stove. "Can you teach me how to light it?"

"You want to learn?"

"Of course."

"Then I'll teach you."

Mary Elizabeth, as it turned out, was a patient teacher. After the fifth try, Avery finally got the hang of it. Then Mary Elizabeth showed her how to put the grounds into the pot and boil the water to make the coffee. Avery sighed. Tomorrow morning she'd have fresh coffee. Even if she had to make it herself.

"Is this how you make coffee when you are at your home?"

Avery shook her head. "I don't usually make coffee, but I think there's an electric coffee maker."

"You *think*?"

"I don't go to the kitchen much. Our cook." Avery shuddered. "Mean, little Austrian woman. She makes a fine strudel, but don't dare set foot in the kitchen to try and get some for yourself."

Mary Elizabeth laughed, and suddenly stopped. "There is one person who lives with you and all she does is cook?"

Avery nodded.

"Do you have a really big family?"

"Just me and my father."

"And does your father eat a lot?"

Avery hid her smile before answering. "No more than average."

Mary Elizabeth seemed to mull that over. "Who does the cleaning?"

"The maids, I suppose." She'd never really given it much thought.

"And do they wash the clothes?"

"Yes." What didn't get taken to the cleaners.

"Katie Rose does most of our washing. But I help. She's my aunt."

Another Fisher sibling? "It's good that you help."

"I suppose, but—"

"But what?"

"Do you know how to cook?"

"No."

"Do the washing?"

"No."

"Can you iron?"

"No."

Mary Elizabeth sat back in her chair, the look on her face both horrified and fascinated. "How long did you attend school?"

"A long time," Avery answered, not wanting to give the details. She held two bachelor's degrees and a master's, but there were times when she'd never learn. She could speak three languages. She had charmed foreign diplomats and helped her father seal multi-million dollar deals, but none of that mattered here. She couldn't light a stove. Couldn't prepare a meal. What good was book learning in the Amish world?

"I don't think any education is wasted." Avery hated the defensive edge that had crept into in her voice.

Mary Elizabeth's expression turned wistful. "I guess not. But it is prideful."

Avery had never really thought about it that way, but to a certain point, education and what a person did with it was on the braggart side. Parents wanted doctors and lawyers for their sons and daughters, whether by learning or marriage. The average cocktail party greeting started with who you were and what you did for a living. Framed diplomas and class ranking . . . what did it matter here?

"I suppose," was all she could manage in reply. Instead she poured herself another cup of coffee, enjoying it all the more since she had made it.

"You're very pretty."

"Th-thank you." Mary Elizabeth's sweet comment caught her off guard. She didn't feel very pretty wearing Gideon's castoffs and no makeup.

Avery raised a hand to the matted mess atop her head. She had used a rag the night before and wiped at the blood and tangles, but she had been trying to figure out a way to really wash it. The bucket by the fireplace could only hold so much water. And since the snow had melted away, Gideon had stopped making a fire altogether.

"Mary Elizabeth," Avery started, almost ashamed of herself. She was supposed to be keeping her presence a secret, but she had shared cookies, learned how to light the stove and make coffee. Now she was about to ask for the biggest favor of them all. "Can you help me wash my hair?"

Surprise lit her angelic features. "Wash it?"

"It's just that the water is cold. I thought maybe I could heat some, and you could help me. You know, pour it and such."

"Oh, that's right. Uncle Gideon doesn't have a heating unit for his water."

"Heating unit? You mean that some Amish families have hot, running water?"

"Of course. We're not hillbilly. We're just Amish."

"And you have hot running water at your house?"

"*Jah*. And at *Grossmammi's* too. Most of the families around these parts have it."

"But electricity—"

"Isn't needed. We use windmills to pump the water to the house and propane to heat it." She shrugged as if to say, *It's as simple as that*.

"So how does your uncle heat his water?"

"I don't think he much cares." The statement was sweet and melancholy. "Not since . . . I'll help you. Wash your hair, *jah*. You light the stove, and I'll get a towel from the washroom."

In no time at all, Avery was bent over the sink while Mary Elizabeth poured the warm water over her head. She quickly cleaned her hair with the shampoo the young girl had brought in with the towel. Ramon, her hairdresser, would faint a thousand times over if he could see her now—discount shampoo, no conditioner, and rural water heated on a wood-burning stove. But her hair was clean and felt better than it had in days.

"The family that owned this house—before *Onkel* bought it—jumped the fence." Mary Elizabeth dried Avery's hair with the fresh-smelling, snow-white towel.

Avery frowned. "Whose fence? The one in the backyard?"

Mary Elizabeth laughed out loud, but Avery didn't see anything humorous.

"*Jumped the fence* means they left the community." Mary Elizabeth mopped her eyes with the tail end of her apron. "They turned Mennonite."

"You can do that?"

"*Jah*. Of course. Not many leave though. And fewer still join up. Most *Englischers* have a problem leaving their luxuries behind."

"What made them leave?"

"Well . . ." Mary Elizabeth paused. "It's a sin to gossip, but I heard that the missus had a hankerin' for a few of the finer things. Her husband tried to appease her, but she had a sister who turned Mennonite, and she wanted what her sister had. He built her a bathroom and got running water to the house, but she convinced him to leave before he could do much else. I heard tell they live in Missouri now."

"And your uncle bought this farm from them?"

"After he sold . . ." She paused. "Maybe we should give your puppy a treat."

"Louie V. is spoiled enough." Avery folded a crease in her pants, mulling over ways to turn the conversation back to Gideon and the house.

"Louie V. is a cute name, but odd."

"He's named after . . ." Confessing her dog carried the name of her favorite designer seemed shallow and superficial, even for a socialite from sin-city Dallas. Avery shook her head. "Never mind."

"I should go." Mary Elizabeth gathered up their coffee mugs and took them to the sink.

Avery had a feeling the young girl was doing her best to steer the conversation away from her uncle and the farm. She followed after her. "What's your hurry?"

At the sound of Gideon's voice, they both whirled around.

# 4

The last thing Gideon expected to see when he returned home from town was Mary Elizabeth's bicycle parked out in front of his house. That wasn't entirely true—it was the second to last thing. The actual last thing was his houseguest in the kitchen swapping stories with his niece.

He'd known he wouldn't be able to keep her presence a secret for long, but he thought for sure and for certain it would be more than a day and a half.

"*Onkel.*"

"Gideon."

Gideon tipped his head without making eye contact with either one of them. "Mary Elizabeth. Miss Hamilton." He could barely look at his guest. Mary Elizabeth must've helped wash her hair. It looked silkier and darker than it had this morning and the kitchen smelled like apple shampoo. And fresh coffee. Both aromas were nearly irresistible.

"*Kaffi* smells *gut*." He waved toward the stove.

Mary Elizabeth fell over herself trying to fetch a mug and fill it with the hot brew.

"I didn't know you liked coffee," his houseguest said.

There was a lot about him that she didn't know. Like the fact that every time he closed his eyes last night, her image swam to the front of his mind.

Gideon tried to act as if nothing was amiss as he set the bags down on the floor next to the table and pulled out a chair. But he didn't feel easy. He was *naerfich*, like a skittish horse.

Looking from one of them to the other, he took a sip. Caffeine surely wasn't going to help, but he hadn't had a cup of coffee in so long he'd almost forgotten what it tasted like.

"I-I was just leaving." Mary Elizabeth tied the strings of her *kapp* under her chin, like *that* was going to make up for her staying longer than she should have. She glanced from him to Miss Hamilton. "*Grossmammi* made you some roasted chicken. And some bread."

"And some cookies." Miss Hamilton held one up for him to see.

They acted skittish, like he was going to bite their heads off. That in itself made him wonder what they had been up to all afternoon—besides hair washing.

"Speaking of cookies." He bent down and retrieved one of the bags. "This one has the things you asked for. You might want to put the yogurt in the refrigerator. Mr. Anderson packed it in a brown paper sack with some ice, but it won't stay fresh for long."

"How clever."

"Oh, they always do that," Mary Elizabeth chimed in. "It takes a little while to get home in a horse and buggy, so we have to find ways to keep the perishables fresh. *Grossmammi* takes a ice chest and—"

"That's enough, Mary Elizabeth. Miss Hamilton didn't come here for lessons on Plain living. She's not interested in such things."

"Actually, I'm very interested. Don't you have an ice chest, Gideon?"

He didn't remember giving her permission to use his Christian name and yet it rolled off her tongue like honey. "No." Thankfully, she let the subject drop and instead retrieved her yogurt and placed it in the refrigerator. She looked at the cookies as if she had changed her mind about them, then set the unopened package next to the bread box.

"I guess I should be going now. *Dat* wanted me to till up the vegetable garden today." Mary Elizabeth made a face that let Gideon know exactly how she felt about growing vegetables. *Poor child.* The older she got, more and more was expected of her. Even with Katie Rose there to help, Gideon knew that taking care of Gabriel and the five boys had to be an overwhelming task.

He walked Mary Elizabeth to the door, Miss Hamilton beside him every step. On the porch, his niece hugged his houseguest as if they were longtime friends. Then she hopped on her bike, gave them both a wave, and pedaled toward the road.

It would do no good to ask her not to tell her father about Miss Hamilton, but he could only hope she didn't rush home and spill it first thing. Maybe he'd have a couple of days before he had to explain why he had an *Englischer* living in his house, when he didn't exactly know why himself.

It was after six by the time Gideon finished brushing down Molly and tossing out some fresh hay for the barn animals. He couldn't put it off any longer. It was time to go inside. Find some supper.

Check on his houseguest.

Gideon scooped up some food for the pure-blood rat she called a pet and walked to the house with the tiny beast trotting along beside him.

He hesitated on the front porch, trying to decide whether to knock or just go in. It was his house, so he turned the knob without warning and went on inside.

The front room looked much as it did every day, except there was a woman in it. A violet-eyed, almost-pixie curled up on his couch fast asleep. She looked peaceful lying there, beautiful in her own *Englisch* way. She was a strange mix of her world and his with her too-short hair and his old clothes. Gideon resisted the urge to wake her. Instead, he fed her dog, then went to the kitchen.

Mary Elizabeth said that she had brought roasted chicken, and she had. No one made the dish like his *mudder*. Gideon pulled the meat from the bones and piled it, white and dark alike, on a plate. There were potatoes and carrots, too, and a fresh loaf of sourdough. He sliced the bread and arranged it on a plate. Then he poured them some milk and set everything on the table.

That's when he noticed it. The front room was clean. Well, at least cleaner than it had been this morning. The mantel gleamed in the waning sunlight from the kitchen window. The floor had been swept, the rugs shaken out, and the china hutch dusted. The place hadn't looked this good since he'd moved in.

No wonder she was asleep. She had been bee-busy this afternoon.

He debated with himself whether he should let her sleep or wake her up. She was his guest, and he couldn't rightly sit down at the table and leave her to fend for herself.

*But she looked so peaceful.* He stood over her and stretched a hand toward the soft, dark hair that gently curled against the nape of her neck. Then he thought better of it and nudged her shoulder.

She jumped as if she'd been poked with a prod, and jackknifed into a sitting position. "What time is it?" She rubbed her eyes and yawned.

"Suppertime."

"I must have dozed off."

"Come eat," he said, and turned back toward the table.

They ate in silence. To Gideon, the food tasted better than it had in months, but he wouldn't let himself believe it had anything to do with the dark-haired woman sitting across from him. No, the food tasted so good because of the physical exercise he'd done that afternoon. Mucking out the stalls and spreading clean, fresh hay all around on the barn floor. If he was going to sleep in the barn, the very least he could do for himself was to tidy it up. He supposed it was good for a body to move around and work. Just like his pampered companion.

He ducked his head over his plate, then cut his gaze back up to her. She looked dead on her feet despite her afternoon nap. She wasn't used to such physical chores.

"Room looks nice." His voice sounded gruff even to his own ears.

"Thanks. The dusting gave me a headache. I must be allergic."

"You want some more of Sister Clara's tea?"

She shook her head. "Some Tylenol should help."

He scraped up the last bite off his plate and walked to the sink.

Side by side they washed the dishes, dried them, and put them away.

She poured herself a glass of water while he fetched the headache pills.

A long moment stretched between them as he watched her down the Tylenol. She rinsed out her glass and placed it on the drain board.

"I guess I'll wash up before bed."

He braced one hip against the table and watched as she took out a big pot, filled it with water, and lit the stove to heat it. She looked as if she had been doing it her whole life. If not for her clothes and hair, she would have looked like any other Amish woman.

Well, maybe not *any*.

There was something special about Avery Ann Hamilton. Could the people in her life see it too? Maybe not. Maybe that's why she wanted to stay with him and hide out on his farm.

She looked at him expectantly.

He hastily straightened up and cleared his throat. "I think I will too. Clean up. Before bed." He stumbled over his words like a tongue-tied schoolboy. He was tired. That was all.

"'Night," he said.

"Good night."

She was yawning heartily when Gideon headed for the barn.

The sun was barely above the tree line when Gabriel pulled his buggy to a stop in front of his brother's house. He hadn't believed his ears yesterday afternoon when he'd come in from the fields and heard Mary Elizabeth telling Katie Rose about Gideon's houseguest. An *Englischer* woman running 'round in barn door trousers and a man's shirt? It was too unbelievable, but Mary Elizabeth knew better than to lie. That meant one of two things: either Gideon had completely lost his mind, or Gabriel's level-headed daughter had.

He said a silent prayer for his brother, for there she was, sitting on the porch as if she belonged there. She had her bare feet propped up on the railing and a little dog at the base of her chair.

She stood as he got down and gathered the reins to lead his

horses toward the watering trough. But they were both spared comment as Gideon came out of the barn.

Gabriel tried his best to hide his shock. Gideon had gone and done the unthinkable. He had shaved his beard.

"Brother!" Gideon called, but sheer surprise kept Gabriel's own words from leaving his mouth.

Gabriel cast a sidelong glance at the woman, then grasped his brother around the arm and pulled him to one side.

"*Ach*, man. What are you doin'?" He continued before Gideon could open his mouth to reply. "I come to your house after hearin' tales that you have a woman livin' here, an *Englisch* woman, and I find that it is true. And your beard!"

Gideon's arm twitched, no doubt a knee-jerk reaction to his words, resisting the urge to run a hand across his smooth-shaven face.

Gabriel watched his brother's eyes, so much like his own, cloud with misery, then harden with resolve. "I do not deserve to wear a beard."

"The bishop is not goin' to allow this."

"Then shun me."

"It may come to that, brother."

He had hoped his words would shock some sense into Gideon, but he just looked away.

Gabriel would have to say an extra prayer for Gideon tonight. He needed more than God's guidance, he needed God's intervention.

"I don't want that," Gabriel said, "I just want—"

"Everythin' to go back like it was before. It can never be that again."

Gabriel's stomach dropped at the pain and grief etched across his brother's face. He and Gideon had been so close growing up, nearly inseparable. Best friends as well as siblings. But Miriam and Jamie's deaths had changed all of that. His brother's body was still standing there, for the most part he looked the same. But his heart was missing.

Gabriel understood. He was a widower himself, but he and his Rebecca had been blessed with five fine sons and the most faithful daughter a man could ask for. They alone had kept him from going out of his mind when he lost his wife. Gideon didn't have that kind of support. It was as if his soul had died with his family and all that was left was an empty shell of a body that walked and talked but no longer really lived.

And now this *Englischer*!

He glanced toward the porch. "How did she get here?"

"Miss Hamilton?"

"Is that her name?"

"*Jah*. She wrecked her fancy car in that big snowstorm. I helped her out of the cold."

"She's been here for *four* days?"

Gideon's eyes narrowed. "What are you tryin' to say, Gabe?"

"I'm worried about you, brother."

"Worry is a waste of time."

"I think I have good reason." He nodded back to the *Englischer*. Anyone could tell that she came from a different world. Privilege rolled off her in waves. Why she wanted to stay on an Amish farm was anybody's guess, but Gabriel couldn't help but be protective, if not suspicious. "She doesn't belong here."

"That may be, but I've invited her to stay."

"You *what*? It is not enough that you . . ." he stopped, unable to form the words. He knew Gideon was hurting, but the good Lord said there was a time for everything. Time for healing had come, but his *bruder* seemed to be sliding further down the slippery path of grief instead of pulling himself up from its depths. "I don't think that's a good idea."

Gideon shrugged.

"So be it." Gabriel tamped down his protests. This was far from over.

"Did you come here for a reason, Gabriel?"

"I came to see if it was true." He nodded again toward the *Englischer*.

Gideon nodded in return. "*Jah.*"

"Simon has a little more time on his hands now that school is almost out for the summer. He can come help you plant."

"*Nay.*"

"You need to put somethin' in the ground, *bruder*. All this land layin' fallow."

Gideon shook his head.

How many times had they had this conversation over the last month? Gabriel had lost count. He loved his brother, so much that he couldn't allow him to go to waste. But nothing he said to Gideon made him change his mind about living again.

Maybe he should send Simon on over and see if Gideon could refuse his nephew. It was underhanded, but a man had to do what a man had to do if it meant saving the life of one near.

So for now he'd let it drop, but soon, really soon . . .

Avery couldn't take it anymore. To her best guess, the brooding man standing in Gideon's driveway had to be his brother. The two were nearly identical in appearance, but whereas Gideon had a mournful expression, his brother wore a permanent scowl. Or maybe it was just for her. She had seen him glance back toward her several times. Although she couldn't hear their words, she didn't need a slide rule to figure out they were talking about her.

She had almost gone over and introduced herself a couple of times, but thought better of it. The other Fisher looked like a big bully, holding Gideon's arm and glaring at her.

Instead she decided to wait until she and Gideon were alone, then she would offer to leave. It seemed her presence here was not sitting well with his family.

Oh, well, there was always Aruba.

Yet she had grown to like the quiet here. It was a different kind of peaceful, serene and steady. She heard the moo of Gideon's cow coming from the barn, and smiled. Maybe not so quiet, but the sounds were gentle and comforting.

Even if she felt there was more she should be doing to help Gideon. Maybe it was the mournful look in his eyes or the sluggishness of his footsteps, a delay that seemed to say he would rather be in someone else's shoes.

But helping him seemed like a moot point after the looks his brother had given her. If she had to guess, Avery would say that the other Fisher did not approve of her being there. Not one bit.

The last thing she wanted to do was cause problems for the kind man who pulled her in from the snow.

Avery settled back in the chair as Louie scampered down the porch steps to flop at Gideon's feet. She still couldn't hear what Gideon and his brother talked about, but at least the topic of conversation had turned from her to something else. Something that kept the other Fisher from shooting death stares her way.

She watched the two men for a few more minutes, then Gideon's brother hopped in his buggy. With a tip of his flat-brimmed straw hat, he set the horses in motion in the opposite direction.

Gideon turned slowly as his visitor disappeared, then walked back and climbed the steps to stand on the porch next to her.

"That's Gabriel. My brother." He braced his hands on his hips.

"I could see the resemblance."

Gideon nodded. "He—"

"Doesn't approve of me being here."

He shrugged, but the rigid set of his jaw belied his uncaring attitude. "It's not his farm." Then he walked into the house without another word.

Avery stood and followed him inside.

Louie ran over to get a drink of water as soon as the screen door slammed behind them. "I can leave," she said, addressing the Y-strap of his suspenders and the broad expanse of his shoulders. He stood facing the window that looked out over the backyard.

She didn't want to go home, but neither did she want to be the cause of problems between Gideon and his family. "I'll leave tomorrow. If you'll take me to town."

"You don't have to leave."

"I think I should."

"I want you to stay." He spoke the words so softly she almost didn't hear them at all. Then he yanked open the back door without a glance her way, and disappeared into the sunshine.

Avery was surprised when Gideon showed up to eat supper with her. She was rummaging around in the refrigerator when he knocked on the front door and let himself in the house. Without a word, he hung his hat on the peg inside, and gave a scoop of dog food to Louie before making his way to the sink to wash up.

Avery set the containers of food on the table, and they ate in a companionable if not stilted silence. It seemed like he had something on his mind. Something weighing heavily.

She had just taken the last bite of her chicken when Gideon pushed his plate aside. "I'm goin' to town in the mornin'."

She looked at him, realizing her time on the farm had come to an end. "I'll get my stuff together." Maybe from Clover Ridge she could rent a car to take her to the airport in Tulsa. Surely she'd be halfway to Aruba before her father realized she wasn't already there.

But Gideon shook his head. "I told you before that you don't have to leave. I just wanted you to know where I was goin' in case . . ."

She had thought he was going to say in case she was worried about him. But that would be too familiar.

"I'm goin' to town," he repeated. "To get some seeds to plant."

Avery couldn't stop the frown that wrinkled her brow. "Okay, then." Maybe Gideon just needed to hear the words. "I'll be here when you get back."

Gideon spent the next afternoon—like he had the one before—avoiding Miss Hamilton. Something about her unsettled him, made his stomach light, and his hands tremble. He had said he wanted her to stay, not realizing until he said the words that he meant them. He *did* want her to stay. And that was the very reason to avoid her.

But unlike the afternoon before, he plowed while waiting for the sun to go down.

He'd had no intention of growing anything this year—or ever—but she was in his house, sitting on his porch in his own favorite spot. A man could only stay in the barn so long before he needed a change of scenery, and Molly and Kate seemed eager for the exercise. Even after the spur-of-the-moment trip into town, the mares were more than willing to pull the plow through the soft earth. The snow had made the ground easy to turn. Moisture-rich, black earth just waiting for seeds.

Corn. He'd plant corn. He'd never been much of a farmer. He'd grown hay and alfalfa for feed. Miriam had planted vegetables and flowers like all Amish wives. The bulk of their money had come from the sheep, but after the accident, he'd sold them all. He couldn't bear to take care of them. Never would again. For months he had wanted nothing more than to join his family on the other side, but if he wasn't going to die, he might as well farm.

Gideon pulled off his hat and dragged his sleeve across his forehead. Louie dropped to his haunches, tongue lolling as he waited for Gideon to continue. The tiny beast had been his constant companion in the fields, running alongside him, romping through the fresh earth and snapping at bugs. The sight of the pampered dog going country made Gideon smile.

It was a fine day for plowing. The sun was hot but not unmerciful. The sky was blue, and the Oklahoma wind blew just enough to keep things cool. Gideon lifted his face toward the sun and closed his eyes.

Yes, a fine day for plowing. He slapped his hat against his leg, placed it back on his head, and clicked his tongue to start the horses again.

Gabriel pulled his wagon in front of Gideon's house the following afternoon. The Lord had led him here—that was his only excuse. Simon sat next to him chattering away about things only a ten-year-old boy could recount. Maybe with Simon there, Gideon wouldn't be so quick to say *nay* about planting and such.

"Is that her?" Simon pointed to the dark-haired *Englischer* kneeling in the overgrown garden at the side of the house.

"*Jah.*"

She was still there, this *Englischer*, bent over in the strawberry patch, yanking out what looked to be perfectly good plants. She grabbed hold of another one, ripped it from the earth, and tossed it over her shoulder.

"Oi!" She spun around evidently so engrossed in her task that she didn't hear them pull up. "Where's Gideon?" he said without preamble. She didn't belong here, and he wasn't about to act like she did.

The bright sun glinted off her dark, dark hair as she turned and waved toward the field across the road from the house. "Plowing."

Gabriel squinted and sure enough he could make out man and horses. He'd been trying to get his brother to grow something— anything—for nigh on a month to no response. But there he was finally taking an interest in life again.

He raised his hand in greeting. *God is good*. What a difference a day made. Gabriel wanted to believe he was the reason his brother had finally decided to plant, but he feared it had more to do with the woman who had invaded their midst.

Gideon waved back, then started across the field toward them. The *Englisch* woman stood watching his brother as he crossed the road and headed across the yard.

"*Onkel*," Simon waved his arm up high in the air, then typical of his hyper, ten-year-old nature, started chasing one of the dogs around the yard.

The little pup that had been sitting at the woman's feet yesterday joined in the romp, yapping and running, its pink tongue hanging out the side of its mouth.

"It's a fine day for plowin'," Gabriel said when Gideon got close enough to hear.

"*Jah*. That it is." He slipped his hat from his head and ran his sleeve across his sweaty forehead.

"We're goin' over to Bishop Riehl's service on Sunday. *Mamm* was hopin' you would come along with us." He had promised their mother he'd ask Gideon, and either one of them would do anything for Ruth Fisher.

But Gabriel couldn't imagine his younger brother showing

up for the church service barefaced. It was just too shameful. Or maybe that's what he needed. To be shamed into knowing that God was in charge and only He was all powerful. If only Gideon could understand that Miriam and Jamie's deaths were part of God's will, that God had different plans for Gideon. It was a hard lesson. And painfully humbling for a man, but necessary all the same. He had done it when Rebecca had died giving birth to Samuel. Why couldn't Gideon?

Gideon shook his head. "I don't think so."

Gabriel stared at his brother a good long time before changing the subject. "Your roof needs some repairs."

"It's held up this long."

"*Jah*, but when the spring winds come, it won't." As if to reinforce his words, the air stirred strands of his hair close to his collar. "Matthew, Simon, David, and me, we're all goin' over to Hester Stoltzfus's place next Saturday. She needs a new roof. We'll come do yours the week after."

Gideon nodded.

"She doesn't belong here." Gabriel couldn't stop the words. "Look what she's doin' to your strawberry patch."

She had returned to pulling up the strawberry plants, discarding them like weeds. Thankfully she hadn't come over to join their conversation. *Smart woman on that aspect, even if she couldn't garden.* Gabriel didn't think he could handle that kind of familiarity with her.

His brother didn't even turn to look at her. "I don't like strawberries much anyways."

"You're vulnerable right now. You need to *geb acht*." Be careful.

"It's not your concern."

Gabriel glanced back toward the *Englischer*. "You're my *bruder*. Of course, I'm concerned."

"Help me plant my corn or leave."

Gabriel shrank back, unable to believe what he heard.

"It's my farm, and I've invited her to stay."

"I think you're makin' a big mistake."

"So you've said." He nodded toward Simon. "Grab the *bu* and a bag of seeds, brother, and I'll return the favor come harvest time."

Avery seized another weed, and felt her fingernail scrape against a rock. "Ow!" She jerked her hand back and studied the damage. Broken straight across, but not salvageable. And it had only been a week since she'd had them filled. Normally, she would have dropped everything and hurried to the spa to have it fixed. She couldn't stand the thought of ragged nails, but she was miles from the nearest salon.

She sighed as she splayed dirty hands in front of her. They looked terrible, but she was pretty certain no one in Amish country cared about the state of her fingernails. Probably for the best. With all the crazy chores she had been doing around Gideon's farm, it wouldn't take long before they were all in this shape anyway.

Still, she'd spent too many years parading around with all eyes on her not to care how her hands looked. Surely Gideon had clippers. She could trim them down and at least make them presentable. When she returned to Dallas, she'd buy a whole new set.

She only wore them because she bit her real nails down to the quick. Her father considered it a sign of weakness, so she hid it from him and everyone else with a thin layer of pink and white acrylic.

Funny thing, but out here she no longer had the urge to chew her nails.

Nor did she have the responsibilities she had at home. There were no children with cancer who needed a new hospital wing, no benefit dinner for high-risk teenagers, and no walk for a cure. No eyes watched to make sure she looked and acted her best, and raised enough money to wow the press.

Gideon hadn't asked her to help with the garden, or clean his house, or any of the other things she had done to repay him for his kindness. Nor would he. Even though her being at his farm did not sit well with his brother—it was obvious Gideon had a problem with her as well. She wasn't about to worry about it now. In a couple of weeks, she would be on her way back to Dallas.

Nails or no, she would do what she could to help. And when the time came for her to go home, she could hold her head high and say that she had given as good as she got.

Gabriel's words were still ringing in Gideon's ears at suppertime. *Ach*, but he didn't want to hear his brother say again that she didn't belong here. He knew that. She knew that. What was the harm in being neighborly and allowing her the time she had asked for?

She was only staying for a few more days. Monday, maybe Tuesday, he'd take her into town and get on with his life.

Still, his brother's echoing voice made him surly. Or maybe it was sitting across the table from her that had him on edge.

He'd thought by giving her some clothes to wear that she wouldn't stand out so much, but all it did was make her stand out more. His clothes were much more modest than her sparkly little *frack*, but he hated seeing her in them. She looked ridiculous, small and fragile. Like a bird pushed out of its nest too soon.

Now he was the one being ridiculous. She was an adult. She had a father who was worried about her. Maybe a suitor. Pretty thing like her had to have beaus vying for her hand.

His stomach pitched, and he took a quick sip of milk to steady it.

He stole a glance at her as she ate. Back in her world, she probably had all kinds of clothes to wear. Yet she seemed to like it on his farm.

She looked up at him, their gazes connecting. "I don't know how you live like this."

Her words cut like a knife—even though they shouldn't have. It didn't matter what she thought about his way of life, because all too soon she would head back to her reality. Maybe she'd be going home sooner than he'd thought. But he still couldn't account for his anger.

"I'm Amish, Miss Hamilton." He tossed his napkin on top of his half-eaten *natchess*. "This is how we live. We don't have electricity and fancy clothes and cars. We're simple people."

She eyed him as if he'd sprouted another head. "Like *this*." She waved a hand over the table. From where he was sitting all he could see was a platter of cold chicken and his mother's homemade loaf of sourdough. "You've been out planting all day in the hot sun, working so hard. Then you come in after all that and eat a sandwich?"

Gideon shrugged, trying not to feel the relief flowing through him. "It's enough."

"And will you stop calling me Miss Hamilton? That's what the headmistress called me at school when I was trouble. Quite frankly, I don't like it."

"Then what should I call you?"

"Avery."

"No." He hated her name. It didn't suit her at all. "It doesn't matter," he said. "You'll go home in a few days anyway."

She paused, staring at him. "Yes." Then she looked away.

Gideon tried not to be touched that she cared enough about him to worry over what kind of food he ate, but he didn't understand why she cared. Especially since he didn't. Food was just the means to get through another day. What he ate was of no concern. Or when. In fact, he'd eaten more since she had been on his farm than he had all of the week before.

"Come." He stood and grabbed up his plate. "I'll help you with the dishes."

"I can do them. You were out in the sun all day."

"And so were you."

"I weeded the garden." She took his plate from him. "You plowed a field."

"An acre," he corrected.

She smiled, the curve of her lips lighting up her face. She had a tinge of pink on her cheeks from her "weeding." He tried not to notice how becoming it was.

"My point exactly. Now, shoo." She waved him toward the door. "Go smoke your pipe. I've got this."

"But I don't—"

"Smoke? Uh-huh. Then go out to the barn and do barn things. I'll do the dishes."

Gideon started to protest again, but changed his mind. With a smile on his face, he headed out the door.

Avery ran the warm, wet sponge across her neck and down one arm. It felt so good to wash the dirt of the day from her body. Like starting over. She dipped the sponge again, treating her other arm and the nape of her neck. Droplets raced down her back and fell onto the towel under her feet.

How she would love to soak in the big claw-foot tub, but this was good enough. Cleansing.

Tomorrow she would figure out a way to wash her hair again. It didn't need such constant attention since she hadn't put so many hair-care products in it. But it still needed to be washed in the worst way.

She toweled herself dry then padded into the bedroom, Louie right behind her. An oil lamp burned with a golden glow, soft and comforting.

She had decided to take Gideon up on his offer of the bed. Since he was sleeping in the barn, there was no sense in both of them being uncomfortable.

She shrugged on the clean shirt she had found in the closet earlier. This one, too, a beautiful blue. It was forward, she knew, to go digging around in someone else's things, but no way could she wash herself clean and then put back on the shirt she'd worn all day.

She pulled back the covers and crawled beneath the sheets, cool, crisp, and smelling like sunshine. And Gideon. That alone brought a smile to her face as she extinguished the lamp the way he had shown her and settled down for the night. Louie V. snuggled up next to her and gave her hand a loving lick.

All in all, it had been a good day. She had weeded most of one garden and tomorrow she would start on the other. If it didn't take her too long, maybe she'd have time left over to give Louie a bath. She was fairly certain there wasn't a doggie spa within fifty miles, and her pampered pooch was starting to smell like a dog.

$\sim\!\!\otimes$ 5

Every muscle in her body protested as Avery dragged herself upright the following morning. Weeding and cleaning were a better workout than she had ever gotten from her personal trainer. It was a good sore, the kind that came from accomplishment.

She pulled up the quilts and folded them across the foot of the couch. Sometime around 2:00 a.m. she had given up trying to sleep in the bed and wandered back to the couch. There was just something too familiar about lying where Gideon slept. It made her uncomfortable and unable to sleep. Now the clock read half past nine.

Usually up and about very early, Gideon was nowhere to be found. As tired as she had been when she finally drifted off to sleep, he could have easily come into the house, gotten his breakfast, and left again without disturbing her one bit.

*That must be what happened.* Avery pulled on her borrowed pants and headed for the kitchen to make coffee. She took a mug from the cupboard and turned to find Gideon stepping into the house, his eyes bright, as if he'd been awake for hours. He carried a plastic sack in one hand and a piece of paper in the other.

"'Mornin'." He hung his hat on its peg. "I take it you didn't get my note." He handed her a piece of paper that had been taped up somewhere. "I had to go to town for a few things. I didn't want to disturb you."

*Town again?* Mary Elizabeth would be impressed.

"Coffee's ready." She pulled down a mug for him and filled it with the hot brew. "Have you eaten?"

"At my brother's."

Avery nodded. She was starving. Must be from all that work she did yesterday. Normally she would have a carton of yogurt and call it good, but not today.

She rose from the table and poured herself a bowl of milk and added in the granola mixture she had been eating for the last couple of days. It was delicious and filling, and she would need all the energy she could muster to tackle the other garden plot this morning. She still wished she had some eggs, maybe some bacon or ham. Turned out Amish life required a lot more fuel than city life. This would have to do for now.

"Your brother doesn't like me," she said once she had returned to the table with her breakfast.

"It's not that."

"Okay, I'll be fair." She dug her spoon into the cereal. "He doesn't like that I'm here."

"It's not his house." Gideon took a sip of his coffee, but refused to meet her gaze.

Honestly, the man could be so stubborn. "Gideon, I don't want to cause problems between you and your family."

"You're not."

"I'm enjoying my time here. I don't want to leave, but I will."

Gideon shook his head. "You don't have to leave. I invited you to stay, and I'll stand by my promise. But I do need somethin' from you."

At the seriousness in his voice, Avery's heart gave a hard pound. "Of course." *Anything* was on the tip of her tongue, but she bit it back.

"As you know I've planted corn, and corn brings crows."

She hadn't really thought about it, but that sounded logical enough.

"When you have crows, you need a scarecrow."

She raised one brow in question. "And how do I play a part in this?"

"I need back those clothes."

He grimaced, and Avery still wasn't certain as to where this conversation was going. She supposed she'd look a little odd planting vegetables in a cocktail dress, but she had spent half her life wearing one, and it hadn't slowed her down yet. The shoes on the other hand . . .

"O-kay."

"You can wear this instead." He handed her the sack.

Avery was almost afraid to look inside.

"There's a *frack* in there. One of Mary Elizabeth's old ones. Katie Rose is just too tall. And when I told them what I needed, they insisted we go into town to the general store and pick up a few more . . . personal items." He cleared his throat, and Avery looked up to see the faint tinge of pink rise to his cheeks.

How refreshing to find a man who wasn't so bold that a package of women's panties could make him blush.

"Just while you're here," he added. "I know it's not exactly what you're used to, but—"

"They're perfect." Any other man she would have hugged in thanks, perhaps given a quick peck on the cheek, but that didn't seem the right way to show her appreciation to Gideon. She would just have to find other means to show what his gesture meant to her. "I'll be right back."

She fairly ran to the bedroom and dumped the contents out onto the bed. In addition to the dress, there was also some kind of an apron, what looked like a cape, and a few other things, but Avery had no idea how to work them. Instead she concentrated on the items she understood.

The dress was a pale shade of blue, almost lavender. It had snaps in front that were hidden from view, and a narrow waist band. A far cry from the labels she was accustomed to wearing, but beggars and choosers . . .

She pulled it over her head, enjoying the fresh scent of clothing dried outdoors. The sleeves settled below her elbows, the hem a few inches below her knees. Serviceable, if not a little big around the waist, but a much better fit than Gideon's castoffs. Still, she hadn't worn something so modest since elementary school.

He hadn't bought her a bra, though, which was probably just as well. An item that familiar might have given him a heart attack.

Avery couldn't help but smile. He was so different than the men she had known in her life. So unassuming. He wanted nothing from her, and yet he gave. He had opened his home to her—though she knew at first he had thought it a mistake. That's why she was trying so hard to help. It just seemed the right thing to do.

She had been washing out her undergarments every night in the sink, so a new pair of panties felt downright heavenly. Maybe the fact that he had given her some clothes to wear meant that he was willing to let her stay a little longer than he had originally planned.

She ran her fingers through her hair to fluff it back in place, scooped up his clothes, and headed back to the front room, a smile on her face.

"What do you think?"

Gideon blinked once, then nodded. But no smile. He grunted out some sort of response, snatched up his clothes, and scuttled to the door, muttering about scarecrows as he went.

~⊙ ⊙~

Gideon didn't show up for lunch . . . dinner, but Mary Elizabeth did.

She breezed in, that big cherub smile on her face. "Wow! Look at you. *Dat* wouldn't let me come yesterday."

"I'm glad you came today."

"Do you like the *frack?*"

"I do. Thank you." The garment was comfortable, and she was pleasantly surprised to discover how easy it was to get around in.

"*Danki.*"

"I beg your pardon?"

"We say *danki*. That's thank you."

"Well then, *danki*, Mary Elizabeth. I like the dress very much. Would you like some lunch, er, dinner?"

The girl nodded enthusiastically, and before long, the two of them had the table all set with leftover chicken made into sandwiches and cold roasted potatoes.

Avery looked at Gideon's empty chair. She had set him a place at the table, hoping he'd come in from whatever he was doing and eat.

"He's at my house," Mary Elizabeth said, taking another bite. "You know what this needs? Applesauce." She got up and rummaged around in the refrigerator. "Ah-ha." She turned around with an unmarked jar. "Have some." She scooped a big helping onto her own plate, then gave Avery's the same treatment.

Avery had never been one for applesauce, but she hadn't been given the choice—it appeared that life with Mary Elizabeth was like that—and tried it anyway. "It's delicious."

Mary Elizabeth smiled. "Aaron's Rachel's Sarah made it."

"Aaron Rachel Sarah . . . that's an interesting name."

Mary Elizabeth laughed out loud. "Her name is just Sarah, but the Amish like certain names more than others, and we tend to use them a lot. Sometimes it's easier to refer to someone by other people in the family. Aaron is her *grossdaadi*, or grandfather, and Rachel is her *mamm*. Her given name is Sarah. So she's known as Aaron's Rachel's Sarah."

"Well, she makes good applesauce." She took another bite, then eyed the younger girl thoughtfully. "Do they call you Gabriel's Mary Elizabeth?"

"No. There's not another here named Mary Elizabeth. And so I'm always known as that. But I wish . . ." She looked down at her plate. "Never mind."

"You wish what?"

"I wish I could be called something different."

"Like?"

She took a deep breath and held it. "Lizzie."

"And no one will call you that?"

"*Dat* won't allow it. My mother named me, and she's gone now."

"She named you after herself?"

"No, but she liked my name just like it is." Mary Elizabeth grimaced. "I miss her, but I wish I could be called something else."

"Then you shall. At least around here anyway."

That seemed to brighten the child back to her normal sunshiny disposition.

"It looks like *Onkel* has been planting."

Avery nodded.

"That is *wunderful-gut*."

"He is a farmer."

Lizzie gave her a strange look. "He has never planted more

than he needed to care for his sheep and barn animals. But once, I mean, he sold them. No one knew what he would do this year. I overheard *Dat* and *Grossdaadi* talking. They were worried that *Onkel* had not planted anything this year. Not even hay for the cows and horses."

"He planted corn."

"That is *gut*," she said again.

"He's been very working hard."

"*Jah.*"

*Too hard to come in from the fields and eat cold leftovers every night.* She had it! The perfect way to show her appreciation to Gideon for all that he had done for her.

"M-Lizzie, could you help me cook something?"

The young girl dimpled at the sound of her new nickname. "Are you still hungry?"

Avery hid her smile and shook her head. "For your uncle. For supper."

Her eyebrows rose. "I have a little time before I have to go back home."

"I want to surprise him. He's been so kind to me, and I'd like to say thanks."

Lizzie smiled. "Then you will. I'll show you how to make his favorite—chicken pot pie. He'll be so shocked!"

Gideon had nothing in his pantry, so Lizzie left to get the ingredients for the meal. Once she returned, she showed Avery how to boil the chicken and pull it from the bone, peel the vegetables, and roll out the dough that would eventually become noodle-like.

And then she left. Lizzie had been gone from home all afternoon. Surely she would be in trouble if she stayed away from her chores for much longer.

Avery ran the back of her hand over her brow. Who knew rolling out dough could be so strenuous? No wonder the Amish ate such hardy meals filled with lard and butter and all the fat the rest of the world avoided. They burned up the calories just trying to cook the stuff!

And that's just what Gideon deserved—a meal that would stick to his ribs.

Amish chicken pot pie, it turned out, looked nothing like pie. Instead it was more like the chicken and dumplings Avery had eaten once in Georgia. The part about the pot was correct, but it didn't seem right to give him just the one dish. So as it bubbled on the stove top, Avery dug around for some side dishes to accompany it. She found the applesauce that she and Mary Elizabeth had eaten that afternoon along with a jar of homemade pickles and another jar containing something called peach chow-chow. Once she sliced the last of the sourdough bread, they would have themselves a fabulous meal!

Gideon was bone weary by the time he finished brushing down Molly and Kate from their trip to Gabriel's. It was a *gut* way to be. The exercise had done him right, though he didn't really want to admit it. As tired as he was, he felt better than he had in days.

He tried not to smile as he remembered pulling up and Miss Hamilton running out onto the porch to tell him that they were having "something special" for supper. But the sight of her in that pale purple dress made him grin in spite of himself.

He'd tried all day to forget how the color had made her eyes seem bigger and more like gumdrops than ever before. And that her hair seemed darker and silkier than it had yesterday just after she had rinsed it clean. Even if it was too short.

He pushed the image from his mind as he washed up in the rain barrel. He brushed the dust from the road off his pants and went into the *haus*.

It was hot inside—near stifling. The biggest pot he had ever seen bubbled on the stove. Was that even his pot? The table was set with plates, silverware, and two large glasses of fresh milk. A jelly jar sat in the middle of the table, serving as a vase for a couple of late-blooming daffodils and a few unfortunate weeds.

"Surprise!"

*Jah*, surprise.

He hung his hat on the peg and tried to think about what to say. His little pixie princess had made him *natchess*. Such a *wunder-baar* surprise. Such a sweet accomplishment. Such a . . . mess. All he could manage was, "*Danki.*"

"You're welcome." She grinned at him. "Come on. Come eat." She pulled out his chair and stood there waiting expectantly, that huge smile still on her face.

He sat down, trying not to let his doubts show. It didn't look like any helping of pot pie he'd ever eaten. But looks don't mean a thing. For sure and for certain, chicken pot pie wasn't the purtiest dish ever made, but it was tasty. His favorite.

He scooped up a bite and immediately wished it had been smaller. Much smaller. The dumpling seemed to grow the more he chewed it. And the more he chewed it, the more he felt like he needed to—it was lumpy and tough and tasted like school paste.

But she was so pleased with herself, and it was generous of her to cook for him.

He managed to swallow the bite, the knot of food slowly sliding down till it hit his stomach.

"How is it?" She looked as eager as a child at Christmas.

He swallowed again, hoping to choke out a response. "It's gut." He'd been taught his whole life not to lie, but this one was necessary. He couldn't hurt her feelings for all the properly cooked pot pie in Oklahoma.

She beamed at him.

Somehow he gathered a smile and sent it back to her.

"You've been working so hard, and I hated to see you eat nothing but sandwiches. You deserve more than that."

"*Jah. Danki.*" Maybe if he concentrated on the chicken. He forked up a bite and chewed. And chewed and chewed and *chewed*. It was like eating a piece of harness. The vegetables were overcooked, even by Amish standards, and the soupy part was as thick as gravy.

Miss Hamilton watched him expectantly, her untouched portion cooling on her plate.

He bravely took another bite. She smiled, and again he managed to return it.

She laughed. "Oh, I was so busy watching you eat, I forgot to eat for myself." Her eyes twinkled as she forked up her own bite, but the more she wallered the food around in her mouth, the less enthusiastic her expression became.

Finally she swallowed. "Does it . . . does it always taste like this?"

Time to tell the truth. "No."

She looked crushed, her big gumdrop eyes melting. "But Lizzie . . . Mary Elizabeth said it was your favorite. And I wanted to make it for you."

"*Jah*, that you did."

"But I wanted it to taste good."

"Then you should've had Katie Rose to come help. Mary Elizabeth is the worst cook in three districts."

She looked like she was going to cry. Gideon reached across the table and covered her hand with his.

And immediately wished he hadn't.

Her skin was soft as a late spring breeze, warm and sweet. Just touching her made him think of so many things he never thought he'd think of again. Long walks, sitting on the porch swing and drinking lemonade, hot summer nights and long winter days.

He allowed himself to run his thumb over the thin, blue vein on the back of her hand, feeling it jump beneath his touch, then he retreated. He released her hand and sat back in his chair.

"It's not so bad." He scooped up another bite.

"You're lying."

"*Jah.*" A chuckle escaped him, then another. He couldn't help himself, and soon she joined in. "Annie, this is a meal to stick to your ribs."

She giggled, and he noticed the start of a line of freckles across the curve of her cheeks.

"Annie?" she asked.

The named had slipped naturally from his lips. To him she seemed much more an "Annie" than a sticker label.

"*Jah.*" He nodded to back up his decision. "Annie."

And her smile grew a little brighter. "I like it."

He didn't know what to say, so he filled his mouth and used eating as an excuse not to answer her at all.

---

"Why are you pulling up the strawberry plants?"

Avery sat back on her heels and twisted around to face Mary Elizabeth. "Because they're weeds?"

The young girl shook her head in mock sadness, smiling the whole time. "These are the plants." She pointed to a tear-shaped, jagged-edged leaf. "The rest are weeds."

Avery pushed herself to her feet. She should stop before she did any more damage to Gideon's garden. She was just trying to help. She didn't even know there were strawberries planted in the little plot of ground.

Maybe it was time for a break.

Mary Elizabeth gave her a kind smile. "Strawberries come back year after year. The rest have to be replanted."

Avery looked back to the larger plot that she had spent the morning "weeding."

Mary Elizabeth followed her gaze. "Oh, don't worry. I don't think *Onkel* had anything planted there."

Avery smiled in relief. "I just wanted to help."

"You are kind, Avery Ann."

They smiled at each other, the bond of friendship growing stronger between them each day. When it was time for Avery to go back to Dallas, she was going to miss the girl.

Mary Elizabeth hooked her arm through Avery's and turned toward the house. "Come. Let's make some tea, and you can tell me how supper went last night."

Soon they were seated in the kitchen, sipping tea and eating the thick slices of angel food cake that Mary Elizabeth had smuggled over.

"Where's Louie?"

Avery shrugged. "Wherever Gideon is, I suppose. He follows that man everywhere."

Mary Elizabeth smiled. "Gideon's that way with animals. They all like him. That's why there're always so many dogs out front. They just seem to naturally want to be around him."

She could understand that. There was something special about Gideon Fisher, something that went beyond his conservative upbringing. There was a goodness about him, a fairness and a noble spirit.

"So how was supper?"

Avery made a face, not wanting to actually say the words that described their meal.

Mary Elizabeth frowned. "I don't understand. I told you everything Aunt Katie Rose said to tell you."

"Maybe I'm as bad at cooking as I am at gardening."

"I'm sorry. I wanted the two of you to have a nice supper together."

Avery smiled. "We did."

"But the food—"

*Isn't the only part of a nice meal.* Avery waved away her protests. "Maybe next time."

"You'll try again?"

"Of course."

"It might be better to start with something a bit easier to make."

"Or perhaps I should ask for the amazing Katie Rose's help."

Mary Elizabeth's eyes grew wide. "That's a great idea!"

"I was being—"

"Brilliant!"

"Sarcastic." She finished in a small voice.

"We'll have to do it next Saturday so that school's out."

"School?"

"Katie Rose is our teacher. Oh, and the work frolic. We'll have to wait until after that."

"Work frolic?"

Mary Elizabeth nodded enthusiastically, still caught up in the plans to teach her to cook. "Hester Stoltzfus needs a new roof on her house and barn. Dat and the boys are going over there to build it for her. It shouldn't take long."

"Really?"

"*Jah.* Aunt Katie Rose is the sweetest person you'll ever meet. I know she'd love to help you learn to cook."

Avery shook her head. "Your dad and brothers are going over to a neighbor's house to replace her roof?" She tried to imagine her upper-crust Dallas neighbors crawling around on her roof with shingles and hammers. The image would not come into focus.

"*Jah.*"

"That's . . ." Kind. Amazing. The way it should be.

"The Amish way," Mary Elizabeth supplied with a shrug.

"Gideon?" They sat across from each other, between them a cold supper of sausage and sauerkraut that Mary Elizabeth had brought in with the cake.

"*Jah?*" He looked up from his meal.

"Mary Elizabeth mentioned a work frolic next Saturday."

"*Jah.*"

"Will you eat here before you go?"

His expression shut down. "I'm not goin'."

"You aren't going?"

"No."

"But I thought—"

He shook his head and turned his attention back to his meal.

"Mary Elizabeth said her dad and brothers are going."

"*Jah.*"

"But you're not." It wasn't quite a question.

"No."

"Isn't that sort of un-Amish?"

He looked up at her, slowly, his gaze hard as glass as it bored into her. It didn't take Avery long to realize she had crossed the line.

"I am not goin'."

"Well, you should." She wasn't sure what had put those words in her mouth, however true, but once they were spoken, she couldn't take them back. She plowed on. "What are you going to do? Just cut yourself off from everybody . . . your family and friends? And for what reason?"

He got up and dumped the rest of his supper into the bucket of scraps they saved for compost. "I think it's time you went home." He stood at the sink, his back to her, his arms braced against the counter.

They had agreed to a couple of days and that time had long passed. It was time for her to go. But she didn't want to. She couldn't leave him like this. She didn't quite understand why, but she couldn't.

She sat back in her chair and crossed her arms over her middle. "No."

He turned around to face her. "No?"

"No. In fact, I think you should to go to the work frolic. And I want to go too."

His jaw tightened, and a little vein pulsed in his neck.

She stared right back at him, her gaze unwavering.

Long minutes ticked between them. Then Gideon looked away.

A smile crept to her lips. And Avery felt she had won a victory of sorts.

"*Ach*, the *Englisch*."

"So we can go?"

"We'll go." He shook his head, staring at her. "Too bad you didn't save any of the pot pie. It'd come in handy for repairin' Hester Stoltzfus's roof."

Avery clapped her hands together, unable to stop her smile. They were going to a work frolic!

# 6

Mornings were her favorite, definitely. And this Monday morning was no exception. Never before had Avery hopped out of bed at the first sign of the sun, and readied herself for the day. Of course, preparing for a day here was far different than what she had to do in Dallas. Every morning in the country, she put up the quilts she used for her bed and changed into the *frack* so graciously loaned to her by Mary Elizabeth. She splashed water on her face, ran her fingers through her hair, and made coffee for Gideon. No steamy shower followed by morning facial, a layer of makeup, and whatever armor she needed to face her father's plans for the day.

It was liberating to jump out of bed, and with minimal effort, be ready to go.

No pressing weight of responsibility either. Oh, there were things that needed to be done, and she knew that she did a fraction of what the Amish women accomplished each day. But she found satisfaction in the fulfillment of a job that was worthy and worthwhile. Putting food on the table to feed a family, wash clothes, clean house, till a garden. The fruits of her hard work were right in front of her each day. Not a wisp of a deal, or the knowledge that someday someone might benefit from her efforts.

Today she was going to do something extra special: she was going to make Gideon breakfast. Not a cold breakfast, but a real one. Well, a better one, at least. Eggs, bacon, and toast. Something more than granola to fuel his work in the fields.

This morning she was prepared. She knew what she had to do. Lizzie had already told her that she had to get the eggs out of the hen house. Who would have known?

Avery snuck out the back door and cautiously made her way across the yard. The green flip-flops she had commandeered slapped against her heels, making way too much noise. This was supposed to be a surprise, and though Mary Elizabeth hadn't said so, Avery felt it was probably a good idea not to make too much noise around the chickens.

She slipped the flip-flops from her feet and tiptoed toward the hen house. More than anything she wanted to surprise Gideon. And she wasn't going to let one less-than-successful meal deter her from her goal. She wouldn't allow herself to call her chicken pot pie a failure. Failure was not trying at all. And she'd tried. Her dinner just hadn't succeeded, that's all.

The hen house was one of the little faded buildings next to an empty pen that should have contained goats or pigs. Judging by the smell, she was betting on pigs. The squat building had a ramp that led inside and a small opening that she had to stoop to get through. She slipped back into the sandals and ducked inside.

Fingers of sunshine shone inside the henhouse, their staggering rays of light streaming through the wire-covered windows lining the top of each wall. Dust and feathers danced on the beams as she made her way inside. It smelled almost as bad as the pig pen.

Almost. Dank and stuffy, she didn't know what the chickens saw in the place. But they had eggs, so in she went.

What was it Lizzie had said? *Just go up to the chicken on the roost. Stick your hand underneath her and take the eggs like they belong to you.*

Like they belonged to her.

Avery wasn't exactly sure what a roost was, but she had to assume it was some sort of Amish word for nest. If that were true, then all of the chickens were on the roost.

She looked around until she spotted a hen, a pretty, rusty-orange colored one that looked nice. At least her beak didn't turn down as much at the corners as the others' did.

"Good morning." She nodded toward the bird.

At the sound of her voice, the hen jerked her beak back and forth, then turned her head away as if she had better things to do than deal with a lowly human.

"I just need to get a couple of your eggs." The green shower flops slapped against her heels as she stepped nearer. The chicken jerked once again. Avery inched closer, doing her best not to lift her feet and make any more noise than necessary.

"Aren't you a pretty . . . chicken?"

She reached out a hand, slowly as to not disturb the hen. Fingers shaking, she hoped the fat, red bird wouldn't notice. Avery was supposed to act like she knew what she was doing. Wasn't that what Lizzie had told her?

But when she got near enough to the chicken, so near she could almost touch the tips of those rusty-colored feathers, the bird moved with lightning speed.

In a flash, Avery drew back, cradling her stinging hand close to her chest. "Ow."

An angry welt had already started to form between her thumb and forefinger. Luckily, no blood.

She propped her hands on her hips and eyed the fat hen. "So that's how this is going to be, is it?"

The chicken stared back with blank eyes.

Avery reached out again, proud of the fact that even though the hen had pecked her once, her fingers were steady. She could do this.

Lightning speed. Another welt. This one on the back of her hand.

"Ouch."

But she needed those eggs.

She inched her fingers close to the hen, but the crazy bird lifted herself up in her nest, flapping her wings and squawking. All the other hens started flapping their wings, too, and screeching, the cacophony almost more than she could stand. Avery backed up a step, and the hen followed, hopping down to the planked floor of the henhouse. Avery screamed, and fled from the building, the hen viciously pecking behind her.

Wishing she had shut the door to the henhouse, Avery neither stopped nor looked back until she was safely on the porch.

She pressed a hand to her thumping heart and took a deep breath, finally turning around to see if she had been followed. *Whew*. No rogue chickens snapping their way across the yard. Safe for now.

"Annie, what's all the commotion back here?"

She peered up to find Gideon watching her. "Uh . . . nothing." She clasped her hands behind her, hoping she didn't leave a smear of blood on her dress. She couldn't stop the flush of heat that filled her cheeks. *Some surprise this was turning out to be.*

"It is a sin to lie."

Why did he have to employ the same tone that he used with Lizzie? He even lifted his eyebrows in that *Isn't there something you want to tell me?* look she had seen often enough.

She let out a discouraged sigh. "I wanted to cook you some eggs for breakfast."

He nodded and crossed his arms as if he were settling in to hear her tale. "*Jah.*"

"Before I could cook the eggs, I had to get them."

Gideon's eyes widened. No sooner had the words left her mouth when Gideon jogged toward her, pulling her hands from behind her, and holding them in his own. He turned them this way and that, examining the peck marks left by the angry red hen. He ran his thumb over one of the marks, his touch alone soothing the reddened skin.

"I should wring her neck and let Katie Rose make a fine Sunday supper from what's left," Gideon said, still holding her fingers in his own.

"Please don't." Avery tugged her hands away. She feared that with a little time she would get entirely too accustomed to his touch. "Lizzie said I had to take charge when I went in there. I guess the hen could smell my hesitation."

"That hen is a menace. Should have eaten her months ago." His eyes grew more serious, his mouth a thin line turned down at the corners.

He looked so stern that Avery couldn't stop the giggle from bubbling up inside her. She slapped a hand over her mouth in an attempt to stop it from escaping, but too late. The laugh burst forth, followed by another.

She held her sides, laughing, with Gideon chuckling right alongside her. The tension in her body drained away, and the silliness of the situation shone clear.

Hearing Gideon's laugh revived something in her, but it sounded rusty, as if it hadn't been used in awhile. She hadn't had anything to laugh about in quite some time, herself. The pleasure that she could share this moment with him overwhelmed her.

She wiped tears from her face, her giggles finally subsiding. "There are eight hens in there. How do you know which one pecked me?"

"It was the fat red one for sure and for certain."

"Nope, it was the black one."

"It is a sin to lie, Annie."

*Maybe the fat red chicken was a menace after all.* "Promise me we won't eat that hen."

He twisted his mouth as if trying to decide how to answer.

"Promise me, Gideon. She was only trying to protect her eggs."

A full minute passed before he answered. "*Jah*, then. We won't eat the hen."

Avery nodded, satisfied.

"For now," he said before ducking into the henhouse.

Not a squawk could be heard. Avery waited, her breath held. Then Gideon returned holding four fresh eggs in one big hand. "Come. I'll show you how to make dippy eggs."

Avery tilted her chin. "Dippy eggs?" She followed behind as Gideon led the way into the house.

Gideon nodded. "But first." He directed her toward the sink, then washed her hands gently, his warmth heating her fingers despite the coolness of the water. The angry, red wounds needed to be cared for to keep them from getting infected, but Avery couldn't look Gideon in the eye as he dabbed the marks with antibiotic cream and covered them with plain, beige bandage strips.

"There," he said, standing up. "Now for breakfast." Avery noticed he had trouble looking at her squarely as well.

"Thank you," she murmured, grateful when the intimate moment passed, and yet sad at the same time that it was over.

Dippy eggs turned out to be eggs over easy. To Avery, they tasted a lot like heaven. Or perhaps it was the company. As much as she enjoyed spending time with Gideon, she preferred to believe that the fresh eggs were the reason this morning's breakfast had seemed so special indeed.

Gideon sat back in his chair. "Today I'm going to plow the fields across the road."

Avery scooped another forkful of eggs. "Where my car was?"

"*Jah.* Gabe and Simon will be here this afternoon to help as well. It should go quick."

She nodded, wishing once again that she could cook so she could make him something more substantial for supper. "Lizzie is coming by to help me clear the garden plot so we can plant vegetables." *And strawberry plants.* She hoped the small gesture could repay him for all the kindness he had shown her.

"You needn't do that."

"I want to." That was the truth. She found it relaxing to dig in the dirt—even when destroying perfectly healthy strawberry plants. There was something special about connecting to the earth, a holiness in gardening, and a uniqueness about time spent outdoors with nothing but the ground beneath her and the sun shining on her shoulders.

He gave her a quick nod and a lingering smile. "There are stakes in the barn for when you need them."

"Stakes?"

"To tie up the plants. Tomatoes and string beans."

There was more to gardening than she knew, but she would learn. For as long as she stayed here, anyway. Just how would her father take her newly-found love of gardening once she returned to Dallas? He might actually approve. Her love of the outdoors would save him a fortune in landscaping.

The days before the frolic were filled with chores and visits from Mary Elizabeth, but seemed to drag by just the same. Avery was excited to be able to witness the Amish working together.

"It's no barn raising," Mary Elizabeth explained as they hoed rows of the recently cleared garden plot.

"I've heard about those. That really happens?"

"Of course. The whole district comes. This weekend, there'll only be a few families there."

"I'm still impressed. If we need a new roof, my father's assistant calls a roofing company."

"I'm impressed that you talked *Onkel* into going."

Avery stopped hoeing and turned to the younger girl. "It was strange, you know. Like some voice inside me saying not to let him stay at home. Crazy, huh?"

Mary Elizabeth smiled. "That's the voice of God."

Avery cocked her head to one side and gave the idea some thought. "Really?"

"I'm sure of it." Mary Elizabeth began a new row, and Avery started across from her.

She let the idea sink in, then took a measured breath. "I'm really grateful your aunt is willing to help me learn to cook."

"You'll like Katie Rose. Everybody does."

"She sounds wonderful."

Mary Elizabeth smiled. "She's the kindest person I know."

They worked in silence for a few minutes before Avery broke the country quiet once again. "You're sure it's okay for me to go without any shoes?" She looked down at her bare feet, half-buried in freshly-turned earth. She couldn't remember a time when she had gone barefoot like this. Maybe on the beach, but this was different. She had been barefoot for days, inside and outside the house. She liked the freedom of it. She would never ever go without shoes in Dallas, but out here, it felt right.

Mary Elizabeth smiled. "Of course. But I will see if I can find you a pair, if'n you want. There's just not much need to wear shoes in the summer."

"I suppose not." She glanced down at her grimy feet. She felt free and breezy, but she'd have to give them a good scrubbing tonight just the same. Avery straightened and looked down the lines of mounded dirt. "What are we going to plant again?"

"Food for the table." Mary Elizabeth counted on her fingers. "Peas and tomatoes. Watermelon, cantaloupe, okra, cucumbers, some string beans. Oh, and a couple rows of corn."

"But Gideon planted fields of corn."

Mary Elizabeth shook her head. "Feed grade for the animals, and to sell to other farmers to feed their stock. This is sweet corn."

Avery nodded and went back to her task. "Do you really think Gideon will keep up the garden after I leave?"

Mary Elizabeth frowned. "I do not like to think about you going."

"I'll have to, eventually."

"But I prayed for you."

Avery stopped and eyed Lizzie curiously. "You did?"

"I asked God to bring someone to help Gideon, and He sent you."

She didn't know what to say to that. Her shoulders slumped. "I can't stay here forever."

Mary Elizabeth scrunched up her brow. "Why not?"

"I have a family and obligations." The thought of staying here, at least awhile longer, kept creeping back into her mind. She wanted to stay and watch the miracle of the garden, the little seeds they had planted turn into food large enough to feed them.

To sit across from Gideon . . . every day.

She shook away that thought. The Dunstan Pro-Am was less than two weeks from now, and she needed to be there. The weight of that responsibility settled heavy on her chest, uncomfortable and stifling.

All her life, she had been her father's show pony, her makeup always just right, the finest clothes, an expensive car—everything to illustrate her father's success to the world. Until now, she had not realized the strain this materialistic lifestyle had put on her. Now that she was away from all that, she felt relaxed. Free. Amish life seemed so natural, so unassuming.

She had once wondered why anyone would live the way the Amish do—separated from modern society without electricity or cars—but after these past few days with Gideon, she understood. The serenity among the Amish was unparalleled. Avery could see why the Plain people lived in this manner and couldn't help but wonder what it would be like to live like this the rest of her life.

She pushed the thought away. Sooner or later she'd have to return to Dallas. Until then . . . Avery lifted her face to the sun, its golden rays warming her cheeks.

Until then she would enjoy this gift she had been offered.

The day of the work frolic dawned with blue skies and a light breeze out of the north. A perfect day.

Avery jumped off the couch, both excited and nervous as she folded the quilts she used as a bed, washed her face, and donned the new *frack* Mary Elizabeth had brought for her to wear. This dress had shorter sleeves that puffed a little at the shoulder and ended with an elastic band just above the elbow. It was the most beautiful shade of green—not quite emerald, and not quite jade.

She tucked her hair behind her ears, fluffed it back out again, and studied her reflection in the small mirror above the sink. Her skin was starting to tan and freckle, but she wasn't at all unhappy with the results. In fact, she thought she looked better than she had in years. Healthy and unburdened. Unfettered.

The front door creaked open, and she tried not to race to greet Gideon. She was afraid he might've changed his mind about the work frolic, but he was there, dressed and ready to go.

"*Guder mariye*, Annie."

She smiled at the sound of his name for her. "Good morning to you. I made some coffee."

Gideon nodded.

"We'll leave right after breakfast?"

"*Jah.*"

They sat down to eat, comfortable in the silence. What would it be like to sit down like this with him day after day, without the threat of returning to her world hanging over them?

For now she wouldn't say a word. She didn't want to ruin what had started out to be such a perfect day.

Ruth Fisher placed the stack of cups next to the big, blue water cooler. A work frolic made for a busy mornin', totin' water, layin' out food to feed the men, and waitin' on them to finish the job at hand. But she didn't mind. Her family was here. Her husband, Abram; her youngest boy, John Paul; Gabriel and his sons. The only male Fisher missing was Gideon.

She sighed despite herself. Gideon would come around on his own. It had been a hard year for him after losing Miriam and Jamie. Every night Ruth prayed that Gideon would find his way back to himself. She didn't know why he couldn't accept that losing his family was God's will. Couldn't say herself how she would feel if she stepped in Gideon's shoes.

"Would you look at that." Beth Troyer, Hester's closest neighbor, stopped arranging plates and napkins and instead watched a familiar buggy pull up alongside the rest.

Could it be?

Ruth's breath caught in her throat as Gideon jumped down from the seat, went around in front of the horses, and held out his hands. She had been so gripped with the sight of Gideon that she didn't see that he had brought someone with him. A woman. A petite thing with *Englisch* cut hair and an Amish *frack*.

So the rumors were true.

Before they pulled up, the yard had been bustlin'. Men going about readying to tear down the damaged roof and replace it with new, stronger shingles. Women hurrying about after children and food. But now everyone stood stock-still, their collective breath held as they waited for her Gideon and the outsider to come nearer.

Even at this distance she could see that he had done the unthinkable—he had shaved his beard. She knew he had been hiding himself. She had been worried about him for a long time. But she had turned her worries to prayer, and her prayers to the Lord. She hadn't told a soul of her concerns, not even her Abram, but she feared that Gideon would only find peace again when he joined God—and his family. As much as the thought pained her, she knew if he could choose, that's where he'd be now.

They'd been close, he and his Miriam. They had grown up together. Miriam had been a fine wife. Ruth just hadn't realized how much her son had grown to care for her. Amish couples didn't always marry for love. Devotion and strength of spirit were much more important. Love came later. Not always, but usually. And Jamie, sweet child. He was smart and funny, bright and carefree, the apple of his father's eye. Most Amish families had five or more children, but Gideon and Miriam had only been blessed once. Yet Gideon poured enough love on that child for six others to boot.

She closed her eyes and sent up quick words of prayer and grace. Gideon was hurtin' mighty bad. If she could take the pain from her son, she would. But she could only ask for the Lord's help. And show that she still loved and supported him.

She took a deep breath and purposefully walked across the quiet yard toward him—toward *them*—and tried not to give too much attention to the fact that they both wore green, like they had matched themselves as a sign. Nor that her son had this *Englischer's* hand tucked inside his own.

"My son." She swallowed back her tears. This was the time to be happy. Maybe this was the first step in his healing.

"*Mamm*." He bent down and kissed her on her forehead just under the edge of her bonnet. He pressed his smooth cheek to hers, then pulled away. "I need you to meet someone. This is my guest, Annie Hamilton. Annie, this is my *mudder*, Ruth."

Ruth reached out a trembling hand and took that of the young woman standing at her son's side. "So pleased to have you with us today, Annie. Won't you come join the women while the men ready up to work?"

Annie let out a long breath as if she had been holding it for some time. "I'd like that very much."

Her smile was enchanting, her eyes a strange shade of violet. Dark hair curled softly around her face in a becoming way that seemed both worldly and innocent. She appeared small and fragile standing next to her Gideon, and suddenly Ruth grew afraid. More so than she had ever been in her life. She sensed a connection between them, some sort of bond, an invisible hold that pulled them together like metal and magnets.

And she could tell that Gideon could feel it as well.

*No, no, no,* she prayed. *Don't let him fall in love with this woman.* His heart was so recently broken, barely starting to heal. An outsider like Annie Hamilton would destroy him in a matter of days. *Lord, please protect him, protect his heart and make him strong. Aemen.*

Mary Elizabeth rushed toward them. "Hello, Annie." She threw her arms around Avery, giving her no choice but to embrace her in return or fall over backward.

Avery smiled, her gaze trailing behind Gideon as he walked toward the men. Her hand still tingled where he had touched it, given it one last squeeze before he surrendered her to his family.

The young girl's eyes sparkled as she pulled away. "I want you to meet everyone." She hooked her arm through Avery's and led her toward the women and children.

"This is my *aenti,* Katie Rose."

A pretty young woman with honey blonde hair and jade green eyes reached out a hand and took Avery's much like her mother had. "So pleased you are here, Annie. I hear we have a cooking lesson this afternoon."

Avery could tell why everyone liked Katie Rose Fisher—she was just that likeable.

Next came Hester Stoltzfus, the young widow who owned the house; her neighbor Beth Troyer, who was also her sister-in-law, though Avery couldn't remember on whose side. Then Lizzie pointed out her brothers. Matthew, the oldest, was the very image of his father. Then came Simon who had been with his father once when Gabriel had come by to see Gideon. Simon had the same green eyes as the majority of the Fishers, but he was blond like Lizzie. David and Joseph both had their father's dark hair, but deep blue eyes they must have inherited from their mother. And then there was Samuel.

Four-year-old Samuel touched Avery the most. Green eyes, red hair, and freckles, he was so different from the rest. His widely-spaced, almond-shaped eyes, moon face, and flattened nose could not overshadow his sweet, sweet smile. He hid himself in the folds of Katie Rose's skirt, only peeking out when he thought no one was looking.

"*Mamm* died giving us Samuel," Lizzie whispered. "He doesn't talk much."

Lizzie didn't state the obvious—Samuel had Down syndrome. Avery's heart went out to the child, so touching and shy. She wanted to scoop him up and rain kisses all over his freckled cheeks, but he retained a firm hold on Katie Rose's skirt.

Katie Rose seemed not to notice that he never let her go, making Avery wonder if this was how they always were.

"The lady in black under the sycamore tree is my great-*grossmammi*. Everyone calls her Noni." She frowned. "I'm not sure why. But she's very wise."

As Lizzie said the words, Noni turned toward them. Avery could see the wit and intelligence in her clear green eyes. She might be pushing ninety, but she looked as sharp as someone half her age.

Yet, Avery wasn't sure what the look meant. Maybe Noni was checking her over, trying to figure out how exactly an Englisher came to be among them this day. Before either of them could say a thing, someone called the group to prayer.

And then the work began.

What a sight! All the men dressed in similar clothing and crawling around on the roof. Avery was enthralled by the cooperation and togetherness they displayed.

The other ladies either sat in the shade, or chased their children, otherwise accepting the miracle unfolding before them as an everyday occurrence. To them, this was probably just another Saturday of pulling together to help a neighbor.

But to her, this was so much more.

She had been a little concerned when she and Gideon had pulled up. The yard full of people stopped and stared. She didn't know who they were staring at the most—Gideon or her.

There were reproving looks all around. She knew the Amish tried not to judge and reserved that right for God. But she could almost see the wheels of their minds turning, trying to decide why one of their own had gone wayward, and why a chosen son had brought a stranger into their midst.

She had not planned on standing out quite so much. Back at the house with Mary Elizabeth, she hadn't noticed the differences. But standing in a yard full of women, all properly dressed, her makeshift attire was glaringly obvious. Shoes weren't her problem at all. Most there were barefoot, women and children alike. She wished, though, that she had taken the time to figure out how to wear the apron that Mary Elizabeth had brought over with the dresses.

And she was the only adult there with a bare head. Men and boys alike wore their wide-brimmed straw hats. The women wore bonnets or what Lizzie called a *kapp*. Avery felt strangely vulnerable without one of her own.

Which was ridiculous. In a couple of weeks or less, she'd be heading back home to Dallas. She only wore the dress she had on now because she had nothing else to wear. It wasn't like she was joining the Amish . . . merely visiting them.

Mary Elizabeth sidled up beside her and handed Avery a glass of lemonade. "It's something, *jah*?"

"Very."

"I love to watch them work." Lizzie shaded her eyes as she scanned the roof covered with family and friends.

"Anyone of them in particular?"

She blushed. "No. *Dat* wouldn't allow it. Not until I'm sixteen."

Which really didn't answer her question, but Avery didn't call her on it.

"Mary Elizabeth!"

She winced. "Yes, *Dat*."

"Stop standin' around and tend to your brother." Gabriel pointed with his hammer toward the sycamore. Eight-year-old Joseph, who was not allowed on the roof, had decided to get a better look from the branches of the tree.

"Yes, *Dat*." She shot Avery an *I'm sorry* look and turned away to get her brother.

Avery had a feeling Gabriel's command had nothing to do with Joseph's safety—and everything to do with her.

———

In a day and a half, everyone in the district—maybe the entire settlement—would know that his son had shaved his beard. Maybe sooner since Beth Troyer knew. She was a good woman, but she talked too much at quiltin' frolics.

And picnics.

And Amish baseball games.

Abram chanced a look at Gideon where he skimmed off the ruined shingles and pitched them over the edge of the roof. By now Gideon's beard should have been long and full. Instead, he was barefaced. Shamed. Once the bishop found out, he was sure to have Gideon shunned. The problem was, Gideon hadn't been around much. He'd stopped coming to church, and rarely, if ever, left his property.

Shunned or not, Abram didn't think his son would care much either way.

But a *meidung* would also mean not giving him food. Ruthie would fret if she couldn't feed him. She had herself convinced that if she didn't provide him with food, he wouldn't eat at all. Abram hadn't protested, because he was scared she was right.

He had raised Gideon better than that. Had given him the same life lessons as Gabe. When Rebecca died, Gabe didn't hole up and grieve like an *Englischer*. He'd pushed on, raisin' his children and accepting God's will.

Not Gideon.

'Course, Gideon had lost more than his wife. He'd lost his son. Abram was afraid that he'd lost his faith in the Almighty as well.

Perhaps if he talked to the bishop on Gideon's behalf. The *Ordnung* was clear, but maybe Rueben Beachy could see his way to giving Gideon a little more time to get his mind back right. The bishop knew Gideon's devotion. He knew what a good man Gideon was. And Abram had faith that, with a little time and direction, Gideon would find his way back.

There was still life left in him.

Abram had seen his son's hands linger a bit too long on the *Englischer's* waist when Gideon had helped her down from the buggy. The act was familiar, almost intimate. He hoped Ruthie hadn't noticed, but he knew there wasn't much his wife missed.

They had prayed separately and together that the Lord would bring Gideon around. And He had. Abram should have been a little clearer, but it was done.

There had just been so much to pray about lately, what with Gideon's grief and Ruthie's doctor appointments.

Abram stopped hammering. He closed his eyes and lifted his face to the sun, allowing the glory of the Lord to wash over him. Faith was believing that God would take care of the problems they faced. And he had faith. But there were times when faith became stretched too thin with barely enough to go 'round.

Unfortunately, this was one of those times.

Abram opened his eyes, readjusted his hat, and started back to work.

"Annie!"

Avery turned, amazed at how accustomed she had become to being called by her middle name.

Gideon's mother, Ruth, strode across the yard, her steps purposeful.

"Can I have a word, please?"

The urgency in Ruth's voice made Avery pause. "Of course."

She had decided not to try and fit in with this gathering, nor did she try to separate herself. She simply moved around, watching the men work, the children play in the sun.

Ruth linked her arm with Avery's. "Walk with me."

They set off around the house and strolled between the rows of fruit trees growing out back. The concerned light in Ruth's eyes had Avery tamping down the questions that filled her mind.

Ruth leaned her head closer. "I don't know how you came to be here."

How should she respond to that?

Ruth continued. "It doesn't matter. What matters is you are here. I've heard that you are stayin' with my son."

Avery nodded.

Ruth stopped. "Don't break his heart."

Avery nearly tripped. "I—"

"From one woman to another." Ruth's eyes implored her. "Please. Please."

"I'm only staying for another week or so."

Tears welled up in green eyes so much like her son's and spilled down Ruth's cheeks. "He's already so sad. When I saw him pull up, I thought he'd finally come to himself. But then I saw you, and how he . . ." She lowered her chin. "He's already lost so much." She wiped her tears away, took a deep breath, and gazed into Avery's face. "I shouldn't be talkin' about this."

Avery saw strength and resolve in Ruth's face. "It's okay." Her heart went out to Ruth and the entire Fisher family. They'd lost so much. Gideon had lost his partner, and his faith. Ruth had lost her son.

Ruth took Avery's hand in hers, the calluses and roughened palms testimony to the years of caring for her family. Lines etched across her forehead. "Promise me, Annie. You seem like a good woman. I know you mean us no harm, but promise me, you won't break his heart. He's just now startin' to heal."

Avery's throat tightened with emotion. "I promise."

How could she say anything else?

"Did you enjoy yourself?" Gideon chanced a sidelong glance at Annie, before turning his full attention back to the road. But in that quick second, he took in every detail of her appearance— flushed cheeks, smiling lips, windblown hair. She brushed against him with the natural sway of the horses, the sensation both sweet and unsettling.

"I did." She tucked her hair behind her ear. He wished it was long enough for her to pin back. It was just so distracting all over the place like that. "Your family is very nice."

"On average, you mean?"

She shrugged. "Katie Rose is wonderful. Your mother welcomed me like I was her new best friend. I love Lizzie like a sister."

"Lizzie?"

"Mary Elizabeth."

"Better not let Gabe hear you call her that."

"That's what she wants to be called."

"Regardless." He gave her his best *Do not push me on this* look, the same one that always had his Miriam hushing up in a hurry.

Again, she tucked a strand of flyaway hair behind one ear. "I think a person should be addressed the way they would like, and not just told what they can be called."

*So that's what this was about.* "You don't like bein' called Annie."

"I didn't say that."

"Then what did you say?"

"Your brother frowns too much."

*Jah*, it was the truth, but he couldn't blame Gabriel. He had a lot to deal with and not much patience for trivial things—like nicknames.

"He expects too much of Lizzie . . . Mary Elizabeth."

"It's our way."

"She's not those boys' mother."

"Neither are you."

She harrumphed, and crossed her arms over her front, but Gideon had the feeling the matter wasn't entirely closed. She was a mouthy one, this *Englischer* Annie. He smiled and turned the buggy down the dirt road that led home.

"And what of the women folk?" he asked, hoping to take the scowl off her face.

"Beth and Hester are very nice. They kind of . . ."

"Kinda what?"

"I know these two women. They're friends of my dad. Beth and Hester remind me of them—always busy, always finding something to get into."

Gideon chuckled. "That is for sure and for certain."

"A little on the annoying side, but you love them just the same."

"Sounds like you really got to know them this mornin'."

She nodded, the sunshine playing off her face and hair. "I think they're just like that, you know."

"It is our way," he said again. "We don't have anything to hide."

"What about when the bishop finds out about your beard?"

He turned so sharply that he almost spun the buggy around. Then he straightened out the horses and acted like nothing was wrong. "It's no matter."

She put a hand on her chest. "I heard them talking. I don't think they knew I was listening."

"Hester and Beth are always goin' on about somethin'."

"They said you'll be shunned."

He grunted, searching around for a way to change the subject.

She cocked her head. "What exactly does that mean?"

"It doesn't matter."

"It does. It worries your family and your neighbors."

He didn't reply. He hated that his *mudder* was concerned, but there was nothing he could do about it. The deed was done. They could shun him all they wanted, but Miriam and Jamie were still gone.

"Is it because you've been skipping church?"

"Let it go, Annie."

"But I—"

"Let it go."

She sat back. "For now," she said. Something in his tone must have gotten through her stubborn streak.

Gideon choked back a relieved sigh.

No one had questioned him since he had moved out here. Since the accident. No one but this *Englischer*. No one had asked him how he was doing, and no one knew the part he played. And he surely didn't want Annie to know. She looked at him with awe and wonder. If she knew the truth, would she ever look at him that way again?

"Whoa, now." He pulled the horses to a stop halfway between the barn and the house, then turned on the bench seat to look at her.

She stared back at him.

He wanted to touch her wayward hair, trace a line between her newly-earned freckles. She was too close and too far away all in the same moment.

She could feel it too. He knew it. Her eyes flared with recognition.

"Annie, I . . ." He didn't know what to say, but in the quiet moment that stretched between them, he needed to say something.

"Yes?" She leaned toward him, the combined scents of lavender and woman filled his senses.

He wanted nothing more than to give into temptation, to lean in and taste the tremble of her lips. "I—"

"Yoo-hoo! We're here." Mary Elizabeth pulled in behind them.

Gideon and Annie jumped apart. They clambered down opposite sides of the buggy as if it had caught fire.

Gideon ran his thumbs under the edge of his suspenders, avoiding eye contact with Annie. "I'll take care of the horses."

"Fine, fine." She smoothed down the sides of her skirt. "I'll go . . . learn how to cook."

"*Gut, gut.*" He gathered up the horses' reins and led them the rest of the way to the barn, giving his sister and his niece a half-hearted wave of welcome.

# 7

By the time Avery turned in, the nighttime sky was littered with stars. She snuggled into her makeshift bed and closed her eyes with a contented sigh.

All in all, it was a good day. *Wunderbaar*, Gideon would say. She was dead tired, but in a satisfying way, her head filled with all the new things she had taken in.

She shifted and received a nudge from Louie in return. "Sorry, baby." She scratched him behind his ears, and he settled into the crook of her knees. Despite her exhaustion, she couldn't settle down. Events of the day kept replaying in her head.

The work frolic was an amazing sight, everyone pitching in to help a neighbor in need. Too bad the rest of the world didn't work that way. If it did, civilization would be a much better place.

At first everyone had been a little standoffish, but by the time they broke to eat, Avery almost felt like she belonged. She watched the children play, and listened to the women talk about quilting and canning and what the deacon said at church last Sunday.

It was the best Saturday morning she had spent in a long time, filled with rest, work, and meaningful conversation.

Then came the afternoon. Not only was Katie Rose Fisher likeable and a good cook, she had the patience of a saint. She worked tirelessly, teaching Avery how to cook with Samuel sticking to her skirt like a half-eaten lollipop. Plus, their time together had given Avery something to think about besides Gideon and what almost happened between them. She had forced herself to let the cooking lesson take over and pushed the rest aside.

Avery punched down her pillow and sighed again. It was infinitely satisfying to eat a meal she had prepared—even if it came with a lot of help. Between the three of them—Avery, Lizzie, and Katie Rose—they made oven-fried chicken, creamed potatoes, green beans, and sourdough rolls.

Gideon had been so surprised to see what she had done. That is, when he finally returned from the barn. Avery couldn't blame him. She had practically thrown herself at him in the buggy. She wanted to apologize for her behavior, but since the matter had been pushed aside, she didn't want to bring it up again. He probably thought she was extremely forward. But it had seemed so natural to lean in closer to him, so right.

Still, whoever said her instincts were good? Her track record where men were concerned was proof of that.

So she had let her efforts in the kitchen serve as her redemption. And tomorrow she'd do it again. Katie Rose had written down detailed instructions on how to prepare a roast, mix biscuits from scratch, and fry bacon. Avery was excited to accept the challenge of preparing a meal all on her own. Maybe too excited.

She couldn't say that was the only reason she was still awake. She shifted on the sofa, trying to find a comfortable spot while not disturbing Louie.

Avery growled in frustration, threw back the covers, and

swung her feet to the floor, just too keyed up to sleep. Maybe if she read awhile. She turned on the gas-powered lamp at the end of the sofa and tried to remember where she had put the stack of books she'd found when she was cleaning. Maybe something in there would keep her interest.

In the china hutch. That's where she'd put them—four in all. One on natural fertilizers, another on getting the most out of your vegetable garden, a book on basket weaving, and a soft-bound copy of the Bible. By far the best of the four.

She returned the others to the cabinet and curled up on the end of the sofa. She opened the Bible in the middle, planning on starting at whatever page it happened to be, but was surprised to find that it was written in German. Not that it was a problem. As a child, she had picked up a working knowledge of the language from their housekeeper. Then she had gone on to further study while in college. She wasn't exactly fluent, but she could manage. It had been a long time since she had read anything in a foreign language. Maybe the challenge would keep her mind occupied enough to calm her thoughts. Half an hour tops, and she would be sleeping like a baby.

Two hours later, she was still reading, making a list of words she didn't understand and marking passages she wanted to return to later: the amazing story of Noah and his ark, Daniel in the lions' den, and the entire book of Psalms.

Louie whined. Avery stuck a scrap of paper in the Bible to hold her place, then scratched him under the chin. "All right, baby. We'll go to bed now."

She turned out the light and settled back down on the sofa, a peace settling over her. Tomorrow was going to be a wonderful day. She had a great breakfast planned for Gideon, and a great supper too. She would truly show her talent as a cook. She smiled to herself as she finally drifted off to sleep.

꧁꧂

Sunday dawned beautiful and sunny. Gideon straightened up his bed in the barn and threw down fresh hay for the horses and Honey. For some reason he felt better than he had in months. It felt good to climb on a neighbor's roof and repair damage done by the unpredictable Oklahoma weather. It felt fine to get out amongst his family and friends, something he hadn't done in a long, long time. It felt good despite the stares and the whispers behind his back.

His only regret in shaving off his beard was how it affected his mother. She had seemed downright heartbroken as she pressed her palm to his smooth cheek. How could he explain to her that it was no more blasphemous to shave his beard than to wear it now that his family was gone?

He trimmed the hair from his upper lip, then put his razor away and walked the distance from the barn to the house with a smile on his face. His sister had spent the better part of the afternoon teaching Annie how to cook. It amazed him that she had reached her age without knowing even the basic principles, and that despite her wealth and privilege in the *Englisch* world she was willing to learn how to survive in his.

He wondered what treat she had in store for him this morning. Bacon? Eggs? Hotcakes?

As Gideon opened the door, Louie barked and jumped down from the couch. Annie rubbed her eyes and struggled to awaken.

"Good mornin'."

She sat up, her voice groggy. "What time is it?"

"Mornin'."

Her eyes popped open wide. She threw off the covers and jumped to her feet. "But I . . ." She ran a hand through her already rumpled hair. "Oh, no."

"What's wrong?"

"I wanted to make you breakfast." She frowned. "I wanted to have it waiting for you when you came in. Biscuits and bacon and—"

"But you overslept."

She nodded. "I couldn't sleep last night so I started reading and the next thing I knew it was late and . . ."

Gideon looked to where she pointed. The Bible he'd received when he joined the church rested on the small table at the end of the couch. "You were readin' that?"

She gave another small nod.

"But it's in German."

"It took awhile, but I got most of it."

He tried not to shake his head at the wonder of it all. Annie, of the *Englisch* world, could understand German. Why was he so surprised?

"I made some notes." She reached for a pad of paper. "I was hoping that Monday . . . maybe you could take me to town. I'd like to stop by the bookstore, look for a couple of things. I mean, it's not like it's a secret that I'm here, right?"

"I s'pose not."

"And I wanted to get some flowers. For the front flower bed. Lizzie said it should be filled with bright colors."

He gave a quick nod. "I'll take you, but on one condition. Tomorrow you make me that breakfast you just talked about."

"It's a deal." She smiled.

And Gideon felt like he'd been kicked by a horse. The large shirt she wore covered her from neck to knees, but clung to her curves. He cleared his throat. "You can go change now."

She glanced down at herself, her cheeks reddening. "Right."

And she hurried off.

After Annie was dressed, they ate a quick breakfast of granola and milk, along with slices of fresh peaches he'd bought at the store. He sure hoped that last snow hadn't killed off all the Green Country fruit trees. Local peaches were so much better than the ones grown states away.

"It's Sunday," she said, an entirely too innocent expression on her face.

"*Jah.*"

"I heard your mother talking about going to a different church district today."

"*Jah.*"

She dipped her chin and cut those big gumdrop eyes toward him. "It sounded pretty special."

*Just what did she mean?*

"Your mom would be really happy if you went with them today."

"Did she tell you that?"

Annie shook her head, her dark hair brushing against her neck. "She didn't have to."

Gideon laid his spoon in his bowl and took them both to the sink, glad he had finished his meal. His appetite was sure gone now. "Leave it be, Annie."

"I don't think I can."

"Try."

He heard the scrape of her chair legs, and then she was beside him at the sink. "I like your family."

He grunted.

"They're worried about you."

He took her bowl from her and turned on the faucet, plunging his hands into the sink without heating any water to mix with the cold.

"Want to tell me about it?"

"No."

"Sometimes it helps if you talk about it."

"You wanna tell me why you were out on the worst night of the year with no coat and no luggage?"

Her eyes darkened and narrowed, and for a second he thought she might start yelling. Then she took a deep breath and expelled it. "I was only trying to help."

He paused. "I'll make a deal with you. You quit tryin' to help, and I'll let you stay as long as you want." He didn't know why he said that. To get her to stop?

Or to get her to stay?

She stuck out her hand to shake his. "Deal."

He looked down at it, and then took it into his own.

She smiled, perhaps remembering yesterday when he took her hand and led her across the yard toward his family and friends.

Or maybe to her, this was just a victory won?

He turned her loose. "I'll be in the barn if you need me."

Avery couldn't stop smiling. She could stay as long as she wanted. Now if she could just figure out a way to get out of going home for the Dunstan Pro-Am. Maybe if she got someone to take her place . . .

She stopped peeling potatoes and stared off into space. She had several friends—female friends—who would jump at the chance to take her place at the tournament and possibly meet a handsome, single pro golfer. Right after she got carrots sliced and the roast in the oven, she'd dig out her phone and make some calls.

She wasn't fooling herself—she'd have to go home eventually. But right now the peace and solitude were worth more than trying to figure out when. Most of her life had been planned out for her from start to finish. It felt good to just let it roll and not worry. When the time came for her to go home, she would, but until then . . .

She had a flower bed to weed. And supper to fix.

She washed and dried her hands then slid the large pan containing their dinner into the oven. Katie Rose had said to cook it long and slow, and it would be as "tender as a mother's love." After the disaster with the pot pie, she'd settle for edible.

Then again, as long as she was eating with Gideon, it would be a great meal.

She smiled to herself and went in search of her phone.

"What are you doin'?"

Annie jumped.

Gideon didn't mean to scare her, but could tell he had taken her by surprise.

She dusted off her hands, then stood and brushed off her skirt. "I'm weeding this flower bed. Lizzie showed me what to pull up. I'm doing it right, aren't I?"

"*Jah.* But it's Sunday. We don't work like that on the Lord's Day."

She propped her hands on her hips and eyed him. "When did you get so concerned that it's Sunday?"

"When you started rootin' around in the dirt."

"But"—she crinkled her nose—"I want to get some flowers when we go into town tomorrow."

"You will. And you'll clean out their beds tomorrow too. Come."

He took her by the arm and led her up to the porch. Louie followed behind them panting as he found himself a bit of shade under one of the wooden chairs.

"Sit." He pointed to the seat closest to the door and took the other for himself. He propped his feet up on the railing and leaned back in his chair. Little by little, Annie relaxed at his side.

This was all he had wanted from his life. A little piece of land. A Sunday afternoon to laze in the shade. Someone special to share it with.

The woman at his side was special, but she was not his. He let out a long, low breath. He'd had his opportunity at happiness, and it had been snatched away.

There had been a time when he thought he'd be able to sit on the porch and watch his children play while the wind blew through the trees and the grass grew. But that wasn't God's plan for him. To tell the truth, he didn't understand what God wanted from him. He hadn't asked for much. Land, wife, children. They weren't a lot to ask for, but were out of his reach just the same.

After they pulled into town, Gideon dropped off Avery at the library. Although she'd expected many stares, no one gave her a second glance. Town residents were accustomed to seeing the Amish among them.

She had originally thought she would pop into the bookstore and pick up a copy of whatever she needed, but there were two problems with that—there was no bookstore and her father would know where she was if she used her credit card. The library was the next best thing.

Avery's stomach fluttered as she walked through the big glass door into a foyer that smelled of old books and new carpet. The only experience she had with public libraries were dedications— not books. She *had* frequented the ones at her high school and college, so how different could this really be?

The woman behind the front desk nodded to her as Avery passed by. She entered through another set of glass doors and into a gigantic room of books. Well, maybe not gigantic, but it seemed that way. She only needed one book, and there were thousands to shift through to find it.

She turned back to the woman at the counter. Her name tag read, *Joyce*. "Can you help me?"

Joyce smiled and stamped something on a piece of paper. "Of course."

"I need a German-to-English dictionary."

"Right this way."

Joyce led her through the reference books, Avery trailing behind, thankful she had a guide. "These must remain in the library," Joyce said, pointing to a large shelf of leather-bound books. Most were big enough that Avery couldn't imagine anyone actually wanting to carry them across the room, much less all the way out to their car. "And these you can check out." She pointed to a different shelf, this one filled with books of a more manageable size. "Let me know if you need anything else."

"I do need a couple more things. Gardening books."

Joyce nodded and gestured in another direction. "Second shelf down that aisle right there."

"And cookbooks?"

"Across from gardening."

Everything she needed right at her fingertips.

Joyce smiled and headed back to her desk.

Avery watched her go before turning toward the books. She chose a couple, and then sat at the nearest table. She opened her handbag and pulled out the list of words she wanted to translate along with their Bible verses. She got the gist of most of what she read, but she wanted to know all of the words. She hadn't had a challenge like this in years.

She snapped the bag shut, the click of the clasp louder than she expected in the quiet of the library. She looked up and found one of the other library patrons openly staring at her. The woman shook her head, then went back to her reading.

Avery supposed she did seem a little odd, wearing a Plain dress and the green rubber flip-flops she had found under the bathroom sink, and carrying a Swarovski crystal-studded evening bag. Maybe she could find something else to bring with her on the next trip. She placed the bag in her lap, out of sight to those around her, then started her translation.

She read awhile, enjoying the quiet and solitude of the library, knowing that soon Gideon would be done with his errands and ready to go back to the house. She stacked up the books she wanted to check out in one pile and the others in a second pile to return to the shelf.

Now all she needed was a couple of gardening books and a cookbook to round out her reading. She wanted to make sure she planted the right things in the flower beds surrounding the house. Lizzie had told her that impatiens would be good. She also needed a row of marigolds in the garden plot to help keep the bugs out of the vegetables.

She chose a couple of books on annuals and perennials—whatever that meant—and turned to the cookbooks.

Last night's dinner with Gideon had been a huge success. Not like the parties that her father hosted, but she had cooked a nice meal, and had good company to share it with. She loved the feeling of accomplishment when preparing the meal from start to finish without anymore help than written instructions. That success gave her the desire to do it all again. It was the least she could do to repay Gideon for his generosity.

Who knows? Maybe she would prepare the food for the next dinner party at her house in Dallas. She smiled, unable to imagine her father's friends eating slow-cooked roast and potatoes instead of paté and shrimp. Then again, a home-cooked meal might do them some good.

Gideon, too. He had started to eat more. Whether because she was becoming a successful cook or something else, she didn't know. She would like to think it was all her doing, but she knew that plowing and planting made a person hungry. And since she had been on his farm she had noticed that his clothes didn't hang as loosely on his frame. Grief could do that to a person, but he seemed to be coming out of it.

She had heard the others talk at the work frolic. The whole community was worried about Gideon and his "wayward" attitudes, and were surprised that he had shown up at the frolic at all. Somehow that, too, gave Avery a sense of achievement.

She was just about to go back to the front desk when another book caught her eye. *Alpacas: A Beginner's Guide.*

A beginner's guide to *what*?

She picked up the book and looked at the back. *The first book you'll need to get started raising alpacas. Care, nutrition, harvesting the wool, and marketing the products.*

She didn't know why, but she added it to her "keeper" stack, then took her finds to the circulation counter. "I'd like to check these out."

Joyce smiled. "Do you have a library card?"

"No."

She took a clipboard out of the top drawer and handed it and a pen to Avery. "Then I'll need you to fill this out so we can issue you one."

Avery sat down in the chairs across from the desk and filled in all the information: address, phone number, birth date, and on and on. She stood and handed the paper back to the librarian.

"Now all we need is—" Joyce looked up from the form. "I'm sorry, you have to be a resident of the county in order to get a library card."

"I'm staying with friends here."

Joyce shook her head. "I'm sorry." She smiled in a way that let Avery know that, though she was sorry, rules were rules.

"Even if I have him come in and vouch for me?"

"No. But if he has a library card . . ."

Not likely.

"Annie?"

Avery swung around. Lizzie stood behind her, a blush on her cheeks.

"Hello, Mary Elizabeth." Joyce greeted her with a warm smile of recognition.

"Hi, Miss Joyce."

"Just give me one moment, dear, and I'll check you out."

"That's all right. Annie can use my library card."

"You know her?"

"Yes, ma'am."

"That's very neighborly of you, Mary Elizabeth."

"Yes, ma'am."

Joyce gathered up all the books, scanned them, and gave them back to the women.

At the door, Avery turned to Lizzie. "Thanks for helping me."

Lizzie frowned. "You're welcome." She lowered her voice. "Now can I ask a favor of you?"

"Of course."

"Don't tell my *dat* you saw me here."

Avery hid her smile. "Isn't that a lie?"

"Not if he doesn't ask you."

She doubted he would. "I won't tell."

"And *Onkel* Gideon. Please don't tell him either."

"I promise."

Lizzie let out a visible sigh of relief. "He just doesn't understand."

"Your uncle?"

"*Dat.*"

"Understand what?"

Lizzie shook her head. "I gotta go now." With that she turned and walked away.

Avery watched her go. Just what secrets did the young girl hide behind her sparkling blue eyes and innocent smile?

Once the supper dishes were washed, dried, and put away, Gideon went out to "not smoke" in the barn, and Avery settled herself on the couch with one of her library books. She needed to skim the cookbook to get a new recipe for tomorrow's supper, or glance through the gardening book to learn more before she planted the flowers they'd bought. But it was the calm face of the alpaca that drew her in.

She picked up the beginner's guide and started to read.

Tuesday brought cloudy skies and a good, soaking rain. Avery made bread from scratch using one of the recipes in the cookbook from the library. Gideon spent the day in the barn sharpening tools and repairing the horses' tack.

It was a good day, but the one thing that Avery really missed was Lizzie. Since Avery had come to the farm, the girl had come over every day after her German lesson at school. (It seemed she didn't know all there was to know.) A couple more weeks and even that would end. When the subject came up, Lizzie seemed sad, like a piece of her life was gone, and there was nothing to take its place.

But there was. According to Gideon, Lizzie would continue to help with the farm and with her brothers. Wash clothes, bake bread, and tend to the garden. In the late summer, she would can food for the winter: pickles, jellies, and all sorts of relishes to get them through the non-growing season. But for some reason, Avery didn't think this was where Lizzie's heart lay.

She was a good girl, and she would help, but Avery had the feeling she'd rather be doing something else.

Despite missing Lizzie, Avery enjoyed the rain. Gideon helped her pop corn on the stove top, and she curled up on the couch, a big bowl of snacks in one hand and a book in the other. Louie, too, seemed to enjoy the break, taking turns sitting on either side of her and snatching up any kernels she happened to drop.

"Did you know that Spanish settlers nearly killed off all the alpacas?" Gideon had come in from the barn and was now using a sharpening stone to "put the blade back on" the kitchen knives.

"The rest—the ones they didn't kill—hid out in the mountains. It says here that they are tough and strong."

He grunted his typical response and Avery smiled. That meant he didn't want to talk about it, but he was too polite to tell her so.

*Thank you, Ruth, for raising such a well-mannered son.*

"That's why they make such a good investment. They're hardy, gentle, and don't require a lot of land. How many acres in your pasture, Gideon?"

"Twenty-five."

"On that much land you could have . . . one hundred and fifty alpacas. That would be amazing."

"I do not want one alpaca, much less one hundred and fifty."

"I'm just saying." She looked back at the book, but she wasn't really reading. The idea had come to her as softly as the rain falling outside. Gideon could raise alpacas. His farm needed more purpose than just feed corn, and alpacas seemed to be the logical solution.

Except Gideon didn't think he needed a solution.

She cut her gaze back to him, and he was watching her.

"What?" she asked, her eyes wide in what she hoped was an innocent-looking expression.

"Why do you think I need livestock?"

"Isn't that what all gentlemen farmers need?"

"And what do you know, Annie Hamilton, of farmers?"

"Well . . . I know you are a gentleman. And—"

"How do you know that?"

"You saved my life." She shrugged as if to say, *We've already covered this.*

"I did not save your life."

"I could have frozen to death out there, but you rescued me."

"Someone would have found you."

"It could have been days."

"You had a cellular phone. Once you woke up you could have called for help."

She shrugged. "And I've seen how you treat Molly and Kate and the cow."

"Honey."

A ripple went through her. "What?"

"The cow's name is Honey."

"Well, that just proves it. Any man who names his cow Honey—"

"I didn't name her. Miriam did."

"Oh." Avery didn't know how to respond.

"I didn't rescue you."

She crossed her arms. "I beg to differ."

Gideon looked out the window, the rain still coming down in a soft drizzle that would last for hours. "*Ach*, the rain is good."

"It'll help your corn."

"That it will."

"I wanted to plant the flowers today."

They had left the plastic buckets of impatiens and marigolds on the porch along with the petunias, zinnias, and all the other flowers they had chosen. Gideon had acted like he didn't care one way or the other about the flowers, but when they got to the nursery, he started picking out different types and colors with as much enthusiasm as she.

"The rain will make the weeds easier to get out of the ground. The new plants easier to put in," Gideon added.

"I suppose you're right, but . . ."

"But what?" He turned to face her and for some reason, Avery didn't want to say the words. *Soon I'll be going home, and I don't want to waste a day of it.* "We need to get the marigolds in the garden before the bugs eat my tomatoes."

Gideon laughed, most probably picturing the tiny little tomato-less plants in their neat little row. "I'm sure your tomatoes will be all right 'til the morrow."

They *were* all right, a little soggy, but fine all the same.

Lizzie arrived just before lunch as Avery had expected her to, and the pair set out to clean the flower bed and get the flowers into the rain-soaked earth.

"In a couple of weeks, the colors will be full and lively."

Avery surveyed the plants with a critical eye. "Are you sure they shouldn't be closer together?"

"Positive. You have to give them room to grow."

Which was something Gabriel Fisher had seemed to deny his daughter.

"Lizzie . . . what were you reading at the library?"

She studied the ground. "Nothing."

"Lizzie. Tell me."

"I . . ." She looked up, her eyes pleading, needing a friend in the worst way. "You have to promise not to tell anyone."

"Who am I going to tell?"

"*Grossmammi. Dat. Onkel.*"

"Okay, okay. I promise not to tell."

"I was reading up on animal husbandry."

"Like being a vet?"

Lizzie glued her gaze to the floor and shrugged one shoulder. "I know it is prideful, but I can't help it. I want so bad to go to school and learn to take care of animals. To heal them."

"But?"

"*Dat* would never allow it."

The image of the sour-faced, frowning Gabriel Fisher swam into focus. Of course he would never allow it.

"It is against the *Ordnung*."

"I don't understand."

Mary Elizabeth smiled thorough her welling tears. "The *Ordnung* contains our rules."

"Like the constitution?"

She shrugged.

"And it's written down in there that you can't go to school past the eighth grade?"

"It doesn't have to be written, it is understood."

"And if you go to school anyway?"

She took a deep shuddering breath "Then they will shun me."

Avery's heart went out to the girl. It was one thing to pursue your dreams and quite another to do it at the expense of your family and friends.

"I'm sorry, Lizzie."

"It's okay." She said the words, but Avery knew they weren't the truth. Lizzie's heart was breaking. She was torn between what her heart wanted to do and what her community expected from her.

Avery feared that one day Lizzie would have to choose between her family—and her dreams.

# 8

"Why did you sell all of your sheep?" Avery asked this question of Gideon two days later on another trip into town. She'd told him she had forgotten a couple of key "girl" items and needed to go back to the store. She hated lying to him, but if she explained that she wanted to learn more about alpacas and their care, she knew he wouldn't take her.

"Who told you I sold my sheep?" He set his jaw. "Never mind, it was Mary Elizabeth."

"Don't be mad. I don't think she meant to tell me."

He grunted his usual response that Avery took as either a yes or a no, depending on what she needed from him.

"So why did you sell them?"

He took his gaze off the road for a split second, using the time to glare at her before returning his attention back to the front. "I didn't want to take care of them anymore."

"Why?"

"I sold my farm, and I didn't have enough room at the new place."

"Why?"

He tightened his grip on the reins. "What are you gettin' at, Annie?"

"Nothing," she innocently replied. "It's just that you planted corn in the fields, but the pasture is empty. You've got a lot of good grazing land just going to waste."

A smile twitched at the corners of his mouth. "What do you know about grazin' lands?"

"Not a lot," she admitted. "But I'm learning. It's good land for alpacas."

"Llamas?"

"Sort of." She tried to make her answer seem nonchalant, but she wasn't fooling him. The Amish might only go through junior high school, but she had learned that living in a close-knit community gave a person a lot of "people smarts."

He narrowed his eyes and gave her a scowl. "No."

"If you don't want to raise them yourself, you could lease that land to a neighbor—"

"I'll not have a bunch of strangers trompin' around my farm all day long."

"They wouldn't be strangers." She watched his cheek twitch as he kept his eyes toward the road as if the subject were closed. "At least give it some thought. It would be a good business."

"I think you need to mind your own."

He had her there.

But she wasn't about to let this drop. She'd be leaving soon—sooner than she probably wanted, and she couldn't stand the thought of Gideon locked up on his own farm, exiled from the others by his own choice. He was alive, breathing, and walking, but parts of him acted dead. She wanted to see those parts come back to life before she returned to Dallas.

She had planted the seed. Now all she could do was bide her

time until she could bring it up again. And bring it up, she surely would. "Can you take me to the library too?"

"I thought you needed to go by the general store."

"I do, but I wanted to get a few more books to read." More books on alpacas—but he didn't need to know that.

"We should have time. I need to order some wood and such to fix my barn. I'll go talk to the man at the hardware store, and then I'll meet you back at Anderson's."

Anderson's was the epitome of the old-fashioned general store. Maybe that was the reason Gideon preferred to shop there over the big-name stores that were pushing their way into Clover Ridge. Or maybe it was because Anderson's had a little bit of everything and what they didn't have, they could order. Coln Anderson, the store's owner, seemed to be able to get almost anything a body could need: fancy soaps, fabrics and zippers—even low-fat strawberry yogurt and Oreo cookies. The service alone was enough to make the community store the hub of the town. Most folks walked through whether they needed something or not. Sometimes to say a quick hello, sometimes just to pick up a piece of candy for the young'uns. Anderson's kept everything together in Clover Ridge.

"Gideon Fisher." Anderson greeted Gideon as he entered the cool interior of the store. The hard soles of his black boots thunked against the planks of the floor, a sound so familiar it was comforting.

"Coln." Gideon tipped his hat and headed over to the drink cooler. The day was turning out to be a warm one and cold lemonade would sure hit the spot. Somehow it felt right to be back in the general store with so many others of the district, everyone bustling around to get things readied up for spring. An invigorating smell permeated the air. The latest fabric, fresh straw hats, and new beginnings.

Gideon twisted the cap off a bottle of lemonade, and took a sip, enjoying the tangy taste and the memories of better days.

"Your sister and brother were in a little bit ago."

"That's *gut*." Gideon nodded. "Gabe needs time away from the farm."

"Not that brother. John Paul," Coln corrected with a flash of a smile.

It was amazing to Gideon that when someone spoke of his *bruder*, it was Gabriel who came to mind first. They had been so close growing up, practically inseparable. But since the accident, Gideon had pushed everyone away, including Gabe.

The smell of new wafted over him again. Time to start again, right old wrongs, correct past mistakes.

No doubt that "to town" trip had been taken to get the house and Gabe's young'uns ready for the growing season. John Paul could no longer be considered among the *kinner*. He was seventeen and in the first year of his *rumspringa*. Though he kept himself pretty close to home. It'd be the same when Mary Elizabeth's time to run around came. Though uncle and niece, she and John Paul were as close as two could be.

"Gideon, have you ever met my granddaughter, Carly? Her parents finally let her come visit for the weekend. I hope they'll allow her to come back in the summer and help out until school starts."

Gideon took another swig of his lemonade and followed Coln to the candy counter. It took everything he had not to stare longingly at the gumdrops and beg the man to sort through the mess of them and gather him a bag of the grape ones.

Instead he focused his attention on the pretty, dark-haired girl behind the counter. Her deep brown eyes held a definite slant, her skin smooth and just slightly darker than his own.

Coln's son and daughter-in-law weren't able to have children of their own and had adopted a little girl from China. Gideon remembered the story, he just hadn't realized it had been that long ago. But the truth stood before him smiling patiently while he gathered a polite greeting.

"It's mighty fine to meet you," he said, though he had been introduced to her once before. She had been only knee high to a post stump then. Though a lot more grown up, she was still not bigger than a minute.

She smiled shyly and tucked a strand of her silky black hair behind her ear. "Likewise." Her eyes dropped to the magazine on the counter in front of her.

Had it not been for the bashful reaction, Gideon may never have noticed what the young girl was reading. But it happened, and he did notice: a magazine with glossy pages and detailed pictures . . . and a vaguely familiar face.

His heart gave a thump as her identity seeped through his consciousness.

*Annie.*

He might not have known her except for those violet eyes. She looked so different in the shiny pictures. Her smile brightened the whole page, but she was dressed in *Englisch* clothes, her hair falling at all angles around her pixie face. She looked at home and at ease.

Gideon pointed toward the magazine. "May I?"

Carly nodded, and he pulled it toward him, turned it right side up, and tried to focus on the pages before him.

The magazine had a story about Annie—*Avery*—and her father and their house, a beautiful three-story structure on the outskirts of Dallas. Gideon had never seen such a place. Gleaming staircase, sparkling chandeliers, and paintings that looked expensive even if he knew nothing about them. He didn't have to know a lot about the cost of the possessions she stood among to know that Annie had everything she could possibly want in the *Englisch* world. Yet right now she wanted to stay in Amish country with him. He couldn't get his mind around the idea.

He flipped the page to see more of her life before she crashed her car in his field. Gold faucet sinks, intricate imported rugs, and polished wood antiques filled the pages.

Even with all the stories that Mary Elizabeth had been begging Annie to tell, Gideon was not prepared to see the extent of her family's holdings.

He tapped his fingers on the counter, a little too loudly—but it beat slamming the magazine shut on the opulence that was her life.

It didn't matter. Not one bit. She was going back to that decadent *Englisch* world real soon. Until then, it was no concern that his entire house would fit twice over into the room the Hamiltons used only to eat.

Not one bit.

❦ ❦

Avery was beginning to love the library. All in all, it was her favorite part of each trip to town. Back in Dallas, if she wanted to know something, she Googled it on her laptop. But nothing compared to holding the words in her hands.

"Good morning, Annie." Sylvia, one of the two librarians, greeted Avery as she walked past.

"Good morning." No one questioned why she dressed half Amish and wore an English hairstyle, but Avery knew they probably speculated about it when she wasn't there. It didn't matter. She was the happiest she had been in years.

"I got that book you wanted on the interlibrary loan."

"You did?"

Sylvia pulled a huge book off the shelf behind her. "*The Complete Encyclopedia of Llamas and Alpacas.*"

"That's great." She wanted to check out other books while there, but this one would keep her reading for a while.

"You've got an extended check-out time, but it has to go back in a month."

"No problem." She'd definitely be back home in a month. The thought made her sad so she pushed it away.

She took the books out of the canvas bag and placed them on the counter. "I'm finished with these, but I want to keep the cookbook for another week." There were still recipes she wanted to try.

"That'll be fine."

Avery smiled as Sylvia scanned the big book out and pushed it across the counter.

A familiar voice sounded behind her. "Avery?"

A voice she hadn't heard in weeks. Her heart gave a thump of dread. She didn't want to turn in case he was really behind her.

But it had to be him. No one in Amish country called her Avery.

"It is you."

She wheeled around, knowing he stood behind her, but still unprepared. Avery braced herself. "Hello, Jack."

He looked the same—handsome, blond, and tan. But he didn't seem as tall as he once had. Was that because she'd been around Gideon so much? Or because she'd grown as a person?

"I'm so glad to see you. I've been looking all over for you."

She tipped her head and narrowed her eyes at him. "Did you check Aruba?"

"Avery. What was I supposed to do? I was worried sick. I called your father to see if you were home. I couldn't very well tell him what happened, now could I?"

"I suppose not." It was impossible to keep the derision out of her tone.

Sylvia looked from one of them to the other, making no attempt to hide her curiosity.

Avery wasn't bothered by it, but she could tell Jack was. He grabbed her book, shoved it into her bag, and then took her arm. "Let me buy you a drink."

"Seriously, Jack."

"An ice cream, then. We have a lot to talk about."

She tried to wrench free of him. "No. We don't."

He half-escorted, half-dragged her toward the doors. Avery only went along for Gideon's sake. And Lizzie's. Everyone at the library knew she and the Fishers were friends. She didn't want anyone to think poorly of them because of her behavior.

Out on the street, Avery managed to tug free of Jack's grasp.

"What do you want, Jack?"

"Ah, Avery." His blue eyes—too blue because they were enhanced by contacts—scanned her. Avery could only imagine what he saw: a touch of sunburn on her nose, a trail of freckles across her cheeks, and her hair hadn't been cut in a couple of weeks, nor had it been properly styled. It curled around her face in a riot of dark locks. She wore another of Lizzie's castoffs, this one brown with cute, little cap sleeves that kept it from being too boring. Her fingernails were all chipped off, her pedicure gone, and she still ran around in those too-big shower flip-flops she had found at Gideon's.

Remarkably enough, she wasn't embarrassed.

"You've been here the whole time." It wasn't a question, but more of a realization. "You've been living with them."

"What I've been doing is none of your concern anymore."

He had the audacity to smile, looking like a used car salesman with a lemon to unload. "Ah, baby. You didn't think I was serious about that waitress." He reached up to tuck her hair behind her ear.

Avery slapped his fingers away. "Looked pretty serious from where I was standing."

"That's why you haven't returned my calls."

"Good-bye, Jack." She turned and started for the general store. It wasn't quite time to meet Gideon, but she wasn't about to stand there a moment longer.

"Avery . . ." He turned around, walking backward in front of her, not bothering to look where he was going. *Same old Jack.* "You and I go back—way back. I made a mistake. Surely you could forgive one little mistake."

She stopped, sputtering. Hot words bubbled up inside her like acid. "Mistake? I came here to tell you that I would marry you. Right away. No waiting, no big ceremony. And I find you in bed with someone else. That's a little bigger than a *mistake*."

"Come on, baby."

"I'm not your 'baby.'"

"Avery."

"Stay away from me, Jack." She pushed past him, leaving him standing in the street staring after her as she made her way into Anderson's General Store.

Thankfully, he didn't follow.

Anger churned inside her as they ambled back toward Gideon's house. Avery kept her eyes straight ahead, her hands twisted together in her lap.

Every so often, she could see Gideon look at her, then turn his attention back to the road.

She knew he had questions, that he was concerned. He was too nice of a man not to care, but Avery was afraid that if she started talking she might never quit. She didn't want to give Jack that kind of power over her.

"Sometimes it helps if you talk about it."

Wasn't that the exact same thing she had told him last Sunday?

"I-I ran into someone I used to know."

"I hope no one was hurt."

She had been, but she'd heal. Then she realized what he said. "I mean, I saw someone I knew."

He nodded, a smile twitching at the corners of his mouth. He was trying to make her feel better.

"It's just—"

"It's just what, Annie?"

"The night . . . the night I came here . . . the night I wrecked my car I'd come to tell my fiancé that I'd marry him. You see, I wanted a big wedding, and he wanted—"

"Whoa." He pulled the horse and buggy to the side of the road.

"Why are we stopping?"

"I have a feelin' this story needs all of my attention."

He was probably right, but she found it easier to talk when his eyes studied the road, instead of intently waiting for her to continue. She looked away, and tucked her hair behind her ear, giving her hands something to do. "I've always wanted a big wedding," Avery said after a minute. "Long, white dress, doves and lilies, the works, you know?"

He nodded, and Avery wondered how elaborate Amish weddings were. She bet they didn't go into debt thousands of dollars and invite half the state. *And for what?*

She took a deep breath. "But Jack, my fiancé . . . my *ex*-fiancé, wanted to elope."

"Run away and get married?"

Avery nodded. "He kept saying he was too busy with his movie and the guest list was getting out of hand. I kept fighting him on it. I really had my heart set on being princess for a day. But then, I decided that maybe he was right. Maybe I was just being foolish. I loved him, and he loved me. Why did we need a big ceremony to prove it? So I grabbed Louie and the first plane I could catch, and I flew up here to tell him I'd changed my mind."

"That was the night you wrecked your car?"

She nodded again. "He borrowed it to drive up here from Dallas. I thought it would be a great surprise for him, for me to just show up. So I didn't call. I figured the town wasn't that big. I rented a car and drove around until I spotted my car at a hotel."

"And?"

"I was the one surprised." That wasn't exactly true. Jack had been pretty shocked when she'd walked in on him and the curvy blonde local. "He was unfaithful to me."

"I'm sorry."

Avery was saddened by her own story, but not devastated. Amazing what two weeks of peace and solitude—and good company—could do for a person.

"You deserve better than that."

Avery smiled. "Of course I do. But I'll never find it."

"Now there's a good attitude." Gideon took up the reins and clicked his tongue at the horses.

"You don't understand." She braced her hand against the seat to steady herself as he pulled the wagon back onto the road. "Jack wasn't the first. I've had a lot of fiancés, but they only want one thing."

He cleared his throat and a deep red color started at his collar and worked its way upward. "I don't think we should be talkin' about this."

"Not that." She laughed despite herself. "My father's money. The Hamilton millions."

"And this is more important to them than bein' faithful and honest?"

"I suppose so."

"Crazy *Englisch*." Gideon shook his head. "And you saw this Jack in town?"

Avery nodded. "He's here doing research for a movie. A motion picture film."

"I know what one is."

"Oh."

"Did you talk to him?"

She nodded. *If you wanted to call it that.*

"And he's why you're angry?"

"Yes. No."

"It has to be one or the other."

Avery sighed. "I guess it's a little of both, but mostly I'm mad at myself." *For falling for his lies.* She was angry with Jack as well, for thinking he could take advantage of Gideon—or any of the kind hearts in the district—like they weren't really people.

"He is gone now, *jah*?"

Avery returned his smile. "*Jah*."

"Then let's not worry about him anymore today."

To Avery, that sounded like a fine idea.

Over a lunch of cold biscuit sandwiches filled with leftover bacon and apricot preserves, Avery watched Gideon. "Is your brother still coming over tomorrow to help paint?"

Aside from wanting to do roof repairs to get Gideon's house ready for the spring storms that would surely hit soon, Gabriel had talked his brother into painting the outside of the house. With the help of the neighbors, of course.

Anyone could see the little house needed a coat of paint in the worst way, but she also had to give kudos to Gabriel for convincing Gideon to let others come and help. One more step closer getting on with his life.

"*Jah*. And *Dat* and the boys. Maybe even a few others."

Avery stopped eating. "A few others? How many people are we talking about?"

Gideon shrugged. "Ten. Maybe fifteen."

"Fifteen people!" Fifteen hungry, working men. Her sandwich caught in her throat. "What will I serve them to eat?" What had Lizzie said? *You can't accept guests without an offering of food.*

There were tables of food at Hester Stoltzfus's house. How ever could she pull that together in under twenty-four hours? Arranging dinner parties had been a talent of hers in the English world, but that was no amazing feat when she had a phone and the Yellow Pages. All she'd had to do was get in touch with a willing caterer and the rest was up to them.

"*Mamm* will help. She and the boys will bring over the tables and meat and such. All you need to do is bake some bread and stir up some lemonade."

Avery smiled. "I can do that."

After they ate, she dragged out her cookbook and began skimming the recipes for interesting breads. She knew she couldn't compete with the deep-seated talent of Amish women and their bread-baking abilities, but she was willing to give it a try. She chose three recipes, an onion cheese bread, a raisin cinnamon bread, and a mayonnaise bread that, if nothing else, sounded interesting.

That she could take something as ordinary as flour, mix it with a few ingredients, and make something to feed the neighbors amazed her.

Still, it was no easy achievement. Her hands and arms ached from kneading the bread, turning it over, and letting it rise again.

The recipe said this break was to give the yeast time to fulfill its duty, but Avery knew it was to keep from killing the bread maker.

Yet the house smelled divine, with a yeasty-rich aroma filling every nook and cranny. A definite satisfaction came from seeing the bread rise and turn a delicious golden brown under her watchful care. She had turned heads and charmed diplomats, but nothing gave her the same satisfaction as this afternoon of baking.

She leaned against the counter, her hands caked with flour and dough. "Are you sure this is all I need to cook?"

Gideon turned a full circle in the tiny kitchen, pointing out each loaf of bread as he went. "There're eight loaves of bread, Annie."

She made a face. "Not enough?"

"Definitely not."

"Really?" She looked around and then glanced at the porcelain clock on top of the china hutch. "I guess I could make a couple more loaves after supper."

Gideon laughed. "There will definitely not be enough men here tomorrow to eat all this bread."

"Oh, you." She swatted him playfully on the arm.

"Maybe we should invite a few more neighbors to help," he said with a laugh.

❧ ❧

Dawn brought with it a beautiful day for painting, the wind calm, and the sun not too hot as it peeked over the horizon.

Gideon and Avery ate a quick breakfast, then readied the house for the frolic.

Shortly after eight, everyone started arriving, and by nine the renovation was in full swing. The women set up the tables under the shade of Gideon's oak tree.

Avery was as nervous as if she were entertaining diplomats and presidents. She wanted to do this right. More than anything she wanted this to go off without a hitch—for Gideon's sake.

"*Guder mariye*, Annie." Mary Elizabeth sidled up beside her and leaned in close so no one else could hear. "Did you make that bread?"

"Good morning to you, too." Avery smiled. "And yes, I did."

"*Aenti* and I were wondering." Her eyes twinkled. "You've been practicing."

"A little." Avery had practically worn out the cookbook. Joyce from the library was probably going to make her pay for it, but that was all right. Maybe she'd use it after she got home.

That'd be a hoot. She could throw a dinner party and invite all her friends. She'd serve them raisin bread and honey butter made from fresh cream and local honey. She tried to imagine her crowd all standing around in sequins and tuxedos eating Amish fare off linen napkins.

The image wouldn't produce. And yet sitting out in the sunshine, watching the men scrape the house and tape the windows seemed as natural as breathing.

"Samuel!" Katie Rose jogged across the yard after Gabriel's youngest. Avery looked up in time to see a flash of blue and black before she was hit full force with an all-body hug from the four-year-old.

"Oof!" She fell back with Sam sprawled on top of her. He sat up, king of the mountain style, straddling her rib cage.

He blinked his big, almond-shaped eyes, his little boy grin melting her heart. "Annie."

"Hi, Sam." Avery ruffled his bright red hair, his hat long gone after his sprint across the yard.

"Oh, my goodness, Annie. I'm so sorry." Katie Rose panted as she caught up with the little boy. She grabbed him under the arms and lifted him off Avery. "Samuel, you are a *bensel*."

"No, he's not." She didn't really know what a *bensel* was, but she knew Sam was not one. He was a sweetheart, so full of wonder despite his challenges, and she adored him. "I don't mind." Avery smiled down at him where he had pushed himself once again into the folds of his aunt's skirt. "That's the best welcome I've received in a long time."

Katie Rose smiled with relief. "It's just that he makes some people uncomfortable."

"That's their problem," Avery stated. "Because he's *wunderbaar.*"

At hearing the word, Samuel peeked his head around his aunt and smiled at Avery. She held out a hand to him. "Come, little Samuel. Let's go see if we can find you something interesting to play with."

Avery watched amazed at the simplicity of Amish children at play. She had never really given it much thought, but as with all things Amish, playtime was simple. No gaming devices, music players, or computers, just children of all ages with a bat and a ball. While their parents scraped and painted, the kids—with Katie Rose serving as both umpire and coach—played a game of softball. Avery sat in the shade with a ball of yarn entertaining Samuel with string tricks. He sat fascinated, watching as she twisted the yarn between her fingers to make the patterns: Spider Web and Jacob's Ladder. Then she taught him each move slowly. He laughed and enjoyed the afternoon.

She had learned string tricks long ago and hadn't thought about them again until today. Hadn't even thought about that summer at camp, the one she had gone to the year after her mother had died and her father didn't know what to do with a ten-year-old girl. At first he'd hired a nanny. When that didn't work out, he shipped her off to summer camp in the hills of Missouri.

She hadn't wanted to go. She had cried, but never in front of him, begged the servants to go to him on her behalf, but she never once told him herself that she didn't want to go. She couldn't stand up to him. Still couldn't to this day. That's why she hadn't called him to tell him she was still in the States. And that she wasn't coming back for the Dunstan Pro-Am. She had called her friend, Allison, and talked her into helping out in her place. Then she had texted her father with the news and immediately turned off her phone.

*Chicken*. But if she talked to her father, he would guilt her into going back to Dallas, and she wasn't ready for that. She needed a little more time. She was enjoying herself too much to return just yet.

"Annie, come on," Lizzie called.

Avery glanced down at Samuel, reluctant to exclude him. "Let's go play some ball, Sammy."

They played for nearly an hour, hitting the ball and running around the bases like their lives depended on it. There was fun and laughter and such a sense of well-being.

Never before had she ever felt such a part of something as she did right then. There was a camaraderie, a family love that seemed to happen when good neighbors and friends got together to help one another.

She could never picture Mr. Alastair Barnes, their closest neighbor, or any of her father's cohorts for that matter, climbing a ladder to help. They might get paint on their Armani suits. The only ladders they climbed were corporate ones.

Sadness for them came over her. Dinner parties and cocktail hour, operas and plays, even their artistic value couldn't compare to the . . . the . . . *togetherness* she felt here.

Love, true friends, and fellowship had all been missing in her life. With Gideon's family, she felt as if a hole inside her had been filled. She felt warm and welcome, more than she did among the people she called friends and family. Her father was always formulating some business deal or heading off to one beach spa or another to keep his soon-to-be wife, Maris, happy. There just wasn't a lot of time left over for Avery.

Not that she minded all that much. She was an adult. She didn't need constant attention. Still dinner with her father—without forty people in attendance—would have been nice from time to time. Maybe she should bring that up to him when she returned to Dallas.

Suddenly that thought didn't appeal to her, not at all. She did not want to return to Dallas, nor stand up to her father. In that moment she just wanted to *remain*. Remain in Oklahoma. Remain with the Amish.

Remain with Gideon.

When the men stopped to take a break, the women fed them, and gave them lemonade to drink. The only problem Avery could see was that the women and men ate separately. She loved the kinship she felt with the ladies that surrounded her—Ruth, Katie Rose, Lizzie, and the rest. But she really wanted to sit with Gideon, find how he was holding up, how it felt to once again be accepted by the people around him.

She found satisfaction in seeing the rough scrape of beard on his cheeks and the smooth curve of his upper lip. He was growing his beard back. He was sitting among the men, talking and sharing stories, every now and then laughing at something one of them had to say. Somehow she felt the light was shining back in his world after being absent for a very long time.

He looked up and caught her watching him. Their eyes held, and Avery couldn't look away. It was almost like that day in the buggy when some unknown force pulled them together, except yards lay between them instead of inches. Instead of them being alone, people were everywhere, family and friends chattered around them instead of the simple call of the birds.

Then someone said something to him, and he looked away.

Avery felt the rush of blood to her face. She wanted to fan herself, run inside and hide, to go over and take his hand and see what would happen all at the same time.

Instead, she took one last lingering look at Gideon. Then she turned to Samuel and tickled his ribs, relishing in the musical laughter of a child.

9

The odor of fresh paint drifted in on the night breeze. It was a good smell, a kind of "new start" scent that said things were going to be different. After today, Avery really believed things *were* going to be different for Gideon.

She had been there three weeks and already his farm looked so different than it had when she'd first arrived. Besides the lack of snow.

Fields and gardens were planted, and flowers started to grow. The house was painted and clean. Now if she could do something about the state of his pasture. If only she could convince him to raise alpacas. Corn could only take him so far. He needed a sustainable crop. Surely, alpacas would provide that for him. They would give him something to care for, a reason and a purpose.

She used a piece of yarn to mark her place in the book on raising alpacas for fun and profit and set it on the table at the foot of the couch. She had learned that the piece of yarn, as well as the one she and Samuel had played with most of the afternoon, had come from Miriam's loom.

Upon first learning this, Avery worried the others might take exception. But seeing the yarn again was like a trip down memory lane for the women. She'd learned a lot about Gideon's late wife through them. Miriam King Fisher was gentle and unassuming—two things she herself was not. Miriam was a fine woman, and well-respected in her community. She worked hard to pull her weight and fulfill what was expected of her. She tended the house and the sheep, and ran her own loom to make yarn and wool goods to sell in the marketplace. She sounded wonderful, and Avery could understand why he missed her so.

A part of her, just a tiny part, was jealous. She knew Gideon had loved his wife, his grieving alone was testimony to that, and that Miriam was admired by his family. Avery wished she had a little of that for herself—the love of a good man and family. She had been young when her mother died, but not so young that she didn't remember life with her. Though her mother was loving and caring, Avery couldn't imagine her in Ruth Fisher's shoes. Her mother just wasn't that . . . motherly.

And Avery could never proclaim that her family was very close. Her father had a brother they hadn't seen in years. Avery knew the two men talked regularly, but neither one carved time out of their schedules to visit the other. Her mother's family lived in Fort Worth, and she only saw them at charity functions they had been mutually invited to attend.

But today . . . today had been amazing. She knew what her friends would think about this new crowd. They would assume the Amish were simple and uneducated, but Avery loved them. The ladies talked about canning and jellies, pickles and diapers. The men worked hard and ate heartily. The sense of community and togetherness was tangible and something she had sorely been missing in her life. She hoped for another work frolic or even a barn raising soon. She wanted more to store up and keep with her after she had gone. From now until she to returned to Dallas, Avery planned on making the most of her time here.

She pulled out the Bible and started to read. It was slow going, reading in German, translating, then looking up the words she didn't know. But it was a satisfying challenge, like a lesson hard won. Maybe when she got back to Dallas she would buy a German Bible and her own copy of the translation dictionary to continue her study. She could get an English copy, but the slower pace helped the meaning sink in, forced her to keep her attention on the words and her mind on the meaning.

Her reading was interrupted by a soft knock at the front door.

Gideon poked his head in before she could bid him to enter. "I'm just headin' off to bed now," he said.

Not once in all the days since she had been on his farm had he felt it necessary to let her know when he was going to bed. *Why had he picked tonight of all nights to check in with her?*

She stood, not missing the fact that he toed the threshold, not setting foot into his own house.

"Okay, then." She closed her finger in the Good Book to hold her place.

He nodded toward the Bible she held in her hands. "Don't stay up too late readin'."

"I won't."

He hesitated as if wanting to say more, then with a small nod and a quiet, "*Gut nacht,*" he closed the door behind him.

"Good night," she murmured after him.

Then she understood. Today meant as much to him as it did to her—the fellowship, the closeness. She wished she could have more of it, and felt reluctant to see it pass.

There would be tomorrow, but how many more days would she have to savor the stillness of Amish life before she had to return to the crazy pace of her life in Dallas?

❧ ❦

Morning came far too early for Avery's taste. Despite Gideon's warning, she stayed up late reading. Still, she dragged herself up and put away her "bed," then staggered to the kitchen to start the coffee before getting dressed for the day.

She poured a cup for herself just as Gideon came into the house, looking refreshed and renewed and *not* like he'd stayed up half the night. She poured him a cup as well, and they sat down at the table to drink their morning brew together before she started breakfast.

Avery looked at him over the rim of her cup. "It's Sunday."

"*Jah.*"

"Have you given any thought to going to church this morning?"

"*Jah.*"

"You have?" She set her cup down so hard, some of the coffee sloshed onto the table. "That's great." She jumped up to get a rag to clean up her mess, unable to keep the smile off her face. His mother would be so relieved to see him in the congregation today.

Gideon squinted at her. "I only said I had given it thought. I did not say that I was going."

"Gideon." She dragged his name out across several syllables. "You should go."

He didn't say anything, just rubbed a hand across the stubble on his chin.

Avery wondered if his beard was itching him since it had been growing back in, or if he wasn't ready to face everyone in the district with his nearly-bare face.

He shook his head. "*Nay.* No. I can't do it. Not with everyone . . ." He pushed his chair back and stood in one jerky motion. One minute he was sitting across from her and the next he stood with his back to her while staring out the window.

"What are you going to do?"

He didn't answer.

"Just hide out here until . . . until—"

"I die, too."

His words were quiet yet they reverberated with heartbreak. It was all about grief.

She moved to go to him, then stopped herself. He wasn't hers to comfort. Never was, never would be.

She sat back in her chair and said the first thing that came to mind. "When you are brokenhearted, I am closer to you."

He turned. "What?"

"When you are brokenhearted, I am closer to you. Psalms, I think. I just read it, so you'd think I'd remember."

"It doesn't matter."

"It *does* matter." She squirmed, but held her place. "You're pushing everyone away. Even God. And right now you need them . . . you need *Him* the most."

He took a deep, shuddering breath, then grew still. "Let's have a picnic today."

She stared at his back. "You're avoiding the issue."

"We could pack some sandwiches and maybe a jar of *Grossmammi's* pickles."

"Gideon, you can't hide like this."

"Go down to the creek. There's a big old tree down there, just perfect for eatin' under."

"It's going to catch up to you one day."

"Louie would love it down there. Dragonflies to chase. Moss to roll around in."

She released a sigh. "All right, all right. A picnic it is. But this isn't over." She knew when she had been beaten, but she wasn't giving up. Even if it was the last thing she did before she left, she vowed she'd get Gideon back to church.

＊＊＊

He was right about one thing. Louie loved the creek. He romped around and pranced through the grass like a big dog. Snapped at the promised dragonflies, chased butterflies, and in general had a high old time while she and Gideon sat under the shade of the giant oak and ate the food they'd packed.

Gideon finished first, and stretched out on his side, twirling a blade of grass between his fingers as he kept watch on Louie who darted back and forth, yipping at one insect or another. She sat cross-legged next to him, her legs tucked under the folds of her skirt. Yet another mark on the "pro" side for Amish attire.

"These are the best pickles I have ever eaten." She took another bite, savoring the crunch and tangy flavor.

Gideon shrugged. "Old family recipe. Or at least that's what *Mamm* says."

"I thought homemade pickles were supposed to taste bad." The episode of the old *Andy Griffith Show* came to mind, where Andy changed out all of Aunt Bea's pickles for store-bought ones.

Gideon shrugged again. "This is all I've ever eaten."

"Really?" That seemed so strange to her, but after three weeks of living among the Amish, she could believe it. They were so self-sufficient, so capable. There didn't seem to be anything they couldn't do—including make homemade pickles.

"'Cept on a fast-food hamburger."

She tried to picture him eating a cheeseburger wrapped in

paper, but the image wouldn't surface. Instead she saw him *chew,* *chew, chewing* her failed attempt at chicken pot pie.

A giggle escaped her, followed by another and another.

"What's so funny?"

"You."

"Me, what?"

"I mean . . ." she struggled to pull herself together, to stop laughing. "When you were eating the pot pie I made. You were too polite to tell me that it was awful, instead you just kept eating and eating and . . ." She sucked in a deep breath. "That's not funny, is it?"

"No, but I like to see you laugh."

Then it happened again. A moment like the one in the buggy, where all the air seemed to stand still, and there was no one in the world except the two of them.

Their eyes met and held.

She reached out a hand to touch his face. Slowly, fingers trembling.

But he grabbed her hand before she could make contact.

"*Nay.*" His eyes blazed with an emotion she couldn't name. She wanted it to be longing, but thought it more like anger. He'd had something special with his wife and even if it was over, he wasn't ready to move on. She had been too bold.

She pulled her fingers from his grasp. "I . . ." She wanted to apologize, but couldn't. It wasn't the truth. She wasn't sorry. He was handsome and gentle and kind. And she had wanted to touch him, kiss him. It felt as natural as breathing, and she couldn't feel sorry about it.

Instead she stood and walked to the water's edge. The wind had started up again, and it ruffled her hair, whipping the growing strands into her eyes.

He drew up behind her. "Annie, I . . ."

Avery didn't turn around. She just shook her head. "It's okay." Thankfully her voice sounded steady and calm, not at all turbulent, like she felt inside.

"But—"

"Louie!" she called, searching the tall grass for signs of her tiny pooch. Anything but to have to turn around and hear Gideon say those words to her. He didn't deserve her rudeness, but she couldn't look into his eyes again, couldn't see that flash of shock when she'd been so forward. It was one thing to realize that she had made a mistake, and another altogether to have him say it out loud. "Louie V.!" She let out a shrill whistle, watching for him with a steady and unwarranted intensity, until he appeared in view.

"I'll get the quilt," Gideon said. "It's time to go home."

He folded up the quilt they had brought to use as a picnic blanket, while Avery picked the strands of dry grass out of Louie's hair. He squirmed in her arms, preferring to run free rather than be pampered. He certainly had adjusted to farm life.

Together they walked slowly back to the house, the only sound coming from the wind in the trees and the occasional cry of a sparrow. They were almost to the porch when Gideon finally spoke.

"Annie, I—"

"Don't say it." She set Louie on his feet, and he immediately trotted over to the group of dogs lying in the shade of the barn. "You don't have to say it. I know you loved your wife. And I know that I'm too bold. I should have never—" she broke off. "Anyway, I'm sorry. No, I'm not. But I should apologize for being so forward. I'm English, what else can I say?" She attempted a smile, but it felt more like a grimace.

He nodded once. "Accepted. I'll be in the barn."

His words sounded so final, even though it was only the middle of the afternoon.

She watched him retreat, his back to her. "What about supper?"

He didn't turn around. "Don't worry about me. I don't think I'll be hungry." Then he disappeared into the barn, taking a chunk of Avery's heart with him.

It was better this way. It seemed callous and unchristian, but he couldn't tell her the truth. It was better that she think he was still so in love with his wife that he couldn't bear to be touched by another. It was for the best that she think she was too bold for him, because the truth was scarier to him. By far. The truth was that he had waited for her touch. Wanted it desperately, and in that desperation knew it had to be stopped.

Gideon stared up at the boards above him, sleep elusive. He had stayed in the barn for the rest of the day. He'd oiled all the leather in the horses' gear. He'd brushed the animals unnecessarily. And he repaired the loose floorboards of the hay loft. That had taken about two hours. The rest of the time he sat and tried not to think about . . . her.

Impossible.

She had no place in his world. She might have on an Amish *frack*. She might have learned how to make *snitz* pie, but she was *Englisch* through and through. It was better for her to think he didn't want her touch when in actuality he longed for it. There wasn't enough of his heart left to be broken a second time.

He turned on his side, and closed his eyes, willing his mind to empty and allow him to sleep. He listened to dogs bark in the distance, and the answer of his own mutts, to the soft breathing of barn animals, and the occasional call of something wild.

Maybe tomorrow he'd go to town and get some pigs. It'd be *gut* to have some fresh bacon to go with his dippy eggs. That had always been his favorite breakfast, and it took only one lesson for Annie to learn to make them.

Once again, she filled his mind as he drifted off to sleep.

By Monday afternoon, Avery was sure the air would crack if the tension between them became anymore brittle. They walked around each other like rival countries, each afraid the other would break the peace treaty first.

She tried to pretend nothing happened between them, and by English standards nothing did, but that "nothing" sure did change things. She hadn't looked into his eyes all day.

He'd made no attempt either, preferring to look down at his plate, out the window, or at the top of Louie's head, rather than at her.

She'd ruined it, she thought as she pulled up the tiny shoots of grass that dared to poke their heads through the rich soil in the front flower bed. She'd had the perfect place to rest and relax—well, at least get away from the city and the demands her father made on her—and she'd blown it.

She probably needed to call her father and tell him she'd be back for the tournament this weekend. Then she'd call and get an appointment to get her hair cut. If she sweet-talked Ramon maybe she could convince him to squeeze her in. She'd have to get a mani-pedi too. She looked down at her hands. All of her acrylics were gone, the nails underneath brittle and short. Not that it mattered. It was hard to weed garden plots and knead bread with longer nails. Back in the real world, though, they'd need protection and show-manship. The thought of all that pampering should have made her smile with contentment. But it didn't.

Because all that pampering meant leaving this world behind.

She had known it was coming. She had understood from the beginning that her time here was limited. But she wasn't ready to leave just yet. She wanted to attend a quilting bee. She still had to convince Gideon to buy some alpacas. And she wanted to get him back to his church family.

He wasn't far. She had seen him in the fields when he didn't know she was looking. He'd stood there, a hoe in one hand, his head bowed. She had taken to saying her own silent prayer before they ate, but she'd peeked once, and Gideon had been praying too.

He only thought he'd lost his faith. It was still there, lurking under the surface of his grief. Just a few more layers, and it would shine through. Unfortunately, she wouldn't be here to see it. With any luck—no, *help* from above—he would continue down this path of recovery.

The soft thud of horses' hooves caught her attention. Avery shielded her eyes from the sun, but from this distance she couldn't tell who approached. She stood and dusted the grass from her skirt and pushed her hair behind her ears. Just another part of the refreshing Amish lifestyle. She didn't have to hurry in and change clothes, worry about the state of the house, or inform the mean little Austrian cook that they had guests who needed to be served.

She wasn't sure what offering she could make them. She still had the unopened package of Oreo cookies Gideon had brought back from town that first day, but store-bought cookies didn't seem right.

The buggy drew closer. At first, Avery thought Gabriel was seated there, but a few more yards closer, and she could see the streaks of silver in the dark beard. Abram, Gideon's father. Looking at the elder Fisher, Avery knew what Gideon would look like a decade from now. Hard-won lines at the corners of deep blue eyes, streaks of silver bisecting a beard that almost touched his chest. Abram Fisher was a broad, solid man, the kind of man a woman knew would provide and protect. But the hard line of his mouth reminded her more of his oldest son. The squint of his eyes seemed more assessing and disapproving, than protection from the bright rays of the sun.

Was that sour expression the norm for Abram Fisher? Or was that glare reserved for lost and lonely Englishers who had outstayed their welcome?

"Good afternoon, Mr. Fisher."

He grunted, sounding so much like Gideon that Avery had to hide her smile. She knew that Gideon's father didn't approve of her being here. He had barely said two words to her at the work frolic. But it didn't matter. Avery wasn't about to let him chase her away. That time was well on its way without his help.

"Gideon's in the barn, I think. Shall I get him for you?"

"I can find him." He set the hand brake and hopped down from the buggy.

Avery held out a hand. "Give me the reins, and I'll get your horses some water while you visit. It's too hot already to be out without a drink."

He paused for a long second, then took the brake off and handed her the straps of leather.

"Maybe after you find Gideon, the two of you could come in and get a drink yourselves. I just made some tea this morning."

Abram nodded, then started off toward the barn, the Y of his suspenders dotted by the brim of his hat.

He stopped and turned back around. "Annie," he said, his mouth still tight, but his eyes softened. "Name's Abram. Amish don't use titles 'cept for those who are chosen by God." Then he touched the brim of his hat and continued on his way.

Although unsure of what he meant by the statement, somehow Avery felt one step closer to the Fisher patriarch.

Gideon heard the soft crackle of straw before his light was blocked.

He didn't want to go into this again, didn't think he was strong enough to stand his ground a second time. He closed his eyes and willed himself to be strong, then he swerved around, a bale of hay held in front of him like a shield.

His father stood before him, not Annie, and it was all he could do not to sigh in visible relief.

"*Dat.*" He tossed the hay to one side and nodded to his father. Then he took off his gloves, slapped them against his leg, and stuffed them into his back pocket before extending his hand.

His father's grip was firm and reassuring, its strength flowing into Gideon. For the first time he could ever remember, Gideon wished to be little again with no more worries 'cept milkin' the cows, gathering eggs, and findin' enough worms to support an afternoon's fishin'. The bygone days of childhood, without so much grief and loss, so many tough decisions.

"Looks good here."

Gideon nodded. The new paint on the clapboard made the house sparkle like a jewel in the sun. The garden was coming in, the strawberries blooming, and the flowers that Annie had planted displayed their riot of color as pretty as you please. The farm actually looked like someone lived there. Strange, for this was the place he had come to die.

Abram jerked a thumb over his shoulder toward the door of the barn. "Seems like your Annie has taken to Plain livin'."

"She's not my anything," Gideon protested, the taste in his mouth as sour as his thoughts. Never had been, never would be.

"That's good to know." Abram nodded. "Our ways aren't for everyone. It's hard goin' for the *Englisch* to try and join up."

Gideon knew that. It was more common for Plain folk to jump the fence than outsiders to climb over onto their side.

"She's just not *unser satt leit*."

He knew that too. She was not their kind of people, but it rankled him to hear his father say it all the same. "Is that what you came all the way out here to tell me?"

Once the words were out he couldn't take them back. His father seemed not to notice his surliness.

Abram shook his head, his eyes growing cloudy, and the thin line of his mouth flattened out even more. "We're havin' a family supper tomorrow night. You need to be there."

It wasn't a *We'd like to have you* or *Come join us* invitation. Not that his father had ever been one for soft words. But there was an urgency in his statement, a "no room for noncompliance" in his tone that made the hair on the back of Gideon's neck stand up.

"What's this about?"

Abram pressed his mouth together before answering. "We'll talk tomorrow. When everyone's together."

Gideon ran a hand around the inside of his collar. "Is this about a *meidung*? Just go ahead. I deserve it. I knew what I was doin'." He wasn't sure if he could say the same about allowing Annie to stay in his home.

"You know as well as I do that shunnin' ain't about punishment."

"I do." Shunning was more about bringing somebody back into the fold. Gideon just wasn't sure if he was ready for that either. "But I've done what I had to do. If'n the bishop's not happy with that—"

"This has nothin' to do with the bishop. It's . . . it's somethin' else."

He opened his mouth to speak, but his father cut him off. "Not now. Tomorrow night. Five thirty."

"Five thirty," Gideon repeated. He watched his father turn and walk back out of the barn.

Something was wrong, and it ate at him to not know what. *You'll find out soon enough*, he told himself. Then he rolled his shoulders in an effort to get those prickly hairs to go back into place.

⚜

Avery was surprised when the door opened at a little after six. She hadn't expected Gideon to come in for supper. He had been avoiding her all day, sneaking into the house to snatch up food while she worked outside in the yard.

It hurt to see him try so hard to keep away from her, but was to be expected. She had overstepped the bounds, and though she had apologized, the action couldn't be taken back.

"Is there enough for two?" He smiled a little sheepishly, the slashes of his dimples nearly gone in his quickly growing beard. It would have taken Jack a month to have what Gideon had grown in a little over a week.

"Of course," she said, relieved that he wanted to eat with her. Or perhaps he had grown tired of cold meals. Whatever the reason, she was glad to have the company. Have *him* for company.

She finished putting the food on the table, and they sat down to eat like so many times during these past few weeks. Avery bowed her head, and thanked God for the food, the beautiful day, and all the blessings she had. She had never before counted her life in blessings, but now she could.

This time she didn't peek to see if Gideon prayed as well.

They loaded up their plates with food and ate in companionable silence, but Avery could tell that Gideon had something on his mind. He usually devoured his food, bite after bite with steady concentration. Tonight he took extra care in buttering a roll. Lingering as if he wanted to say something, but didn't know what.

Avery ate her fill, waiting patiently for him to find the words. She needed to say things too, but didn't want to say them yet. She needed to ask him about going to town—and about going home—but she hadn't even called her father. She just couldn't. As much as she needed to leave, a big part of her longed to stay behind. So she waited for Gideon.

Finally, he looked at her, those smoky green eyes filled with uncertainty. "*Dat* came by."

She nodded. "I invited him to come have a glass of tea, but he seemed like he was in a hurry." She tried to hide her disappointment. She really wanted to get to know Gideon's father, and if she were leaving tomorrow, today was her last chance. Although she hoped to come back and visit, she knew she never would. In Dallas, her life was hectic, filled. If she couldn't find the time to drive over to Ft. Worth to go horseback riding, no way could she make it all the way back to Oklahoma.

"He . . . invited me to supper tomorrow night."

She heard the pause before "invited," but didn't mention it.

He looked down at his half-eaten meal, then out the kitchen window. "I want you to come with me."

"You do?"

"*Jah*." The word came out quietly and heartfelt.

Avery realized that the biggest part of her that wanted to stay in Oklahoma was her heart. And she needed to get back where she belonged before she lost the rest of it. She swallowed the knot of emotion that had formed in her throat. "I think it's time I went home."

Gideon's forehead creased. "Because of yesterday?"

She nodded.

"You don't have to go home, Annie. I said you could stay here as long as you wanted. That offer still stands."

"You don't regret it after . . ." She couldn't say the words out loud.

"No." He turned his gaze on her, and Avery could tell that he was worried about much more than an almost kiss.

"What's happened?"

He shook his head. "I don't know. *Dat* said for me to be there, and so I will."

"But I don't think—"

"I want you there."

How could she refuse him? "All right, then. I'll be there." But delaying her move back to Dallas would only make leaving harder when the time came.

"Yoo-hoo! Annie? You in there?"

Avery poked her head out of the bedroom door, thankful to see Lizzie standing on the porch. "I'm here," she called. She turned back to the garments laid out on the bed and studied them some more.

The screen door creaked open and slammed shut, then the young girl was beside her.

"What are you doing?"

Avery cocked her head. "Trying to decide what to wear."

Three dresses lay across the bed, each one fresh from the line outside. A little wrinkled, but smelling like sunshine and late spring. To an outsider they would have looked the same, but to Avery, there were subtle differences that made each one special— puffed sleeves, a slightly shorter hem, or a more flattering color.

The young girl didn't hesitate. "The green one." She paused. "Where are you going?"

"Supper at your grandparents' house."

Lizzie squealed and clapped her hands together. "Really? That's *wunderbaar*!"

Avery wasn't so sure. She wanted to go, but at the same time, she worried that spending time with Gideon and his family would make it harder for her to leave when the time came. As much as she wanted to deny it, put it off, and pretend that it wasn't imminent, her return to Dallas lurked just around the corner.

She pushed those thoughts away and concentrated on the matter at hand. "I like the green, but . . ."

"Green is *Onkel's* favorite."

All the more reason not to wear the soft, jade-colored dress.

"He'll probably be wearing a shirt that matches and the pair of you will look so handsome together. Like at the work frolic."

This solidified the suspicions Avery had on Saturday morning about their matching outfits. Lizzie was responsible. She looked into the young girl's blue eyes and saw love and hope shining there. It seemed that Amish girls were no more above matchmaking than English ones. "Mary Elizabeth."

"*Jah?*"

"Get that look off your face right now, missy."

"What?" Her expression looked innocent and wide-eyed.

"Quit trying to set up your uncle and me. We're just friends." It was true. They were friends. A friend was someone you could talk to and count on. Gideon Fisher was all that . . . and more. "And that's all we'll ever be." She hated saying the words.

"You can't blame me for trying."

"Sure I can."

Lizzie laughed. "It would be so *wunderbaar* having you around all the time."

And it would be *wunderbaar* to be around all the time. Just not feasible. "Despite your not-so-subtle attempts at matchmaking, I'm wearing the green dress anyway." She sniffed. "It's my favorite, and it has nothing at all to do with your uncle."

"Have it your way." Lizzie's smile stretched all the way across her face.

Avery hung up the other dresses.

"Oh, no!" Lizzie cried.

"What? Look here."

"It has a stain. *Guck datt hie.*" She smiled sheepishly.

Avery studied the *frack*. It did, indeed, have a stain. And the dress was her favorite. She sighed. "Lavender or brown?"

"I like the green best," Lizzie stubbornly replied.

"I do too, but I can't go to dinner at your parents' house with a stain on my dress." Some things just couldn't be unlearned.

"Too bad you don't have a for-*gut* dress."

"Too bad." Avery stared at the stain, wishing it would disappear.

"'Course no one could see it if'n you wore the apron."

"I beg your pardon?"

"The apron. Where's the other stuff I sent you that first day?"

Avery searched through the bottom of the closet and pulled out the bag with the other items Gideon had brought her.

"This is a cape." She took out a garment that looked like a long vest with a point in the back and two narrow flaps in the front.

Lizzie gave it a shake, and then laid it on the bed. "And this is an apron."

Both garments were faultless black. If she wore them, the apron would cover the stain. She hesitated. At the work frolic, it was obvious that Avery was an outsider. She wore the dress, but no prayer *kapp* or apron or cape. And she felt a little odd not dressing like the rest. So though it might not be healthy, for this one night, Avery wanted to do it up all the way.

"Are you sure it'll be all right?"

"Of course." Lizzie smiled, hope returning a sparkle to her expression. "In fact, I think it'll be *brechdich.*"

"Is that Amish for disaster?"

"It's *Deutsch* for magnificent."

"I'm not sure about that," Avery said with a smile. "Especially not with all these wrinkles."

"I don't suppose they taught you how to iron in that fancy school you went to."

Avery shook her head.

"That's okay." Lizzie smiled again. "I'll teach you how."

She turned and made her way into the kitchen, muttering all the while about shoes.

## 10

Gideon rubbed his palms down his pant legs. Why was he so *naerfich?*

Maybe it was his father's attitude about the upcoming dinner. Abram Fisher was a hard man. He'd not been the same since his sister Megan had left. Even though it was customary to allow Amish teenagers to "run around" and experience the *Englisch* world before settling down and joining the church, it was difficult when someone left the fold for the sins and pleasures outside their community. For the elder Fisher, it was as if somehow he had failed.

Gideon took a deep breath to settle the uneasiness in his middle. Or maybe it was waiting for Annie that had him as skittish as a long-tailed cat in a room full of rocking chairs. It had been a long time since he'd had to wait on a woman. He propped his feet on the porch railing and tried to create a nonchalant pose.

The screen door banged against the house. Gideon's boot heels hit the boards with a thud. Mary Elizabeth appeared, her cheeks flushed and a wide smile on her lips. "Are you ready?"

"Been that way, *jah*."

Mary Elizabeth's grin grew wider still, if that was possible, then she stepped to one side and another woman walked onto the porch. Ten full seconds passed before Gideon realized it was Annie.

*Ach*, she looked different. The shock of it rendered him speechless. She wore the green *frack* that she had borrowed from Mary Elizabeth, but she had also put on the black "for good" cape and apron like a proper Amish woman. Even more proper, she had somehow pinned up the short strands of her hair and added a prayer *kapp*.

She took his breath away.

Annie beamed. "Well, what do you think?"

He thought she was the purtiest thing he had ever seen, but what was the benefit in telling her so? She would be gone soon, back to her fancy world. It'd do them no good a'tall to start up something that could never be.

"You look fine." He hated that his voice sounded gruff, like Gabe's . . . or his father's.

"*Danki*," she said.

Mary Elizabeth echoed the word.

Annie looked more than fine from the top of her head to the tips of her polished black shoes. Suddenly, he felt like a heel. He should have given her shoes a long time ago. She was *Englisch*, not used to runnin' around barefoot like an Amish girl. He should have realized that. But instead it was Mary Elizabeth who had brought her shoes to protect her feet and go visitin'. Where she got them, he had no idea, but they looked fairly new.

Now he understood why the young girl was so determined that he wear his green shirt tonight—so he'd match Annie like they had at the work frolic. It seemed Mary Elizabeth had it in her head that she would match them as well, but it wouldn't work. Well, the *matchmaking* would work, but the match never would.

He'd speak to her about that later. No sense in letting her get false hopes.

"Ready?"

The girls nodded.

"Then let's go. Mary Elizabeth, do you want to put your bike in the back of the buggy?"

She shook her head so hard he thought her *kapp* might fly off. "Oh, no. I'll just ride it back to the house." She gave them a little wave, then jumped off the porch and raced to her bicycle as quick as a fox.

She was halfway to the road before Annie turned to him. "Is this bad?" she asked, biting her lip, her mouth a crooked line of indecision. "Lizzie said it would be okay if I wore this. I mean, I can take off the apron and cape and . . ." As she said the words, her fingers flew to the front tie of the apron.

All he could manage was, "*Nay.*"

"Are you sure?" Her big violet eyes filled with a mixture of hope and hesitancy.

Gideon nodded and held out a hand. "We should go."

She dipped her chin and placed her hand in his. Her fingers were warm, her palm starting to bear the calluses of her work on the farm. Gideon had mixed feelings about that. He was impressed with her ability to adapt, yet somehow sad that she had traded her soft, sweet skin for a garden of vegetables and flowers.

Molly and Kate stood patiently by, waiting for the signal to pull the buggy wherever Gideon needed to go. He helped Annie into the seat, and then swung himself up beside her. He clicked his tongue against his teeth, and they started off in his niece's wake.

The evening was warm, the sun creating a golden halo in the sky, the breeze making the rays bearable. Gideon loved traveling by buggy. On the occasions when he had the opportunity to ride in a car, he found it unnerving. He enjoyed the gentle sway of the horses as they clopped along, the fresh air on his face, and the opportunity to slow down and talk to one's companion.

He cleared his throat, feeling like a teenager at his first singin'. "The flowers are coming in nice."

"Yes. Yes, they are." She tilted her face toward the sky, and Gideon could see the tiny beat of her pulse in the side of her neck, and the edge where the sun's color ended and her own began.

"Won't be long now, and we—there should be some vegetables to gather." He had almost said, *We will have some fresh food for the table*, but stopped himself just in time. There was no "we."

"Are you sure this is all right?"

"You look fine," he said again.

"I mean the two of us going to this dinner at your family's house."

"*Mamm* will be glad you came. She loves to feed anyone who will sit down long enough for her to fill a plate."

Annie let out an audible breath. "I feel like I'm meeting the parents. I mean, I *am* meeting parents, just not the parents of a boyfriend. Suitor."

"No."

"I'm just nervous."

"Don't be." His words belied his own feelings.

"Who's going to be there again?"

Gideon shrugged. "*Mamm* and *Dat*, Gabe and his boys, Katie Rose, Mary Elizabeth, and my brother John Paul. You've met 'em all."

"So why am I quaking inside?"

He would like to know the answer of that for himself. "It's just *nachtess*."

"Just supper," she repeated.

Somehow he knew this was something more. Whether it was that Annie had gone all out in dressing like a Plain woman or his father's serious tone when he demanded that Gideon come eat, he wasn't certain.

One thing he did know—this was more than just supper.

Avery's cheeks were flushed, and her heart pounded. She felt like she was on the set of an old black and white movie, except everything was in color—beautiful, brilliant color. The sky was impossibly blue, the trees a fresh green, and the buggy vivid black. Crisp and real, yet surreal all at once. Riding in a buggy along the country road was enchanting too. She could almost imagine she was in a bygone century—except for the couple of times when a car pulled gently around them and sped down the road ahead.

She could hardly wait to eat an authentic Amish meal—especially one she hadn't prepared. She had become quite a chef since coming to Gideon's farm, but she was anxious to try the real thing.

And so many people. The banquets, parties, and benefits she attended for her father were mostly austere occasions for the event of the day—save the whales, send the underprivileged children to college, or build a new basketball court at a favorite park. The atmosphere was always controlled and calm, organized and withheld. Attendees of those dinners were there for one reason—to give money. They ate what they were served at hundreds of dollars per plate. But they didn't come for the food, or the fellowship, or because their father had asked them to come and gather together. They were there because they were wealthy, and someone needed money.

This dinner, she had the feeling, would be different. Maybe that was the reason for her nervousness. She was accustomed to standing before hundreds, giving speeches and asking for funds to complete a project, but this dinner was all about family, something she didn't have much experience with.

In no time at all, the buggy turned down a fence-lined, packed-dirt drive. At least it seemed like the travel time went by fast. Avery still wasn't sure if she was ready.

"This is it," Gideon said, swinging around toward the barn, while Avery turned in her seat to get a better look at the house.

The outside was similar to Gideon's farm with its whitewashed clapboard and a big matching barn. A garden sat off to one side, a clothesline on the other, and tufts of red and yellow flowers grew out front. This house also teemed with life—chickens and horses, pigs, sheep, turkey, and geese. Not to mention the passel of dogs and cats napping in various places around the yard.

Gideon helped her down from the buggy, and Avery noticed that his hands didn't linger on hers a moment longer than necessary. She shouldn't care, but she did.

"Are you sure I look okay?" she asked as they approached the porch steps.

"Are all *Englisch* women this concerned with their appearance?"

Avery nodded. "Most of them."

"Then that must *halt* now. Tonight you are not *Englisch*. Tonight you are among the Plain folk."

As compliments go, it wasn't a very good one, but it calmed some of her insecurities. Tonight no one would judge her appearance. All the women there would be dressed practically identical to her. There would be no sideline talks about someone's dress or shoes or escort. They would talk about quilting and canning and milking and all the other things she heard about at the work frolic. The tension in her body melted away.

Gideon knocked.

Lizzie flung open the door, as if she had been waiting on their arrival, and ushered them inside. "Look, everyone. Gideon and Annie are here!"

A throng of family members greeted them as if they hadn't seen each other in months instead of days.

Avery felt welcome in the Fisher home and more like she belonged. Only Gabe, Gideon's older brother, withheld smiles and conversation from her. Lizzie wanted her to tell stories about her home in Dallas, how they had a cook and a maid and all sorts of gadgets that made life easier. Katie Rose wanted her to recount her cooking experience, and Gideon wanted her to describe Louie chasing butterflies down by the creek.

When it was time to eat, they all took their places down both sides of the long rectangular table and bowed their heads.

Avery asked for peace for Gideon and good fortune for his family. She also offered thanks to be included in such a special evening.

"*Aemen*," Abram finished for them all.

Everyone served themself, and the table sagged under the weight of food. Bowls of sausage and sauerkraut were served to rival the likes of Inga, her father's cook. There were mashed potatoes, green beans, and several relishes, as well as those amazing pickles she and Gideon had eaten on their picnic.

All in all, dinner was a loud affair. So many adults and children all in one place was nearly deafening. The elder Fisher's home was a great deal bigger than Gideon's with a large front room and gigantic kitchen. It was evident that God and love lived in this house.

Avery barely ate. Instead, she watched those around her. Everyone doted on Samuel, made sure he was happy and had everything he needed. It seemed that Katie Rose had taken the place of a mother in his life. The rest of the mothering went to Lizzie, an underage matriarch making sure that her brothers had what they needed and that they were minding their manners. Like that was a big chore. Even as loud and boisterous as the Fisher clan could be, Avery was inspired by their respect for one another.

"It's so good to have everyone here," Katie Rose said.

"*Jah*," Ruth agreed, smiling at those seated around the table.

"Everyone, but Megan," Lizzie said.

Ruth's smile froze, and she glanced at her husband.

Avery could tell from her expression that Lizzie immediately regretted her words. She all but clamped her hand over her mouth to keep more from spilling out.

A hush fell over the table. Abram seemed to shut down, then go into autopilot mode. He blinked once, his eyes staying closed for only a fraction of a second longer than necessary, and then he opened them again and began to eat like nothing had happened.

Lizzie's comment seemed innocent enough, but everyone's reaction sent questions zinging through Avery's mind. Evidently Megan was special to the family, yet somehow gone from them now.

The atmosphere at the table became a bit subdued, but still remained a fun and energetic affair. Avery glanced at the animated faces in the room. What might it have been like for Gideon to grow up in such a spirited family?

"Seven sweets and seven sours is just a myth made up to attract tourists," Lizzie said. She chatted nonstop while helping her grandmother and aunt clear the table. "We eat the same stuff like everyone else."

"Some more than others," John Paul said, pinching her side.

Lizzie swatted his hand. "The Lord loves all creatures great and small."

John Paul opened his mouth to retort, but Ruth broke in. "Now, now," she said gently.

Lizzie shot him a smug look, which John Paul returned with a *just you wait* stare that was all in fun. Suddenly Avery wished that she'd had a bigger family to enjoy, share jokes with, and love.

"Watch out. Coming through." Lizzie and Ruth came to the table, each bearing two homemade pies. They set them in the center of the long table while Katie Rose handed out dessert plates like graded papers.

Lizzie pointed to one of the desserts. "This one's pear pie." She pointed to another. "And this one's shoofly. It's my favorite," she whispered. "Then there's cherry from the ones we canned last summer and pecan." She leaned toward Avery. "I'd like to take that back. Pecan is my favorite."

"At least it is tonight." At last, John Paul got in his word, and Avery laughed.

Pie was served all around and against her better judgment, Avery took two small slices, one of cherry—*her* favorite—and the other of shoofly. That one she just had to try.

The cherry was blue-ribbon worthy. Sweet and delicious, the shoofly tasted like a little piece of heaven. A cake-like top covered a syrupy filling with a bottom crust that flaked under her fork. But even after that treat, cherry topped her list. Maybe next time she'd have room enough to try the pear too.

Avery pushed her plate away, certain she wouldn't be able to eat another bite for days. The food was amazing, the company even better. The evening had been perfect.

"Uh-hum." Abram cleared his throat. The table fell silent, even the youngest of the children turning a wary eye on the eldest Fisher. "John Paul, Matthew, you take the boys outside to check on the horses. Mary Elizabeth, you go with them. Go on." The teens looked reluctant, but didn't argue. They gathered up the smaller children, Samuel included, and herded them toward the door.

Once the youngsters were out of the house, a hush fell over the diners. Ruth bowed her head, and Avery was certain she was praying. Abram cleared his throat again, then braced his elbows on the table in front of him and looked at each of them in turn.

"*Mudder* and I have some sad news to share."

They all waited impatiently for him to continue. He took several deep breaths, and then his eyes filled with tears. "I . . ." He started, but seemed unable to finish.

Ruth raised her head, her green eyes strong and determined. "I have cancer," she said firmly and without emotion as if she had long since come to terms with the news. "Breast cancer. I've asked the Good Lord for guidance, and your father and I have decided that I'm to go to Tulsa for treatments. We felt that you should know."

Energy erupted around the table.

"How?"

"What will we do?"

Avery started to stand. "I don't think I should be a part of this."

Gideon grabbed her hand and squeezed it hard. Other than that, he showed no emotion at his mother's announcement. Like his father had over the mention of Megan, Gideon seemed to shut himself off from whatever was to come next.

"*Nay*." He gave her hand another small squeeze.

"*Nay*," Ruth echoed. "Annie, over these last few weeks, you've become like one of our family. This is a family affair, and you should be here for it."

No one dared contradict her.

Avery sat down in her seat, glad to be included, and sad all the same.

"It's not goin' to be easy," Ruth continued. "But it's not my time, and I'm goin' to fight this. I'll need your help around the house and with the chores. The Bradleys have offered to drive us into town to the cancer treatment hospital. They have lodgin' there when we need to stay."

"What about insurance?" The words slipped from Avery's mouth almost of their own accord.

"Plain folks don't go in much for insurance," Abram explained.

"The Good Lord will provide," Ruth added, that serene quality back in her voice.

"Let me know how much you need," Avery said. "I'll help you with the bills."

Abram faced her. "That's mighty fine of you, Annie. But we can't accept your charity."

"It's not charity. You just said yourself that we're like family."

Ruth smiled and shook her head.

Avery leaned forward. "Then take my car."

"Your car is in no shape to drive to Tulsa." Gideon had found his voice. "And even if it was, who would drive it?"

"It's . . ." She almost hated saying it. "It's a very expensive car. Even sold for scrap parts, it would be worth a lot."

It was Abram's turn to shake his head. "Plain folk take care of one another. There is a fund that will help us pay the doctors."

"Cancer treatments are very costly. It won't be nearly enough. Let me—"

"The Lord will provide for us," Ruth said again.

Avery saw firsthand where Gideon had gotten that stubborn streak.

"But—"

"The Lord takes care of those who take care of themselves," Abram said, shaking his head.

Avery turned to Gideon's mother. "Ruth?"

The Fisher matriarch shook her head as well. "Your offer is generous and much appreciated, but we're Amish. And Amish take care of their own."

Avery felt shut out, that if she were truly Amish, the Fishers would accept her help. Yet she knew that's not what Ruth had meant. They had their own ways of dealing with these matters, ways that kept them close as a community and family.

Still Avery wasn't about to let this rest. She had spent the better part of her life raising money for others in need. She would find a way this time too.

There was a stifled sob from across the table, and Avery looked up to see Katie Rose's shoulders start to shake.

"It's okay," Ruth said, pulling Katie Rose's head down onto her shoulder. "The Lord will provide for us."

Katie Rose sniffed and snuggled her head into the crook of her mother's neck. "I know." She sniffed again. "I know."

Avery wished that she could do something—anything—to take away some of their pain.

Then Ruth straightened and smiled through her tears. "Maybe we should do a Bible readin', huh?"

"*Jah.*" Abram nodded.

Avery looked to Gideon, his hands white from clenching them together on top of the table. Other than that, he looked as if they hadn't been talking about anything more important than the weather. He had shut off. Avery knew. He fought feelings he didn't want to battle. Instead of dealing with them, he had pushed them down and capped them off. Pretty soon they were going to blow.

She just hoped he could get them out before too much damage was done.

"Annie, will you go get the others?" Ruth asked.

Avery nodded.

"Gabe," Ruth said as Avery stood. "I'll expect you to tell the boys and Mary Elizabeth. Tell them how you want, but make sure they understand that God's in charge, and we are doin' His biddin'."

"*Jah, Mamm.*"

"*Dat* and I will talk to John Paul tonight."

Avery opened the door to the warm spring night. The stars

were just starting to sparkle in the indigo sky. The crickets had begun their nightly song. In the distance, she could hear the call of the mourning dove. A beautiful night for such terrible news.

The younger children all stood around outside the barn, the older ones huddled together, no doubt trying to figure out what had happened and why they were exiled from the room.

"You can come in now."

Seven eager and worried faces turned toward her, and then seven bodies of all sizes ran toward the house as fast as their feet would carry them. All but Samuel.

"What happened?"

"What'd we miss?"

They all started asking questions at once, but Avery just shook her head. "Get in there. Abram's about to read from the Bible."

She left them standing half in and half out of the house, then hurried across the yard to get Samuel. He had stopped to look at some clover that grew in a patch between the house and the out buildings. She scooped him into her arms and held him close, loving the clean smell of his shirt and the sweet aroma of innocence. He smiled up at her and handed her the white clover flower he'd picked.

"Annie," he said.

It was all Avery could do not to break down on the spot.

Gideon was quiet the entire ride home.

Avery wanted to comfort him, to touch him and let him know that even if she couldn't say that everything was going to be all right, she understood his pain. Felt it herself.

But he sat in the driver's seat, staring straight ahead as if his life depended on it.

Avery sat next to him, trying to figure out what to say.

When they reached the house, she had no more ideas, but she couldn't let him go to the barn alone. Not like this.

"Gideon, I . . ." she said, as he hopped out of the buggy and came around to her side. "I . . ." she started again.

He only shook his head. "It's been a long day." He set her on the ground as if she weighed no more than Samuel. "I've got to care for the horses, and then I want to get some sleep."

"I'm worried about you." There, she said it. It was the truth. God would care for Ruth and Abram—all they had to do was pray. But Gideon . . . Gideon needed more than that.

What was it Abram had said? *The Lord takes care of those who take care of themselves.* From what she had seen so far, Gideon was in no state to take care of himself.

"It's not me you need be concerned with," he said as he unhooked the horses and gathered their reins.

"But I am."

"In the morning, Annie. We'll talk after we've rested." Then he turned and led Molly and Kate into the barn without another word or glance in her direction.

She watched him, not knowing what to do, unsure if anything could be done. Then she turned in the opposite direction and made her way to the house.

When she walked in the door, Louie was there to greet her, barking out his welcome and begging to be picked up and cuddled. Avery obliged, gathering him to her as she went about lighting lamps and getting ready for bed.

It had started out as such a perfect night. With the exception of the terrible news, the evening had gone well. A loving family, so wholesome and caring, was something she had never experienced. Something she had always missed in her life. Until she met

Gideon and his family, she had never known what she had been searching for.

She sat Louie on the bed and carefully removed all the garments Lizzie had helped her don a lifetime ago. Avery had enjoyed being one of the Plain folk for the night—the fellowship, the Bible reading . . . the *pie.*

She smiled. The Amish sure did love their pie.

Once the borrowed dress was hung back in its place of honor in the closet, Avery slipped into one of Gideon's shirts and padded to the front room, Louie hot on her heels.

She made her bed on the couch, fluffed her pillow, and lay down. Her mind fluttered back to how she fussed over herself while getting ready. Shame over being so obsessed with her appearance enveloped her. There were so many other problems—worthier problems—in the world. She knew now that what she wore was of no consequence. Old habits and all that.

Ruth and Abram had welcomed her into their home. Avery had the feeling that it would have been the same had she showed up in a *frack* or the cocktail dress she'd been wearing when she crashed her car.

She sighed and turned over. And Samuel. He would understand none of what had been announced tonight. Probably for the best. By now, Ruth and Abram had told John Paul. Avery wondered how he took the news. And Lizzie. Gabe was supposed to tell her. Avery couldn't imagine the iron-faced Gabe understanding a young girl's worries about her grandmother. Hopefully, Lizzie would come by tomorrow afternoon after her German lesson, and they would have the chance to talk.

Gideon had promised Avery that they would talk as well, but she suspected he had only said that to get her to go to bed.

Like that did her any good. She was just too keyed up to sleep.

Avery sat up and turned on the lamp. Maybe she would read a little. Surely that would help.

She threw back the covers, ignoring Louie's whine of protest, and went in search of something to read. She still had a couple library books, and the books that were in the house when she got here—and the Bible.

It drew her in, called her name. She picked it up, ignoring the pen and paper she normally kept close whenever she read the Bible, and instead tucked her feet up under her and started to read.

> *Der Herr ist mein Hirte; mir wird nichts mangeln.*
> The Lord is my shepherd; there is nothing I
> lack.
> *Er weidet mich auf grüner Aue und führet mich*
> *zum frischen Wasser.*
> He lets me lie down in green pastures; He leads
> me beside quiet waters.
> *Er erquicket meine Seele; er führet mich auf rechter*
> *Straße um seines Namens willen.*
> He renews my life; He leads me along the right
> paths for His name's sake.
> *Und ob ich schon wanderte im finstern Tal, fürchte*
> *ich kein Unglück; denn du bist bei mir, dein Stecken und*
> *dein Stab trösten mich.*
> Even when I go through the darkest valley, I
> fear no danger; for You are with me, Your rod and
> Your staff—they comfort me.
> *Du bereitest vor mir einen Tisch im Angesicht*
> *meiner Feinde. Du salbest mein Haupt mit Öl und*
> *schenkest mir voll ein.*
> You prepare a table before me in the presence
> of my enemies; You anoint my head with oil; my
> cup overflows.

*Gutes und Barmherzigkeit werden mir folgen mein
Leben lang, und werde bleiben im Hause des Herrn
immerdar.*

Only goodness and faithful love will pursue me
all the days of my life, and I will dwell in the house
of the Lord as long as I live.

A peace like she had never known washed over Avery. God was with her. Always. God was her protector, her champion, her light.

Avery had first heard those words in Sunday school, before her mother had died, when they had gone to church as a family. How many times had she heard them since?

Now they held a special significance. She read them as if seeing them for the first time, their meaning suddenly clear.

Her eyes filled with tears as her heart expanded in her chest.

She'd been saying all night that God would take care of Ruth, but now . . . now she *knew* He would take care of her.

She didn't think twice. She jumped up from the couch and headed out the door, barely taking the time to let Louie out with her. Emotion burst within her and she needed to share her joy with Gideon.

The well-worn path to the barn was soaked in moonlight. Avery didn't hesitate. She flew across the yard to the barn doors and found Gideon sitting outside. Not smoking his pipe like she suspected he would when he could not sleep.

"What are you doing out here?"

He sat in the shadows, his voice thick and hoarse. Avery couldn't see his face. She didn't need to in order to know that tears slid down his cheeks and into his newly-grown beard. He stood when she approached.

"I-I . . ." The elation from moments ago stilled in her chest. "Talk to me."

"There's nothin' to talk about."

"Then what's wrong?"

"Nothin's wrong. Nothin' at all." But his voice was filled with derision.

She had found her way to God, and Gideon was struggling.

"She's going to be okay, Gideon."

"You don't know that."

"But I do."

"No—"

"The Lord will take care of this."

He almost laughed, the sound heart wrenching. "You sound like my mother."

"I'll take that as a compliment. She's a very smart lady."

They stood there, she in the moonlight, he in the shadows, and listened to the crickets and frogs call to one another.

"I haven't asked God for a lot in my life," Gideon said quietly. "And the things I've asked for have been taken away or unanswered. I don't know if I can believe that God takes care of His people anymore."

"That's part of faith."

"Then I'm all out." His clothing rustled as he shifted.

"You're not. It just feels that way."

"*Nay.*"

"Oh, Gideon, I felt the same way when my mother died. I was ten, the time in a girl's life when she needs her mother the most. I felt hurt. Hopeless. It's hard. And you ask why to anyone who'll listen, but no one has those answers. You can drive yourself crazy with questions like that."

"I want to help her."

"You want to save her."

"Is that so wrong?"

"No." She gave her head a slight shake. "It's not wrong. I would have saved my mother if I could have."

"How did she die?"

"Suddenly. In a car wreck."

"So there was nothing you could do?"

"No."

She could hear him breathe and wished again to be closer, close enough to lay a hand on his cheek, intertwine her fingers with his, anything to let him know that he wasn't alone.

"Gideon, your mother has agreed to go to treatments. That's a lot. Some people would just throw their hands up and let the cancer do what it would. But Ruth, she's a fighter."

"There's got to be more."

"You can pray."

"How can that be enough?"

Avery smiled. "Because God's involved."

They sat in silence for several heartbeats. Inside the barn, animals shifted on the hay as they rested in their stalls.

"It's more than that," he said finally.

"Then tell me."

She heard his deep, shuddering sigh, but she couldn't determine if he was pulling himself together or coming apart at the seams.

"I killed her. Miriam's dead because of me."

# 11

Any sane woman would have been terrified to hear a man say those words. Especially a man she was alone with . . . way out in the country . . . with no phone or car or means to get help.

But she wasn't fearful at all.

"Gideon, that's not true." Tears welled in her eyes at his heartbreak. What burden he carried to feel he was responsible for the death of someone he loved—no matter how untrue the self-accusation.

"It is." He heaved a great breath as if gathering himself to continue. "But that's not the worst of it. I killed Jamie too."

"Jamie?" she whispered, afraid to ask.

"My son."

Avery's heart plummeted, her breath caught, and she could barely whisper the words. "You had a child?"

"*Jah.*"

She longed to rush to him, to wrap her arms around him, to take some of that unbearable hurt away. But she knew it was better to give him the privacy he'd found in the dim corners of the barn to tell her his story. She dropped down in the hay, ignoring how it pricked the back of her legs, and moved as close to him as she dared. "Tell me."

He drew in a breath.

She held her own and waited for him to begin his story.

"It was about this time last year," he started slowly. "There was a big storm comin'. Everyone was sayin' it was gonna flood. You could smell it in the air. Miriam didn't believe it was goin' to be that bad. Her family had already planned a sisters' day. They were goin' to make baby stuff for Sarah, the oldest. I told her not to go, but she did.

"When she got home it was rainin' so hard. I was tryin' to get the sheep to higher ground. I yelled at her. I yelled at her in anger." He paused, his voice jagged, raw. "There were just so many of them. The rain was comin' down so hard I could barely see two feet from my nose."

Tears caught in Avery's lashes, then fell to her cheeks, sliding down, down, down until they dropped off the edge of her chin. From the darkness, she heard him move again. He resumed his story, his voice rusty and worn.

"I sent Jamie after the new lamb that had been born that mornin'. There was somethin' wrong with it, and it couldn't keep up with the others."

Avery bit her lips to keep from crying out. She was afraid that if she interrupted, he would stop and recede once again into the shell he had created for himself.

"That's when I told Miriam that she shouldn't have gone to her sister's. She should have been there to help me, and this wouldn't be happenin'. She didn't get mad back. She just lifted her soggy skirts and ran after Jamie." He shifted again. "That was the last time I saw them alive."

Avery's breath caught in her throat, a stifled sob blocking her air.

"Jamie managed to catch the lamb, but he fell into the creek. Miriam jumped in to save him. They found them downstream, the poor animal a few feet away."

A long silence followed Gideon's revelation. In the quiet, Avery froze between her desire to reach out and comfort the grieving man and his quest to be left alone with his pain.

"So you see—I killed her. I killed them both. Just as surely as if I had laid hands on them."

Avery shook her head. Hard. "Oh, Gideon, you don't really believe that." She couldn't imagine the pain he suffered at the loss of both his wife and child, but to believe that he had been responsible?

"*Jah*," he said from the darkness. "I do."

"But it's not your fault. It was an accident. It was—"

"God's will?" His voice, still thick with emotion, had taken on a hard edge.

Avery thought about that. "I can't say that God *wills* bad things to happen to us or to anyone. To a child. But you can't go around your entire life wondering why things happen like they do. It'll eat you up inside. Sometimes it's better to deal with what happened the best way you can and move on. If you want to call that God's will, then yes. It was God's will."

He sat in silence, and Avery hoped he was thinking about what she had said.

He sighed. "I could have done more . . . somethin', *anything* to help them. I should have gone after the lamb myself."

"But you didn't."

"I should have," he repeated.

Avery drew in a deep breath and steadied her nerves. "Some things are left up to God. And the 'hows' and the 'whys', well, maybe someday we'll understand. Until then, the sun still rises in the morning and sets each night. Frankly, I think Miriam would be disappointed to know that you've stopped living all those times in between."

She heard his sharp intake of breath, but he didn't say anything.

She continued. "I came out here tonight to tell you that I understand now. I understand how much God loves me and what He wants me to do. I discovered this all because I wrecked my car and you were gracious enough to let me stay." She pushed herself to her feet. "I've finally found my way, Gideon, to something I've been searching for my whole life, even though I just realized it tonight.

"If you want to stay wallowing in whatever self-guilt you've concocted for yourself, I can't stop you. But I'll not let you drag me down there too."

Without waiting for him to respond, she turned on her heel and headed back to the house.

By the time he made his way into the kitchen the next morning, Gideon's eyes felt raw and scratchy, like they were filled with ground glass. He'd spent half the night thinking about Annie's words—and the other wondering if they were true.

And he knew. It was all true. He *did* feel helpless. He'd wanted to save Jamie and Miriam, and now he wanted to save his mother.

But all that happened in the past, and the present was beyond his earthly power.

He poured himself a cup of coffee from the pot sitting on the stove and took a tentative sip. It was still hot, which meant she hadn't gone far, and she hadn't been gone long. Like it mattered. She probably wasn't speaking to him today anyway. An Amish woman would be over her snit by now. *Nay*, an Amish woman wouldn't have started such a ruckus in the first place—but the *Englisch*. *Ach*, they were a different lot altogether.

"Good morning."

He turned. She stood there, looking nearly as she had the night before at his parents' *haus*. She had donned the purple *frack* with matching cape and a white everyday apron. She had forgone the shiny black shoes for the green flip-flops, but she had done that pinned-up thing with her hair and managed to place it all under the *kapp*.

He couldn't help it—his eyes riveted on that symbol of obedience.

She raised a hand to the *kapp*. "Lizzie told me that Amish women wear a prayer cap out of respect for God, and that they wear them all the time because they don't know when they might be moved to pray."

"*Jah.*"

She gave a quick, jerky nod, then Annie moved past him to the stove and poured her own cup of coffee. "I'm not going to apologize for what I said last night."

"I didn't ask you to."

"Would you like for me to make us some breakfast?"

"I . . . I'm goin' over to talk to my *elders*."

"Your mom and dad?"

"*Jah.*" The idea had been forming all through his sleepless night. Everything Annie had said knocked around in his head mixing up with his fears and worries. The only way to put those concerns to rest was to talk with his parents, especially his *mamm*. Last night didn't leave much time for questions and answers what with the whole family there. But today, with everyone going about their daily routine, he should have plenty of time to visit with his *mudder*.

Annie nodded. "I'll be here when you get back."

She stood on the porch with Louie at her feet while he readied the buggy for travel. He wasn't sure, but he thought he saw her smile before he turned to the front and urged Molly and Kate down the driveway.

Ruth heard the buggy before she saw it. She propped the hoe to one side and waited, wondering who was coming for a visit at this time of day.

She wasn't at all surprised to see Gideon's buggy ambling down the lane toward the house. Of all of her children, Gideon was the one she worried most about these days. She could barely look at his face the night before when she had told them the news about her cancer. Gabriel had been stony-faced as usual, John Paul in his unwavering faith had been hopeful, and Katie Rose had been naturally upset. But it was Gideon whom the news would most affect. She was glad to see him coming to her today, better than her showing up at his house.

As he drew closer, she saw that he was alone. That in itself was a blessing. She'd been glad last night that he'd brought his *Englischer*, but she needed this time alone with him. She needed a chance to make him understand that God was good, and that everything happened for a reason. That there was a purpose and a solution to everything she now faced.

Abram walked out of the barn just as Gideon set the hand brake and jumped down. With only a clap on the shoulder in greeting, Abram took the reins and led the horses toward the watering trough.

Abram turned and looked at her, and her heart tightened. She smiled at her husband of so many years, hoping the one little motion conveyed all the promise and love she felt. But Abram just nodded and turned away. He was having a tough time dealing with the news they now faced, but she had made her peace and prayed that her family would be able to see that only through faith could she truly be healed.

"*Mamm.*" Gideon's quiet voice carried to her on the soft breeze.

"My *sohn.*" She touched his face where his beard was growing back in quite nicely. *God is good.*

He gathered her up in a bone-crushing hug, and Ruth fought back the tears that threatened. Now more than ever she had to be strong.

"There'll be none of that," she scolded, wiping tears from Gideon's face as she spoke. She had wanted to go on holding him for as long as possible, like she had done when he was little. But he was a grown man, and as much as it pained her, she had to let him heal the hurts for himself.

He swallowed hard, seemingly unable to speak.

"Come inside." She lead him toward the porch, propping the hoe in the corner and waiting for him to catch up.

He moved ahead and opened the screen door, ushering her inside.

"Let's have some pie," she said.

He shook his head.

She cut two big slices of last night's shoofly anyway and carried them to the table. Before he could protest again, she poured them both glasses of milk and set them next to the plates.

Reluctantly, he pulled out a chair and sat down across from her.

"Now, tell me what concerns you, *sohn.*"

"Cancer?" he asked, his voice as weak as his faith these days.

She covered his hand with her own, drawing strength from him whether he knew it or not. "The Lord will provide."

His eyes, so much like her own, seemed doubtful at best.

She couldn't help but smile. "You see, Gideon, it's all about faith."

He shook his head, his pie sitting untouched before him.

"I thought I raised you better than this," Ruth admonished. "What awaits the faithful on the other side?"

He paused. "Heaven." His voice was rough, raw with emotion.

"And on this side I have my family. So you see, I win in either direction."

"But—"

"I know it's prideful to believe that I'll automatically go to heaven, but I have faith. And my faith is strong. So if He takes me from this world, I'll go to be with Him. I can't lose."

"I'll sell my farm," Gideon finally said. "You can have the money from that—"

"You'll do no such-a thing." She sat back in her chair, her own pie forgotten. "I'm hearing that you have finally started to work your farm. You can't go back on that now."

"But Annie's right. This will be costly. We'll need every penny we can find."

"*Jah*, that it will." Her heart swelled when he said "we" and not "you." This was a family fight. "But I've already told you, the Lord will provide."

"I can't help but—"

"You can. Everythin' bad that happens to us is just a test of our faith. I'm not about to lose mine now." She worried that he might take offense to her words, but he didn't. Or maybe he didn't see the connection to his own life.

She knew Gideon still had faith. It had been trampled on and nearly taken from him in his grief, but it was still there, shimmering below the surface, just waiting to be rediscovered.

He nodded, and she knew the exact moment when his merely agreeing with her became a testimony of rekindled belief. He might not recognize it now, maybe not ever, but he knew the Lord was good, that He would provide, and all would be well.

"Now eat your pie," she said. Then she gave up a small thanks to God above.

The talk with his mother must have soothed Gideon's fears. He wasn't exactly cheerful when he returned, but he seemed more at peace with himself. And that, in turn, eased Avery's heart. They hadn't yet talked about that revealing conversation in the dark. He hadn't mentioned it, and she hadn't brought it up. Ruth would tell her to let sleeping dogs lie, so that's just what Avery planned to do.

She shook out the quilts she used each night for a bed and laid them over the porch railing. Breakfast had been eaten, the dishes cleaned, and now there were chores to be done. She needed to wash out her dresses, sweep the kitchen floors, then pick the strawberries. But for now, it'd be good to let the covers hang outside for a while and capture the freshness of the sunshine and beautiful spring day.

At the rattle of a buggy, she turned and looked. Gabriel pulled to a stop in front of the watering trough. He nodded to her, then made his way into the barn.

As far as greetings went, his wasn't exactly warm, but then again, she had never topped the list of Gabriel Fisher's favorite people.

With a shake of her head, she pushed thoughts of Gabe from her mind and went in search of her broom.

The brothers planned to attend an auction that afternoon. Gideon had mentioned that Gabriel was looking for a couple of new cows and that he had somehow talked him into going along for the ride. This was a step in the right direction. Just getting Gideon off his own farm was a feat in itself. She smiled at the memory of Lizzie's wide eyes when she told the young girl her uncle had gone into town that first time. And now he was attending auctions. What a difference a week made. The Lord truly was good. He was pulling Gideon back into the living.

She waved good-bye to them as they pulled away in Gabriel's buggy with promises to be back by supper. Porch swept, Avery set to work washing out her borrowed dresses and hanging them on the line to dry.

✺ ✺

Later that afternoon, Avery wiped a hand across her brow and made a mental note to work in the garden earlier in the day next time. Of course, today was unseasonably warm, but Oklahoma was a lot like East Texas, and it was only going to get worse. She dropped another plump berry into the stainless steel bowl she had brought from the kitchen and crawled a couple of spaces down to search for more. Lizzie had told her to be careful about the berries she picked, for once they were off the plant, they would not ripen. And she wanted only ripe berries for the strawberry cake she had planned for tonight's dessert.

The hum of an engine and the crunch of tires on gravel pulled her attention away from the berries. Gideon would be home soon, but surely not in this sort of transportation.

An unfamiliar silver sedan pulled to a stop and a blond-haired man stepped out wearing clothing more suitable for an exclusive country club than the back roads of an Amish district. Sunlight glinted off the frames of his dark glasses as he shut the door behind him.

Jack.

Avery scrambled to her feet, brushing the bits of grass and dirt from her skirt. Louie growled.

How had he found her?

His eyes scraped over her from head to toe, taking in every

detail of her appearance. Every Amish detail. "It's good to see you, Avery."

"What are you doing here, Jack?" She wasn't about to pretend she wanted him there.

"We need to talk."

"We don't have anything to talk about."

"We do."

She shook her head.

"Maybe you could invite me in"—He peered over her shoulder toward the house, as if looking for something. Or someone—"to have a cup of coffee." His attention swung toward the barn. "Or maybe to just sit awhile."

"I don't think so."

"Listen, I know I made some mistakes."

*Mistakes?*

"But if we could sit down, talk it out . . ."

She opened her mouth to remind him that she had caught him in bed with another woman, but stopped. That wouldn't mean anything to him. She, Avery, didn't mean anything to him either. Never had.

"Why are you really here, Jack?" It was a rhetorical question. She knew *why* he was there. She just wasn't sure how he had found her. Or how to get him to leave.

He took a step toward her. "I've missed you."

She crossed her arms. "Try again."

"Avery . . ."

"You have no business here, Jack."

"You're here. *You're* my business."

"Not anymore, I'm not."

He removed his sunglasses with a sweep of his hand that looked so practiced she almost laughed. Might actually have done it if the situation weren't so sobering. "I need you, Avery."

"My father cut off your funding?"

"I need an insider—"

"No."

"Someone who can tell me what it's really like here—"

"No."

"For authenticity." He glanced around. "They're just so secretive."

They weren't. They had welcomed her, treated her like one of their own. Ruth had revealed her emotions, Lizzie had told Avery her deepest desires, and Katie Rose had taught her how to cook. Maybe the reason they didn't accept Jack was that he was out to exploit them. The Amish were sheltered, not stupid.

"These are good, decent people, Jack. God-fearing people. Leave them out of your Hollywood pipedreams."

"And what are you doing here?"

Now there was a question. Her sabbatical had gone beyond rest and relaxation to hiding out. And now?

Now, she didn't have the answer.

She only knew she wanted him to leave. His presence contaminated everything it touched. He didn't belong here, and she surely didn't like the reminders of her real life. She had been just fine pretending that she would never eventually have to go home.

Jack cocked one eyebrow and waited. "Well?"

The rattle of a horse and buggy rumbling along the dirt lane saved her from having to answer. She glanced up, thankful for the familiar rig pulling down the drive.

Gideon was home.

All the joy Gideon felt on the ride home died as his brother steered his buggy toward the barn. They had visitors. Or at least Annie had a visitor. A fancy man with slicked-back blond hair and polished shoes. It could only be one person. Jack. Her one-time suitor.

They stood in the yard just this side of the strawberry patch. Annie wore a frown. He couldn't tell if she was unhappy or if the sun was in her eyes. Surely if she needed something she would holler. But she didn't.

Gideon jumped down from the buggy and caught his brother's eye.

Gabe raised a brow.

Gideon shrugged. He wasn't about it admit it, but it bothered him that Annie had invited someone over. He just wished she had mentioned havin' company this mornin' before he'd left. Of course, she was *Englisch*, and they did things a mite different than Plain folk. Gideon had lost sight of that this week. It was no wonder with her goin' around in an apron and a prayer *kapp* just like a proper Amish woman.

He shrugged again as if this all meant nothing to him and ambled over to where they stood.

Louie met him halfway, barking and yapping at his heels until he picked up the critter and tucked him under one arm.

"Gideon." Annie breathed his name as if truly happy to see him.

Gideon pushed that thought away. "Annie," he returned with a nod of his head.

"Annie?" Jack parroted.

Annie turned to the well-heeled man. "It's . . . what he calls me. Jack, this is my . . . host, Gideon Fisher. And his brother Gabe." She nodded toward Gabriel who stood apart, waiting by the buggy. "Gideon, Jack Welch."

The *Englischer* gave a small wave to Gabe, then stuck out his hand. "Pleasure," he said with a quick flash of his teeth.

"*Jah.*" Gideon shifted the dog so he could shake his hand. The handshake was strong and firm, too much so, like this Jack had something to prove.

But he didn't want to think about Jack, didn't really want to talk to him. He wanted to talk to Annie. He glanced at her. "I bought a mule."

"You did!" She clapped her hands together, those big, grape gumdrop eyes of hers sparkling. "That's *wunderbaar*."

"*Jah.*"

Jack swiveled his head toward Annie, then back to Gideon. "*Wunderbaar?*"

"It means wonderful," Annie explained.

"I know what it means. I just didn't know you did."

*There's a lot about her you don't know.*

Jack turned his attention away from Annie and focused it on him. "Say, how 'bout we all go have a cup of coffee. I didn't see a Starbucks in town, but there's that little diner."

Gideon didn't have time to answer before Annie shook her head. "I don't think that's a good idea."

"Then maybe here. A glass of lemonade?"

"Gideon's much too busy with the farm." She looked at Gideon like she was trying to tell him something. He sat the dog on the ground, wondering what she was gettin' at. "Right, Gideon?"

The farm was busy, but not *that* busy. He had another couple of hours before he had to milk the cow. Even then it was only one cow. He needed to get his new mule settled into the barn, but that wouldn't take more'n fifteen, twenty minutes. The best he could figure, she wanted to be alone with her fancy suitor.

He couldn't say it didn't sting, that she wanted to get rid of him, and that she wanted to spend time alone with an unfaithful man. He couldn't explain the ways of the *Englisch* no more'n they could explain the ways of the Amish.

"I'll just . . . put the mule in the barn." He slapped his gloves against his thigh and walked backward toward Gabe's buggy. "Get your dog, Annie, 'fore he gets stepped on."

He turned and walked to the wagon without another glance.

Gabe eyed him as Gideon started to untie the mule from the back of the buggy. "He's been asking questions around town, that one."

"I heard."

"He seems to have taken a shine to your Annie."

"She's not my anythin'." Gideon grabbed the strap and tugged on the mule to get him to follow him to the barn.

"Long as you remember that," Gabe called after him, then swung back into the buggy.

It took exactly fifteen minutes to get the mule settled in and get back to the house. To his annoyance, the *Englischer's* car was still parked in front when Gideon came out of the barn. Annie and her visitor had moved closer to his car, but that was as near as it came to him leaving.

Gideon ignored them as he walked up the porch steps Louie ran over to him and together they went into the house, the screen door slamming behind them. He went straight to the kitchen and washed his hands in the sink.

It was none of his business a'tall. Well, 'ceptin' this was his property, and Annie was under his care of sorts. She was his guest, anyway. And that bore a certain amount of responsibility. He should check on her to make sure she was okay.

He dried his hands on a dishtowel and made his way back into the living room. He could see them easily from the window. Annie stood with her arms folded across her middle, while her *Englischer* leaned against the front of his car.

He was a slick one, this outsider. His pants gray, his shirt the pale yellow of the butter cream frosting his *aenti* put on the cupcakes she made every Easter.

He shouldn't be spying on them. Annie had made it clear she wanted to be alone with this Jack. He should grant her this request. And he should not feel jealous at the possessive light in the other man's eyes.

But he didn't like how the outsider had treated Annie. Didn't like that any man thought he could treat a woman with such disrespect, and then to come around again like nothing had happened . . .

Gideon tore his gaze away from the pair and went back into the kitchen. He cut himself a wedge of pie and a hunk of cheese to refuel for the afternoon.

He sat down at the table with his snack. The auction had been sort of fun. He hadn't been in a long time, and it was *gut* to see all the folks he'd been missing these last few months. It was *gut* to spend time with his brother. And *gut* to bring a new animal onto his farm. He had gotten a deal on the beast—that was why he bought him. He hadn't gone with the intentions of purchasing an animal, but the mule would help with the plowing and save Molly and Kate's energy for trips to town.

*And church.*

He hadn't made up his mind about going, but he had been thinking about it. Mostly due to his *mamm*. If she could keep her faith even with what was ahead of her, he felt . . . well, he felt like he owed it to her to keep his right alongside. At least try to.

The auction had done something else. It had brought him face to face with the alpacas Annie was always talking about. Once he saw them, he walked over and visited with the man who was selling them. They were everything Annie had said—small, gentle, and docile in disposition. They had thick fleece coats in many beautiful colors, and they would provide for years since they—like sheep—were not slaughtered for their commodity. He'd talked with the man for a few minutes, then walked away, but the lazy eyes and alert ears of the alpaca had stayed with him for the rest of the afternoon.

Louie whined, and Gideon broke off a piece of crust and fed it to the tiny dog. What could they be talking about out there? And how long was he going to stay? Gideon shifted in his seat trying to see out the window, then fooled himself into believing that wasn't his intention at all.

Would the *Englischer* try and take Annie with him? *Would she go?*

He grabbed up his plate and took it to the kitchen, peering out the window as he did. They still stood in the yard, but he could barely see them. He deposited his plate and fork in the sink and eased back over to the window.

The wind ruffled the ends of Annie's hair that had pulled free of the pins she used. She started to brush it back, but Jack Welch beat her to it. There was a familiarity to his touch, and Gideon had to remind himself again that the ways of the *Englisch* were so very different than his own. He had to remind himself again that Annie was *Englisch*.

Their muffled voices told him nothing. He could hear the sound, but not the words. Jack said something. Annie replied. She still had her arms across her middle, but now Jack Welch had taken ahold of her elbows. Gideon couldn't tell for sure, but it looked like she was trying to pull away from him.

*Jah.* That was *gut*.

Annie took a step back and forced Welch to straighten. She said something else, and the blond-haired man replied. Then he leaned down, his intention clear—he was going to kiss her.

But Annie moved just in time, and the kiss fell on her cheek instead.

Although he had no right to be, Gideon was pleased.

The next thing he knew, she was striding toward the house.

Louie barked as if sensing her return. Gideon jumped back from the window, hoping she didn't see him, that she didn't know he had been spying on her.

He hurriedly sat in the rocking chair, barely getting his behind on the seat before she burst into the house, her face like a thundercloud. Cheeks flushed, eyes blazing.

"Of all the—" She saw Gideon sitting in the living room.

He rose to his feet out of sheer habit. "Annie."

"Sorry . . . I . . . I thought you were out back."

"Did you have a nice visit?"

She hesitated a fraction too long before answering. "Very nice. Jack wished he could stay a bit longer, but he had to get back to town." She tucked the loose strands of hair back under her *kapp* and smiled a little too brightly. "A mule, huh?"

"*Jah.*"

"That's really good."

He knew it was *gut*, a step toward healing, but her gushing response was more than the situation called for.

"Are you sure you don't want to talk about it?" he asked.

She smiled again, but the emotion didn't reach her eyes. "There's nothing to talk about. I'll get us something to eat."

He didn't have the heart to tell her he'd just had a snack. Instead, he followed her to the kitchen, scratching his head over the ways of the *Englisch*.

# 12

Avery tried to appear as casual as possible. "Tomorrow's Sunday."

It had been three days since Jack had intruded into her extended vacation. Thankfully, Gideon hadn't asked any more questions about the visit. Thankfully, Jack hadn't returned for round two. And thankfully, she had left her phone off to keep him from contacting her.

Or maybe that was just cleverness on her part.

Gideon nodded but didn't look up from the seed catalog he'd picked up in town the day of the auction. "*Jah.*"

"I heard the service is at Hester Stoltzfus's house."

"Where'd you hear th—never mind, Mary Elizabeth told you."

"Actually, it was your mother."

At the mention of his mom, Gideon stopped, looked up, and gave her his full attention. "*Jah.*"

"I think she would like it if you were there."

"I think Hester likes to have somethin' to talk about."

"Not Hester, your mom."

He grunted, the sound that was neither a yes or a no.

"What's stopping you?"

"I—"

"Your beard's grown back in."

"I—"

"And don't tell me you don't have faith. I've seen you pray. You didn't think anyone noticed, but you're not fooling me." What had started out to be a friendly conversation had turned into an all-out nag fest. Pestering the stubborn man would only make him pull away more. "I'm sorry," she said. "I just—"

"You're right."

"I beg your pardon?"

"*Jah.*" He nodded. "You're right. It's time I got back to church."

※◎ ◎※

Avery had never been so proud in her life as she watched Gideon step up into his buggy the next day. He looked very handsome in his black pants and matching for-*gut* vest. The pale blue shirt he wore underneath made his eyes seem even greener than before. Or maybe it was the specialness of the day, a turning point for him on his way to recovery.

Avery saw this as a personal triumph. His mother would be thrilled. His entire family would be ecstatic. She waved once, still watching as he pulled the buggy around and headed toward the road.

She would have loved to have gone with him, but she understood that just wasn't possible. The Amish were open about showing their religious views, but very closed when it came to their worship. Avery would love to attend an actual service, hear them singing in unison, praying from a book and preaching off the cuff. But she knew she wasn't allowed.

Plus Gideon being gone would give her some much needed time to herself. She knew he felt an attraction for her. Every now and then, she would glance his way only to find him looking at her. Desire burned in his eyes, but she had been around him enough to know that he would never act on it. If he had been English he would have already tried to get her into bed, but he wasn't. He was Amish, honorable and chaste. He wouldn't even kiss her. How ironic that the very virtues she admired in him were causing her such grief.

It was for the best. As much as she liked pretending that she wasn't leaving anytime soon, Jack's visit made it perfectly clear— her time here was coming to an end. She wouldn't be able to keep her "real" life from intruding much longer. Soon her father would come looking for her. Or Maris would. The wedding of the year would require her attendance. Or another benefit, or fundraiser, or golf tournament. Whichever happened first didn't matter. Something *would* happen and force her return to Dallas.

It was bold of her to think about it, but she wished she had kissed Gideon down by the creek so many days ago. Then again, any physical relationship with Gideon would only make leaving harder.

Avery sighed as the black dot of Gideon's buggy disappeared through the clump of trees down the road. She still wished she could go to the service. Maybe next week she would go to one of the churches in town. At least she would be around others for worship and praise.

The Bible said whenever two or more gathered in the Lord's name, then He would be there as well. She looked down at Louie, who sat at her feet, his head tilted to one side as he watched Gideon leave. "Guess what?" She scooped him into her arms. "You'll have to be my two."

And she carried him into the house to get the Bible.

Louie settled at her feet as Avery opened the Good Book and started to read. It was amazing how much her German had improved since she'd started. She was quite proud of herself. Not in a bad way, but in a you-finally-stepped-up kind of way. Just like cooking, cleaning, and planting a garden, there was so much she had never known she could do. She couldn't help but be pleased with herself for all she had learned.

*Lord, thank You for helping me realize my talents, and may I always use them in a way that glorifies You. Amen.*

Annie was on the front porch reading when Gideon pulled up. *Ach*, but he had missed her! He'd enjoyed the church service, and the fellowship afterward, but even as he feasted on chicken and crackers, cheese and pickles, and drank sweet tea, what he had really wanted to do was come home and see his Annie. It wasn't *gut*, these feelings he was starting to have for her. This week just proved it— it wouldn't be long before she returned to her life in the big city. What he hated most of all was that she would probably fall in with the likes of that Jack. She deserved so much more, so much better.

She closed her book as he hopped down from the buggy, and Gideon could see she had been reading the Bible. He smiled. She had gained something from this trip. In truth he had gained so much more.

"Well, hello there." She shaded her eyes with one hand. "I wasn't expecting you back so soon."

Gideon shrugged. "Hester's isn't so far from here. And . . ." *And I ate like the devil was taking away my food, and I talked to everyone I had to as fast as I could so I could come straight home. To you.* ". . . thought I'd better check on my mule. I don't think he was none too happy about sharin' the barn with three ladies."

Annie laughed, and the sound made Gideon chuckle in return. This was why he had hurried home. Because he knew their time was limited, and he wanted every second he could squeeze out of the day. Maybe it would hold him over when winter came again.

"You been there all mornin'?"

She stood and stretched, her back and knees popping with the motion. "I guess I have." She stretched again. "I didn't realize I'd been sitting here so long until now."

Goes to show what the Good Book could do. "Have you had anythin' to eat?"

She shook her head.

"Whadaya say we take us some food down to the creek and let Louie chase butterflies again?"

She tilted her head to one side as her lips curved upward. "You're hungry?"

"*Jah.*"

"You didn't eat after the service? I thought there was a big feast, enough food to feed the masses and whatnot."

He'd eaten just enough so he could say he had. "Come. It'll be fun."

She looked at him for a heart-stopping moment, then she smiled knowingly. "Okay." She nodded. "We'll have a picnic."

Gideon held the door open for her. Annie lifted the hem of her skirt as she crossed the threshold. Louie scampered in alongside them, their furry little chaperone.

As they worked side by side, gathering up leftover chicken, apples, pie, and the bread she had baked yesterday afternoon, Gideon wondered what would happen if she didn't leave.

It was a crazy thought. Amish were more likely to jump the fence than the *Englisch* were to give up their worldly ways. *Ach*, she seemed to like it there well enough. Some would say she had adapted quite well to the ways of the Plain people.

*But for how long?* How long before she grew tired of all the cooking and cleaning and weeding, all the plain old hard work? He heard the stories she'd told Mary Elizabeth. He had seen the fancy pictures in the magazine. Avery Ann Hamilton came from wealth and privilege—the likes of which he could hardly imagine. This type of life was new to her. Might even be considered fun for a while.

But how long?

He tried to shake away the persistent thought as he poured lemonade in a thermos and packed it inside a basket to take down to the creek.

He didn't think she would stay, but he knew she wasn't ready to leave. He supposed they would continue on like this until she grew bored and decided to head back home. It wasn't so bad. She was good company, a fine woman. She was a hard worker, never gave up, and any man would be blessed to have her as his wife.

The thought stilled his hands.

"Gideon?"

The sound of her voice got him moving again. He tucked some napkins in the basket and placed a towel over the top. "*Jah?*"

"Are you okay?"

"Fine. *Jah.*"

He could feel her gaze on his back as he turned toward the sink and washed his hands. He needed something to do other than think about the kind of wife she would be to someone else—and why it should worry him at all.

"Did you hear me?" she asked.

"You said somethin'?"

"I'll take that as a no." Laughter replaced the concern in her voice and once again, Gideon breathed a bit easier. "I said I couldn't bear to take these beautiful quilts down to the creek. Do you have an old sheet or something we could sit on while we eat?"

"In the hallway closet."

"Right." Those green shower flip-flops slapped the back of her heels as she headed for the closet.

The last thing he needed was to be alone with her on a sunny creek bed, but he could think of nothing that he wanted more.

Louie jumped to his feet and let out a yip of recognition.

"*Onkel?*"

Mary Elizabeth stood at the front screen.

He motioned her into the house. "Come on in."

The door slammed behind her, its sound normal and comforting. But his niece's cheeks were flushed, and her breathing heavy, like she had run all the way there.

"Is everythin' *allrecht?*"

She stood with her back to the door as if too scared to take another step.

Louie sat at her feet, stubby tail wagging, waiting to be picked up and cuddled close. The young girl just nodded, her hands tucked behind her back.

"Gideon, these are as exquisite as the rest." Annie came around the corner, a load of quilts in her arms. "We can't sit—oh, hi, Lizzie. I didn't expect to see you today."

Mary Elizabeth didn't smile, or rush to Annie's side, or do any of the other sisterly things he had noticed her do. Despite her declaration otherwise, something was wrong.

"They are what we have," he told Annie without taking his eyes off his niece.

"But they'll get dirty."

"We'll wash them."

"In that wringer washer? You've got to be kidding me."

"Then we'll take them into town and use the coin-operated ones."

"Is that allowed?"

"Yes."

"No," Mary Elizabeth said over him.

A frown puckered Annie's brow.

"What Mary Elizabeth means to say is that it'll be all right for you to wash them in town, Annie."

"Okay," she said slowly, looking at each of them in turn. She sensed the difference in Mary Elizabeth as well.

"I didn't mean to listen in," Mary Elizabeth started, near tears.

Gideon cocked his head. "Listen in on who?"

"The preacher," she said. "And the bishop."

Bishop Beachy had returned earlier in the week, but Gideon hadn't given it a second thought until now.

"We were getting ready to leave, but Samuel had left his blanket in the house. I went in the back door to get it. I didn't mean to listen, but I heard your name. They were talkin' about you, *Onkel*." Her tears flowed freely now. Annie retrieved a towel from the kitchen for Mary Elizabeth to wipe her face.

"The bishop said that it's gone on long enough. They were disappointed that you didn't stay longer after the service and that got them talkin' about other things. He found out you had shaved your beard and that you—"

"Go on."

"You had an outsider staying here."

Annie turned to him, her voice half pleading, half apologetic. "Gideon."

"What else did they say, Mary Elizabeth?"

"They're . . . they're gonna have you shunned unless you confess the errors of your ways."

Just a few short weeks ago, the promise of a shunning wouldn't have mattered to him at all. Now it did. It mattered a lot.

A few short weeks ago, he hadn't known what he was living for. Today he did. And a shunning would mean separation from his family, his mother. That was one thing he couldn't bear, not with the cancer treatments she now faced.

"Stop your cryin'. I'll confess."

"You will?" Annie and Mary Elizabeth spoke at the same time.

"*Jah*. I've done wrong in the eyes of the church and of God. Now, let's go."

"Where are you going?" Mary Elizabeth asked.

"On a picnic." He should have invited her along, but he wanted to be alone with Annie. Today would most likely be the last time they would have this opportunity, and he planned to make the most of it.

Annie shook her head. "Gideon, I don't think we should go."

"Of course, we should."

"But . . ." Once again the girls protested in unison.

"The elders will be by tomorrow to tell me their plan. I'm not about to let what's left of a beautiful day burn away worryin' about what's to come."

Slow to agree, Annie finally nodded.

Gideon smiled, then walked Mary Elizabeth to the door, hushing her protests as he escorted her to her bike.

He came back into the house as Annie slipped the Bible into the basket on top of their picnic fare. She hooked her arm through the wooden handles and headed for the door.

He held open the door for her. "Are you ready?"

"As I'll ever be," she muttered. "Are you su—"

"Shh. Let's just enjoy the afternoon." He left off the *while we can* that hung in the air between them.

❧⟋ ⟍❧

The sun was warm on the back of Avery's neck as she and Gideon made their way toward the creek. He had finally convinced Mary

Elizabeth that she couldn't talk him out of having a picnic, so she reluctantly left for home. Avery wasn't sure a picnic was the best idea either, but it seemed Gideon Fisher had a stubborn streak.

Secretly, she was glad. She had wanted to spend today with Gideon. And she could think of no better way than lounging about on a creek bank watching her once-prissy dog chase bugs through the tall grass.

She shook out the beautiful handmade quilt. "Are you sure this is okay?"

"*Jah*." As if impatient with the whole situation, he took the quilt from her and spread it on the ground. Then he dropped into a sitting position and patted the space next to him. "Come," he said with a smile. "Let's get this picnic started."

Avery knelt beside him, uncovered the basket, and started unloading their food. The afternoon was beautiful—better than beautiful—it was perfect.

They snacked in a companionable silence, intermittently feeding Louie bites before he scampered off after butterflies.

Avery leaned back and raised her face to the sun. Golden rays of sunlight, a cool spring breeze, and good company . . . everything a picnic should be. She picked up the Bible from where she had set it when she emptied the basket. "Shall I read?"

He nodded and lay back, staring up at the sky as she opened to a passage.

"Trust in the Lord with all your heart," she read slowly, translating the familiar message in Proverbs as she went along. "And do not rely on your own understanding; think about Him in all your ways, and He will guide you on the right paths. Don't consider yourself to be wise; fear the Lord and turn away from evil. This will be a healing for your body and strengthening for your bones."

She stopped. Did he know that she had chosen this passage on purpose, waiting for an opportunity like today to share it with him?

Gideon was a smart man. Surely, he knew what she was trying to tell him. Now all he needed to do was heed the words of the Lord.

"Honor the Lord with your possessions," she continued. "And with the first produce of your entire harvest; then your barns will be completely filled and your vats will overflow with new wine. Do not despise the Lord's instruction, my son, and do not loathe His discipline; for the Lord disciplines the one He loves, just as a father, the son he delights in."

She closed the Bible as the wind ruffled through her hair. Gideon didn't say a word, just continued to stare at the sky as if soaking in what she'd just read. He had most likely heard those words many times before, but like she had, Avery hoped that he could look upon the message with fresh eyes, that he could see how it applied to his life now.

Even more so with what he would face tomorrow.

"I saw those alpacas at the auction."

"You did?" Avery straightened up and gave Gideon her full attention. Since she had finished reading the Bible, he had hardly said two words. She could only hope that her message—the Lord's message—had gotten through. "Why didn't you mention it before now?"

Gideon shrugged. "Just didn't."

"Well?" She stared at him. "What did you think of them?"

He nodded. "They're fine, I s'pose. Smaller than I thought. Still bigger'n sheep."

"They're good creatures."

"*Jah*," he said. "They seemed to be."

"Oh, that's so exciting. I wish I could have seen them too. Are they as pretty as in the pictures I showed you?"

He tilted his head to one side and squinted at her. "You don't know?"

Avery shook her head.

"Why not?"

"I've never actually seen one. I mean, I've seen regular llamas at the zoo and—"

"Are you tellin' me, Miss Annie Hamilton, that you're tryin' to get me to invest all my hard-earned money in creatures that you've never even laid eyes on?"

"I've seen them in pictures and in books."

"I'm not sure that counts."

"They say they're very docile and beautiful creatures," she said, attempting to change the subject.

"*Jah*. That they are."

They must have left an impression on him if he was moved to talk about them nearly a week after the auction. Maybe he'd come around to her thinking after all.

She shifted and tucked her legs under her, the green flip-flops abandoned at the edge of the quilt. "Tell me about the service."

"It was *gut*."

"That's not telling me anything. What was the sermon about?"

He shrugged. "Followin' God."

She waited for him to continue. Something in his manner, the slant of his shoulders, the angle of his chin, made her think the service had left shadows behind.

"It's hard to know," he said finally, "what God wants from you."

"I suppose." Before coming to Amish country, she hadn't known what God had wanted from her—hadn't even known that God wanted anything at all from her—and yet here her understanding had changed. Here she could feel God all around.

He sighed, picked at a blade of grass, and tossed it aside. "More often than not."

"Maybe you're just having trouble listening."

"Maybe."

He sat quietly for a moment. Avery wondered if he was think-ing about what she'd said, maybe even what she'd read.

"I guess it's all about faith." Sometimes faith was hard to come by, but she had seen it on Samuel's sweet face, and shining in the eyes of Ruth and Abram as they talked about her condition. "How's your mother?"

"*Gut.*"

A sweet spring breeze whistled through the branches of the tree above them. Birds sang to each other from their perches, and a few yards away Louie yapped at a squirrel.

"How are they going to pay?" They both knew she was talking about the costly cancer treatments his mother had agreed to take. Avery wished the Fishers had let her give them her car or call her father for some money, or even start a fund in Ruth's honor. All their talk about the perils of pride, it was still alive and well in this Amish family.

"The Lord will provide." He sounded so much like his father, so confident and sure, but a frown of worry puckered his brow.

Avery didn't think twice. She reached out and smoothed the wrinkles of his brow, then laid her hand against his cheek. His skin felt smooth against her fingers, his beard springy and coarse against her palm.

Despite all the activity of nature that surrounded them, the world stood still.

His gaze locked with hers, and she could see the want and need, the concern and worry, in those mossy green depths. Then she did what she had wanted to do so many days ago. She closed her eyes and leaned toward him.

His lips were warm, faintly salty and pliant beneath hers. He neither fought her touch, nor did he participate. But she was encouraged by the hitch in his breathing and the sigh that followed it. For all his noble and faithful nature, he had wanted this as much as she had, though she had known all along the first move would have to be hers.

She reveled in the sensation and all the other small differences that made him who he was. That he smelled like laundry detergent and man with a whiff of fresh hay thrown in for good measure.

As if unable to help himself, he kissed her back. He touched her nowhere but her lips, yet she could feel him all around her. When she ran her fingers through the length of hair brushing his collar, hoping to draw him closer still, he cupped his hands on the sides of her face and pulled away from her.

"Annie, sweet Annie." He expelled a breath as he rested his forehead against hers and sighed. "I shouldn't have done that. I'm sorry."

"I'm not." She smiled though her heart was nearly breaking. Was he sorry because he still loved his wife? Because he could never care for her the way he did another?

⁂

He kissed her hard on the mouth, just once, then let her go.

He had to. Otherwise he might go on holding her and kissing her until the sun came up the next day.

He couldn't deny it. He had wanted to kiss her since the first time he'd seen her in that slip of a dress. Even with her hair matted with blood.

Thinking about seeing her for the first time was a sharp reminder that she was from a different world—something he had been able to put aside as long as she was wearing a *frack* and a prayer cap. Soon she would be leaving regardless of the fact that she seemed to be adapting to his world with more grace and eagerness than he'd thought possible.

He stood up on the pretense of looking for Louie who still pranced through the grass after every type of creature unfortunate enough to cross his path.

"Is it because of her?" Her voice was light as a feather, as if the question had slipped out on its own.

"Miriam?" He felt as if he had been goosed with a hot poker. He swung around to face her. "Why would you ask that?"

"Because . . . because she was your wife, and . . . you still love her."

"*Jah*." He nodded, hooking his thumbs through his suspenders, needing something to do with his hands. "I'll always love her. She was a good woman, my Miriam."

"I understand."

He could tell she was lying.

"Time to head back." Her voice sounded falsely bright as she started gathering up the remnants of their picnic and placing them in the basket.

He couldn't let it end this way. It couldn't go on, but it couldn't end like this. His shadow fell over her and blocked out the sun. "Annie?"

"Hmm?" She tried to appear as if nothing was wrong, but wouldn't look at him.

He dropped to his knees on the blanket beside her. "I shouldn't have taken advantage of you like that."

She gave him a wistful smile. "I think it was the other way around."

"Not from where I'm standin'."

"You're a good man, Gideon Fisher."

"And you're a good woman, Annie Hamilton. Now go get your mutt, and let's head back to the house. I've got a cow to milk."

He reached out to help her to her feet. Together, they walked hand in hand back to the house. If it was all he could have, he'd take it. Her hand was warm and tiny in his, and yet he could feel a strength in her he was certain hadn't been there before.

Her time with him had changed her. It had changed him too, for the better. *Ach*, but he would miss her when she was gone.

He squeezed her fingers, and she turned to look at him.

"What?"

"Nothin'." A smile played at the corners of his lips. There was so much about her that he would miss. "What's for supper?"

"Is that all you think about? Eating?"

"*Jah*." It was all he could let himself think about when she was near. Otherwise he might start thinking about things better left alone. "Want to learn how to milk the cow?" He shouldn't have asked, but Honey needed to be milked, and he was reluctant to see Annie go into the house alone. One thing was certain, tomorrow would bring change, and he wanted to hold onto today as long as he could.

"Yeah." A smile split her face. "I would."

The barn was cool and dim when he led her inside. "Grab that bucket." He pointed to the metal pail hanging just outside Honey's stall. "Then wait here."

Then he left her alone.

Avery did as she was told, shifting patiently from one foot to the other as she waited for Gideon to return. He went out the Dutch door at the other end of the barn, the one that led to the pasture. She could hear him calling for Honey, then whistle, followed by the low moo of the sweet-faced bovine.

Without so much as a rope, Gideon led the cow inside.

"How did you do that?" Avery asked.

"She knows what she's supposed to do. Right, girl?" He patted her on the side, but she chewed on a mouthful of hay without batting an eye.

Gideon motioned for Avery to approach. "Come on." He hooked one foot under the seat of a three-legged stool and pulled it closer. "Sit here."

Up close, the cow looked bigger than Avery had imagined. Definitely bigger than she looked from across the pasture. "Are you sure she's okay with this?"

Gideon's mouth twitched, as if trying to hide a smile. "For sure and for certain."

"Uh-hum, okay." She inched closer, each step making the cow look that much larger than before. She could do this. She wanted to do this. She took a deep, fortifying breath and eased herself onto the stool.

Gideon took the bucket from her and placed it on the ground under Honey's enlarged udders. "First thing," he said, "is to get her to let down her milk."

"Okay."

"Ever see a calf come to nurse?"

Avery nodded.

"He doesn't just walk up and start right in. He nudges around on his *mamm*, letting her know his intent. When she feels him, she starts to relax. Then her milk comes down." He spoke, all the while massaging Honey's hindquarters, rubbing his hands down her sides, and gently pressing on her udders with his fist.

"I think she's ready now," he said, guiding Avery's hand to the swollen udder.

The pale pink skin was soft to the touch, barely covered with a fine bit of fur, firm though mushy under her fingertips. "Are you sure this won't hurt her?"

"I'm sure. Now." Gideon held up his hands, pressing his fingers together while moving only his thumbs back and forth. "Hold her teat in between there and squeeze, but don't pull."

"Squeeze, don't pull," Avery repeated.

"Wrap your fingers around and—"

A stream of milk shot down into the bucket.

"I did it!"

"That you did."

Avery tried again. Carefully she grasped the teat in the vee made between her forefinger and thumb. Careful not to pull, she wrapped her fingers around, but this time no milk came. "What did I do wrong?"

"Place your hand here." Gideon demonstrated, pushing his hand right up under the udder. "If you get ahold too low, the milk will go back up."

Avery did as he showed her, and once again, milk squirted into the bucket.

She couldn't help the smile that spread across her face—even though it seemed silly to be proud of herself for something Lizzie had been doing since she could walk. But she was.

Avery Ann Hamilton, city girl extraordinaire, could milk a cow.

Of course, milking a cow was not glamorous, and was in fact, hard work. Her hands became tired long before the milking was complete.

"I'll finish up," Gideon said, allowing her to stand before taking her place on the stool.

Avery flexed her fingers. "That takes some muscles." She watched him milk the cow, his movements steady, rhythmic.

"It's just 'cause you're not used to it. Give it a couple of weeks and . . ."

Neither one of them knew what tomorrow would hold for him. Most likely, she wouldn't be there in a couple of weeks.

Avery crossed her arms, the perfect moment tainted by thoughts of the unknown. Suddenly, the barn felt confining, stifling. She drew in a breath. "I'll just go . . . start supper."

"*Jah*." He turned all his attention to a chore she was sure he could complete in his sleep.

Avery stared at those broad shoulders for a minute more, then turned and made her way back into the house.

# 13

Monday dawned with a bright, blue sky filled with summer sunshine and budding trees filled with singing birds. A beautiful day for a reckoning.

Gideon did his best to act like normal. He went out to the barn while Annie made coffee. He milked the cow. He tended the horses and saw to the mule he'd bought at the auction. It was a day like any other, but it had the sad, sweet sting of endings.

Annie could feel it, too. She was quiet and thoughtful, watching him as if he might disappear without a trace. He wanted to comfort her, to smooth a hand down the silky slope of her cheek and tell her it would be okay.

But he didn't. He couldn't.

Thankfully, Mary Elizabeth came by the house just after breakfast and convinced Annie to go down by the creek and see if any of the wild strawberries were ripe. Gideon could tell that Annie didn't want to leave, but Mary Elizabeth could be quite persuasive when she set her mind to it.

Gideon was thankful for his niece's help. He didn't want Annie around the house when the elders called.

They showed up around ten, came together in one buggy—the bishop, the deacon, and both ministers. Gideon was surprised they all came. Usually the bishop sent the deacon out first to talk to the offender, and if he couldn't make any progress, then the bishop himself would arrive. Evidently Gideon's infraction was serious enough to warrant them all. They were a mismatched foursome held together by the Y strap of their suspenders and the narrow brims of their hats.

Bishop Beachy, the chosen leader of the district, led the men toward the porch where Gideon waited. He was followed closely by the ministers, John Zook and Daniel Glick, and not so closely by the elder deacon, Ezekiel Esh. Beachy, Zook, and Glick walked arrow straight while Esh hobbled forward, bent almost in half with rheumatism.

Wouldn't be long, Gideon thought, before Old Zeke stepped down and another man was chosen by lot to be the new deacon of the district.

The men nodded their greetings all around, but no pleasantries were exchanged. It wasn't that kind of visit.

"Gideon Fisher," the bishop started. "Come down off the porch. We need a word with you."

He did as he was told, standing before the men who stood side by side, the undisputed representatives of the church . . . and God.

"There's been some talk around the district."

Gideon nodded.

"Heard tell you shaved your beard."

"You heard right."

"I'll ask you why you did such-a thing."

"My Miriam's gone." He realized for the first time in months that he could say the words without his heart bleeding. But Jamie's name wouldn't tumble from his lips. Losing a child was a pain that would never ease. "A Plain man's beard is a mark of his family. I didn't think I deserved to wear it."

"And now?"

"It's about followin' God and bein' a part of somethin' greater than oneself."

"That's a big turnaround for a few weeks."

"*Jah.*" He couldn't take the credit himself. That was all Annie's. She was the reason he'd rethought his unworthy state, the reason he had hope and faith again.

"Even been said you had an *Englischer* stayin' with you."

"*Jah.*"

"A woman."

"It's true."

Deacon's eyebrows shot up so high they disappeared under the brim of his hat.

Gideon supposed they didn't expect him to admit to it, but he couldn't lie. "I know why you're here."

No one said anything, but the elders looked at each other and shifted in place. Old Zeke changed his cane from one hand to the other.

"You'll need to be prepared at the next service," the bishop finally said.

Gideon nodded. "I am."

The bishop gestured toward the other men standing with him. "And we think it's time for you to marry again."

"Pardon?" He blinked once, trying to collect his thoughts. This was not at all what he'd expected to hear. He'd been ready for the threat of a shunning, a repentance, a declaration of the wrongs he had committed in the past year.

But a wife?

"You know Rachael Miller." Bishop Beachy's wire-rimmed glasses reflected the sun as he nodded.

*The bishop's niece.* Gideon nodded. "I do."

"She's in need of a husband and a father for her two little girls."

"We think you're the man for that," Esh shouted. Along with his many ailments of advancing age, he was hard of hearing as well.

Gideon hid his shock in the clench of his jaw, knowing it best not to let it show, best not to let his protest turn into outright insubordination. "I wasn't aware the church had started arranging marriages." He had done wrong, and he would change his ways—but this seemed so *drastic*.

"You don't have to marry her," John Zook clarified. "But—"

"We think it best you find a wife," the bishop added. "And Rachael is a fine woman."

"*Jah.*" She was a fine woman. A little on the plain side, but sweet of disposition and not hard on the eyes. She was quiet and obedient and perfect for any man like . . . Gabriel. But if Gideon ever married again, he wanted a woman with more spunk. His Miriam had been a lot like Rachael—good, honest, malleable. If he'd been asked then, he would have said it was a *gut* match. Now he wanted something more in a life mate.

He wanted . . . Annie.

But that would never be.

Pain, like a knife to the heart, twisted in his chest. His breath caught and he had to force the air from his lungs. "I'll call on her." Gideon's voice was just above a whisper.

"What?" Esh hollered.

Zook looked at Esh. "He said he'd call on her."

Esh nodded, his voice louder than ever. "*Gut, gut.*"

Daniel Glick nodded. He was a quiet man, especially for a preacher, and he only spoke when absolutely necessary.

On any other day, Gideon would have laughed at the comedy of it all. But laughter was far from him today because the one he loved the most would never be his.

The men shook hands all around.

Gideon would make a kneeling apology in front of the congregation. He'd confess his ways, promise to repent, and take up with Rachael Miller. For the first time in almost a year he would move forward. He should have been happy, even excited at what was to come.

Instead he felt like something inside him had died.

He watered the bishop's horses. Then he watched the men climb into the buggy and head off back down the road, his stomach a knot of dread.

In Amish cemeteries, there were no flowers, no fancy headstones, just simple wooden crosses to mark the journey of souls from this world to the next. Gideon walked down the rows, passing markers of those who had lived long before him, and those who had recently gone. Two rows down and third from the path were Miriam and Jamie's.

The crosses were painted white, most likely by Miriam's mother. Gideon hadn't been able to come out here since the day they laid them to rest. The markers were identical to those around them except for a piece of blue ribbon tied at the base and nearly buried in the ground to hide it from the eyes of mourners. Blue, Miriam's favorite. The color of her eyes. The color of the dress they'd buried her in. Nearly hidden by the grass, a small wooden pony rested next to the cross under which they had buried his son.

Gideon sat on the ground beside the patch of new grass that covered their graves. Moisture from last night's rain soaked into the rear of his britches, but he didn't care. He'd come out here to say his piece, and that's what he'd do.

Birds flitted from one tree to the next, their feathers ruffling as they matched the rustling of the leaves. Far away and near they called to each other, but Gideon couldn't find the words.

He wasn't sure how long he sat there, the wind brushing against him, the world going on while he just sat. That's how it had been for months now, everything going on around him while he stagnated like poison water.

No more.

"Miriam." His voice came out rusty with emotion. This talk was long overdue. "I've really missed you this past year."

Only the wind answered him.

He reached out a hand toward Jamie's cross, but couldn't find any words to address his son. To say that he had simply missed him was not enough. Words barely covered his grief.

He focused on Miriam's marker. "It's been a long year." A year of sadness, regret, and winter. "But it's over now. And, well, the elders think I should get married again." He picked at the grass closest to the toe of his boot. "I think they're right. You've gone on. I've got to move on too."

He took a deep breath and said the words he'd never thought he'd say again. "I'm goin' to start courtin'. And I'll probably be married this time next year, but I wanted you to hear it from me. You were a good woman. A fine wife to me. A man couldn't ask for better, and I'm not. I'm just goin' on, because that's what we do—those who are left behind—we go on."

From somewhere, he heard a cow moo and the clank of her bell. But there was no answer from above. Not that he really thought there would be. He knew what he had to do, and he knew it was for the best—for everyone involved. Now he just had to have the heart to carry it out.

He took a deep breath, trying to find the words in his heart. "Jamie." His voice cracked on the single word. He ran the back of his hand under his nose, needing a moment to pull himself together before he continued. "The woman I'm to start courtin'. . . well, she's got two little girls. And she needs help with these girls. The bishop thinks I'd do right by them, and I will. But me raising them won't take away from my love for you." He stopped unable to continue. A lump of emotion clogged his throat and made it impossible for any more words to get past. If they had, he'd have told Jamie he would always love him, that he was sorry about that day, and all the other regrets he had. But even holding onto those regrets was a cancer in itself.

And like everything else, he had to let them go, turn them over to God, and pray for the best.

⁓⊙ ⊙⁓

Avery spent a frustrating morning duck-walking through the bushes looking for wild strawberries. On any other day, she would have loved being out in the fresh air with the sun on her face. Today wasn't any other day. The deacon was coming to talk to Gideon. She knew more than anything else—even more than the subject of his beard—that they would talk about *her*.

The last thing she wanted was to be a problem for Gideon. That wasn't entirely true. The last thing she wanted was to leave him, to leave Amish country. Maybe she could move into town, or buy a house on the edge of the community. One thing she knew for certain—she never wanted to go. She had thought of little else since their kiss.

"Annie, wait up," Lizzie called as she tromped through the woods behind her.

"Hurry," she called over her shoulder. "We've been gone for hours. I want to get back and check on Gideon."

"We haven't been gone that long." Mary Elizabeth's face was bright red from exertion.

"It seems like we have. Now come on." It was oh-so hard, but she slowed her footsteps and allowed the young girl to catch up.

The air felt of impending doom. When she said as much, Lizzie pointed to the dark clouds in the distance. A storm brewed. *For sure and for certain*, Gideon would say, but Avery was unsure how much of it originated from the weather.

Finally, they burst through the edge of the trees and headed across the field toward the house. Gideon stood at the edge of the yard. He threw a stick, and the beagle went after it while Louie braced himself up on Gideon's leg and begged for attention.

He waved when he saw them, took the stick from the dog, and flung it again.

Avery wanted to lift up the hem of her skirts and run as fast as she could to Gideon's side, but Lizzie came up next to her and linked their arms together. Side by side they made their way back to the house.

"Glad you finally came home. It's about to start rainin'."

"Told you," Mary Elizabeth said with a friendly smirk.

Avery just smiled. "How did it go?"

"*Gut, gut.*" He nodded, and Lizzie seemed satisfied.

Yet Avery knew there was a lot more he wasn't saying. He wouldn't look either of them in the eye as he threw the stick again.

The dog trotted after it as Gideon motioned for them both. "Come on, niece. I'll carry you home in the buggy 'fore you get caught in the rain."

⁂

The trip to Gabriel's house was quiet, except for Mary Elizabeth. She chatted away the entire time about one thing or another. The constant prattle made Avery anxious. She wanted so badly to talk to Gideon about what the deacon had said, but she knew better than to ask him in front of his niece.

They dropped her off, refused offers to stay for pie, begging off with the excuse of the approaching storm.

Once Gideon started the buggy back toward home, Avery turned to him. "So what did they say?"

He shrugged, but didn't take his gaze from the road. "Not much."

"That's not an answer. Are they going to accept your confession?"

"How did you know about that?"

"Lizzie told me."

He nodded. "Of course."

"Are they?"

"*Jah.*"

"And that will be the end of it?"

"*Jah.*" He answered her the same, but this time the word came out a little softer than before.

"That's good. *Gut.*" She corrected herself with a smile.

"*Gut.* Annie." He straightened. "What do you say we pack up in the mornin' and head into town?"

"Sure. Why?"

"No reason."

A day in town sounded like fun. "I have been wanting to go to the library and check out more books. And Katie Rose helped me pick out some fabric for a new dress. *Frack*," she corrected. "I'm hoping that it's in."

"*Jah.*" He offered his usual reply, but his shoulders were taut, his jaw clenched.

"Are you sure everything's all right?"

"Right as rain."

Gideon never went into town for no reason at all. Still, she had no cause to doubt him. Maybe he had some private errands to run that dealt with his church issues—issues that he didn't want to discuss with her.

But he would. He had talked with her about things he had never told another living soul, and that had to mean something. So she wouldn't mention it again, because in due time, she would know the reason for the impromptu trip to town. For now she would be happy to be by his side.

They made it home before the first fat drops fell from the sky.

⁓◦ ◦⁓

Gideon shifted on the bed of hay he had constructed for himself and listened to the rain patter against the roof of the barn. He should be sleeping. He should have been asleep a long time ago. But dreams eluded him.

Tomorrow would be the last day he would see Annie. He had no choice but to make her go. He'd have to go back on his word, but he should have never made that promise to her, the oath that she could stay as long as she wanted. He wasn't able to make a decision like that. Amish were about community and what was best for the whole. And what was best for them didn't include her.

He shifted again and tucked his hands behind his head. He'd found her phone while she was out in the woods hunting berries. He might not be a man of the world, but he was smart enough to figure out how to work the new-fangled contraption. In no time at all, he had her father on the other end. Gideon stated his name and his intentions and arranged for them to meet in Clover Ridge the following day.

He prayed for the good Lord to help him, because he couldn't look her in the eyes. His sweet Annie, who had brought him back from the edge of grief and taught him how to love again—now he had to let her go.

He had wanted to stay in the house tonight, just to be near her, but he couldn't. Even though she was worldly and going home, he couldn't damage their standing in the community that way. Couldn't have others think poorly of her even if she slept in the bed alone and he on the couch.

He groaned. It wasn't *gut* to tempt his resolve. Every fiber of his faith told him to steer clear of her, but his heart wanted nothing more than to hold her close. And if he did something like that?

He would not be able to let her go tomorrow.

He flopped over again. From one of the stalls, Honey lowed her protest at his restlessness.

Tomorrow, he told himself. Tomorrow Annie would go back to her world and everything in his would return to normal. Or at least as normal as it could be. Tomorrow . . .

<hr>

"Why are we taking Louie again?" Avery struggled to hold onto the tiny bundle of dog. The day had dawned with bright skies and no sign of the evening rain, except the dew sparkling on the green grass.

Having been inside most of the evening and all of the night, the Yorkie wanted nothing more than to run from side to side in the buggy, barking at everything he could see. The horses seemed not to care, but it bothered Avery. Or maybe it was Gideon who had her in restless knots.

She chanced a sidelong look at him, but he stared at the road, the reins held loosely in his strong, capable hands. She had expected him to open up to her, to tell her in depth about the visit from the elders. He had told her some of the morning's events, yet she believed there was more to the story. Maybe because he avoided meeting her gaze all through supper, and that he went out to the barn much quicker than usual. She still had trouble believing they all came—*that* seemed pretty serious to her. But Gideon just shrugged it off. He told her they expected him to repent at the next church service and "that would be that."

Avery thought the punishment harsh. After all, everything he had gone through was due to grief and guilt. He brushed her concerns aside as well, reminding her he wasn't being shunned, and that was most important.

"We're takin' him because he needs to get out of the house too. You brought his bag, right?"

"Yes." She felt strange carrying the designer purse with her Plain clothes. The price of the bag alone could feed a family for a month.

Yet she should be grateful. Jack never wanted Louie anywhere around, and Gideon liked to haul him all over the place. It was a good trait in a man, this love of animals.

Gideon pulled back and the horses slowed as they neared the town. Traffic got a little heavier, though nothing like Dallas. He pulled the buggy into a large parking lot that had once belonged to a movie theater. Now it was used as an Amish market. Many families had already set up their tables and covered them with goods to sell that day.

Avery tilted her head. "What are we doing here?"

He pulled the horses to a stop and turned to face her. "Annie."

Whatever he was going to say next was lost.

"Avery. Thank God."

No one in the district called her that.

She whipped around and saw her father striding across the parking lot, Maris at his side.

She whirled back to face him. "Gideon?"

He just shook his head, his face void of all expression. "It's time for you to go home, Annie."

Her stomach fell, his words so final. "I-I don't understand."

"It's best for everyone."

She grabbed his sleeve, daring him to face her. "How can this be best? Would you look at me!"

He turned his gaze to her, but staring into those green depths did nothing to allay her fears. "I'm goin' to start courtin' Rachael Miller."

His pronouncement landed like a punch to the stomach. "Why?" The word came out in a strained whisper.

"It wouldn't be right to do that with you livin' under my roof."

"I don't understand." Tears ran down her face, and Avery let them flow. "I don't want to go. I want to *stay*."

He turned away from her. "It's time for you to go home."

"Gideon, *no*. Please. I love you."

He didn't respond. Instead he sat there, eyes straight ahead, jaw clenched, and reins still firmly in his grasp.

"Come on, Avery." Her father stood next to the buggy now. "Let's get you home and out of those clothes." He hesitated before saying the last word, telling her exactly what he thought about her Amish garb.

"Gideon?"

"Go on now." Still he wouldn't look at her.

How could she make him understand how much he meant to her if he wouldn't even look at her?

Her father touched her arm, urging her down from the buggy.

Once again she had done it. She had fallen in love with a man who didn't love her back. A man who didn't care about her family's money, but couldn't get past their differences to see what they could have together.

Avery brushed back her tears and let her father pull her from the buggy.

Gideon didn't say anything else, and Avery didn't look back as her father led her toward his car. Her time in Amish country had come to an end.

~⁓ ⁓~

Aside from laying his family in the ground, saying good-bye to Annie was the hardest thing he had ever done. Gideon ground his teeth together as he watched her go. It was best. He knew that.

His mind kept telling him so, but his heart was a different matter.

He slapped the reins, his eyes full of grit, his stomach heavy. She had told him that she loved him. She had poured out her feelings for him, but he had said nothing in return. For all it was worth, he loved her right back. There was so much he had wanted to tell her. How she healed him. How much he loved her. How without her he wouldn't be the man he was today. But he could say none of those things. They would only make this harder.

She didn't belong here, so he had to let her go. He jostled along in the buggy, barely watching the road. It was for the best, he told himself again.

He had made a commitment to God and the church a long time ago, and he intended to honor that pledge. Lately, he had been going down his own path, but no more. Next church service, he would ask for forgiveness, and after the noon meal, he would ask Rachael Miller to go for a ride in his buggy. Life would go on.

Without the violet-eyed *Englischer* who had taken his heart to Texas.

## 14

When she boarded the plane that would take her back to Dallas, Avery was numb. Soon the pain would set in. It was as inevitable as the sunrise.

He had planned it. He'd planned it all. Right down to putting all of her things in the buggy, making sure she had Louie with her, and arranging for her father to meet them in town. She couldn't figure out what hurt the most: his forethought or the fact that she had once again fallen for a man who couldn't return her love.

She pushed the thoughts aside, the situation still too fresh. Maybe later, in a day or two—in a month—she would look at the events of the afternoon in detail. For now, she was going back to Dallas.

Home.

She received more than her fair share of stares as she found her seat. Many more than she ever got in Clover Ridge. She supposed the people in the small Oklahoma town were much more accustomed to seeing the Amish than the travelers at Tulsa

International. Or maybe it was because she dressed Plain, but carried a Louis Vuitton bag and a first-class ticket. What a joke.

She settled into her seat, carefully folded the handles of Louie's bag, and pushed it under the chair in front of her.

She was certain she looked as if she had been run over by a bus. Her *frack* was wrinkled, the apron creased in more places than she could count as she had twisted it in her hands on the ride to the airport. Her eyes were red and swollen, her nose stuffy, and all she wanted to do now was crawl into a hole, and . . . well, crawling into a hole would be enough. The "and" could come later. At least, she had managed to get her tears to stop, but only because crying would do her absolutely no good.

"Good God, Avery, take that thing off your head." Her father waved a hand around, motioning toward the prayer *kapp* she had pinned in her hair a lifetime ago. This morning. She had been wearing it for so long, she had forgotten she still had it on.

She pulled the pins and released the head covering, crumpling it in her hands. She wouldn't even bother to tell her father not to use the Lord's name that way. She didn't have the energy to fight with him.

"And that dress. Is that the going thing in Aruba?" He had managed to keep his opinion to himself on the forty-five minute drive to the airport, but it seemed he couldn't hold his tongue any longer.

"Leave her alone, Owen."

"Come now, Maris. She's put us in quite a bind these last few weeks, hiding out. Lying about where she was." He raised his eyebrows at her in that accusing manner he had perfected long ago, but Avery refused to take the bait. What did it matter now?

"Leave her alone, Owen."

"I'm just saying, we turn our backs for a couple of weeks, and she goes all . . ." He waved his hand again, his vocabulary failing him once more.

"I said, leave her alone." This time the words were pushed between Maris's gritted teeth.

Even Avery's father stopped to stare at his fiancée.

Maris had never been her champion before, and Avery couldn't figure out why she wanted to start now. Maybe the petite blonde knew what it was like to be hopelessly in love with the wrong person.

And Avery was in love. She had poured her heart out to Gideon, and he hadn't even responded. She had all but begged him to let her stay, and he hadn't even looked her in the eyes. She had promised Ruth not to break his heart, and in the end, it was he who broke hers.

Maybe she should have begged. Maybe . . .

Maybe not.

If nothing else, she left Amish country with a few shreds of her pride intact. Not that it would do her any good now. He didn't want her. And he was starting to court another. A proper Amish woman, who wasn't English or mouthy and didn't challenge his decisions and try to force him to raise alpacas. By this time next year, that lucky woman would most likely be his wife.

The thought stabbed Avery's already-wounded heart. She had thought she was in love with Jack, but now she knew she had been in love with the *idea* of being in love. Her feelings for Jack were nothing but a wisp of smoke compared to what she felt for Gideon. This love was real, and she knew she would love him until the end of time. She would do anything for the man. And in the end she had to leave him behind.

Owen Hamilton adjusted his seat back. "Very well." He unbuttoned his suit coat and tried to appear as if backing off was his idea, while Maris stared out the window, a strange look on her face. Avery closed her eyes and tried to pretend that her heart was not broken in two.

Another hour and they would land in Dallas. Sixty more minutes, and they would pull into the gated drive at her father's house. By supper, today would seem like another lifetime. Next week, she'd probably forget the taste of Ruth Fisher's shoofly pie or the exact color of the sky over Gideon's farm.

But it would be a long, long time before she could erase the feel of his lips beneath hers.

*Lord, please take care of him. Lead him where You want him to go. Be with him while we are apart. And Lord, please bless Gideon and his family in every way. Amen.*

She couldn't bring herself to utter even a small prayer on her own behalf.

The house looked strangely empty when he pulled up in front. It *was* empty. Annie wasn't there, making a mess of things, learning to cook, trying to convince him to buy livestock.

Slowly, he climbed down from the buggy, in no hurry to continue on with this day. He'd unhitch the horses for now, as he wasn't planning on going anywhere anytime soon. Maybe tomorrow he'd head over and take a look at the new horses that Gabriel had picked up at the auction, but today he had no desire.

He led the horses through the barn where he brushed them down and turned them loose in the pasture. His body went through the motions, but his mind was on other things. Breathin'. Gettin' through right now. Learnin' to go on.

One day at a time. Isn't that what they said? Well, that's what he'd do. He'd take it one day at a time. Surely in a week or two, it wouldn't hurt so bad that he'd lost love not once, but twice.

Coming back through the barn, he spied the quilts he'd used for his makeshift bed. Better take those on in the house. Maybe throw them over the porch railings and let them air out before toting them inside. He gathered them in his arms and stepped into the bright sunshine.

*One day at a time.*

"*Onkel.*" Mary Elizabeth pulled her bicycle to a stop in front of the house, waving to him earnestly.

He nodded his head in return, unable to mirror her enthusiasm.

"Where's your Annie?" she asked as she set the kickstand. "In the *haus*? I have something for her. It's—"

"She's gone."

"What?" Mary Elizabeth blinked her clear blue eyes.

Gideon was loathe to say the words again. "She's gone," he repeated, this time a little louder.

*One day at a time.*

"I don't understand." A frown puckered her brow, and she looked toward the house, as if she expected Annie to appear on the front porch. Maybe she thought he would tell her he was just playing a joke.

"It was time she went back to where she came from."

"She's gone?"

He nodded. "She has a family, a father." And a beau.

"But I thought she liked it here . . ."

"She couldn't stay here, Mary Elizabeth. She isn't one of us."

"But . . ." He hated the tears that welled in her eyes, spilling across her lashes to slide down to her chin. "She didn't even say good-bye."

Because he had never given her the chance. If he had, he wouldn't have been able to let her go—and *that* would have been the worst thing for everyone involved. Despite the pain it caused, it was best to get it over quickly and move on.

*One day at a time.*

"And Louie . . ."

*Jah*, he would miss her mutt almost as much as he would miss her.

"I—I." She opened and closed her mouth like a fish out of water, but no more words would form. Then she clamped her hands over her lips, and fell into his arms.

Gideon dropped the blankets at his feet. He wished so badly that he could do the same. Rail to the heavens, cry, stomp his feet, and rid himself of the poison of this new grief that consumed him. It would do no good, for the grief would be with him the rest of his days, along with the hole in his heart that her leaving had left behind.

"Why? Why? Why?" Mary Elizabeth sobbed into his shirt front. "Why did she have to leave?"

He wrapped his arms around her more tightly, trying to comfort the sobbing girl, gaining a little comfort in return. The question *he* wanted answered was why he had to go and fall in love with an *Englischer* in the first place.

The first night without her was the hardest. Moving back into the house only made it worse, as it served as a constant reminder that she was really gone. And that he was truly alone.

It was as if she had left a piece of herself in every room. The afghan she had tossed at the foot of the couch. The box of rags he had fixed up for Louie to sleep in. An extra prayer *kapp*, the cookbook from the library, and her scent. That lingering fragrance seemed to float all around him no matter where in the house he stood.

He picked up the Bible she had left on the lamp table along with the German-to-English dictionary. He smiled, turning it over in his hands.

She had been full of surprises, his Annie. Reading in German, learning to cook, trying her best to fit into his world.

Had he been too hasty to make her leave?

Then he remembered the talk he'd had with the elders. He was to start courtin' again. It wouldn't do to have an outsider livin' in his house while he set his intentions on another.

With Annie underfoot, he surely wouldn't be able to focus his attention on Rachael.

With a sigh, he placed the Bible back on the table and headed for his room.

First he had to confess his sins and the errors of his ways. Then he would let Rachael know of his plans. His heart wasn't quite in it, but it would be. Soon, he'd forget the color of Annie's eyes. The scent of her hair. The way she tilted her head to one side when she smiled.

He pulled his suspenders from his shoulders and shucked off his pants, laying them neatly over the back of the chair.

It was best for him and Annie, he thought as he changed out of his shirt. Best for the community and Rachael. He crawled into bed. *Surely God will see fit to help me through.*

One day at a time.

Gideon was bleary-eyed the next morning as he stumbled from his bedroom into the kitchen. He yawned and stretched, pulling the suspender straps over his shoulders as he prepared to go out for his morning chores.

He wished he had a cup of coffee, but none was made. That was something he'd have to do once he came back from milking Honey. He pulled on his boots and stomped to the front door, missing Louie who made the trip with him every morning.

It wasn't like he needed another dog. He had a few of his own and even more that seemed to show up on a regular basis. He just missed the little Yorkie, city dog turned country. And he couldn't help but wonder how the whelp would adjust back to city life.

*Just fine*, he told himself. It was much easier to go back to the *Englischer* ways than it was to embrace the hard, old-fashioned lifestyle of the Plain people. Louie might not have an endless supply of butterflies to chase in all of the concrete and steel that made up the city, but he would find other things to occupy his time that were just as enjoyable.

Just like his mistress.

He would miss his Annie much more than she would miss him. She would look back on her time in Amish country with a faint smile and think *Once, I . . .* while he'd wish every day that she was at his side.

He shook his head and walked into the barn. Those fanciful thoughts would get him nowhere. It was time to move on. One day at a time. But even as he completed the task himself, Gideon had to push aside the memory of her learning to milk Honey.

He headed back into the house for coffee, then breakfast. After that, he would head out to check on the hens and maybe walk down and make sure his scarecrow still stood.

He opened the cabinet, but the coffee tin wasn't in its usual place. He checked the cabinet over, and the one next to it on the other side, and even the one down below. Still no coffee.

He was just about to give up, thinking Annie had used the last of it the day before and forgot to mention it to him, when he spotted a new canister on the counter. Made from some sort of ceramic, it was painted blue with a shiny, slick finish.

Annie.

He pulled the jar toward him and sure enough it was filled with the missing coffee.

He smiled as he filled the straining basket with coffee and started the water to boil. But as he tasted his own brew, his smile disappeared quickly enough. *Jah*, that was the reason he'd stopped making coffee. His efforts were barely palatable.

Still grimacing, he fried up some dippy eggs and ate them, hating that he was alone. He and Annie never talked much at meals. That just wasn't the Amish way. Mealtimes were for refueling the body, not for chatting. But he missed having her across the table from him, just a mere touch away.

He held back a sigh as he finished off the last of his eggs and toast, and took his plate to the sink. His day stretched before him, a chasm of loneliness.

He looked to the clock on the mantel remembering as he did so that it needed new batteries. But it worked—another of Annie's legacies.

At just after six, he had a lot of work to do. That was the Amish way, just part of life in the Plain community. Although it felt next to impossible to put one foot in front of the other to get the work done, it was necessary.

He took a deep breath and started for the door, again noticing the stack of books at the end of the couch.

He sighed again. *Annie.*

She might have gone back to Dallas, but she'd left several pieces of herself behind.

The book on top was the German-to-English dictionary she'd used to look up words from the Bible. Below that was a cookbook, then one on the alpacas she had been telling him about. He picked up the dictionary and turned it over in his hands. With a sad smile he opened it, running his fingers over the title page. Mayes County Library was stamped inside, the name of the library in town. He'd have to return those soon. He didn't have any idea how long a person could keep books from there. Maybe tomorrow he'd run them into town and drop them off at the library. It would give him something to do. For now he had stalls to muck and hay to spread. He gave the tome on alpacas one last look before placing it on the stack and heading for the door.

Gideon took a deep breath; the sweet smell of a Clover Ridge spring filling his lungs. What a beautiful day to be out in the fields. It was May, the most perfect time of year. The grass was green, and the sky that wondrous shade of impossible blue.

He had everything he could possibly want. He took another satisfied breath and tamped down the swell of pride. It was a sin to be prideful. God had given him so much that he turned his pride to prayer and thanked the Lord for the gifts he'd received.

Off in the distance he heard the bleat of a sheep. But that wasn't his lamb. It couldn't be. He had sold all the lambs after the accident.

"Gideon." He heard her voice so soft and yet so near it sounded like she was right next to him. He turned, and she was. So real, he could see the creases in her prayer *kapp*, the neat stitches in her pale blue *frack*.

"Miriam."

"Come," she said, holding a hand out to him. "The lambs need you."

"But," he started to protest.

"But what?" she asked, that sweet smile on her lips, her eyes sparkling.

"There are no lambs." Then again, if she were still there, then surely the lambs were too.

Gideon realized his second chance had come home again. He took her hand, allowing her to lead him toward the pasture. "Where's Jamie?" he asked.

Suddenly rain started to fall. Soft patters at first until it came down in sheets. Miriam didn't answer, just walked on as if the sun was still shining.

"There." She pointed toward the creek.

Gideon turned, expecting to see their son, but Jamie wasn't there. The water had risen with the rain, nearly flooding the banks as it rushed on by. It was dangerous. But he could keep her safe now. All he had to do was keep her at his side—and find his son.

"Gideon!" Annie, his sweet Annie, stood on the other side. She was dressed in a plain blue *frack* with a sparkling red dress on top of the conservative Amish garb. She had on one flip-flop and one high-heeled sandal.

"Stay there," he told her. She'd be safe as long as she didn't try to cross the creek. If she could just stay there until the rains stopped.

She nodded, wringing her hands as if she wasn't as confident in his decision. She inched closer to him, to the swollen banks of the creek.

"Stay there!" he yelled again. But the wind had picked up and carried his words away before they could reach her ears.

"What?" she cried, taking one step more.

He tried to tell her again to stay put, but as he opened his mouth to say the words, she disappeared. She was gone in the blink of an eye. One second she was there, the next she was gone.

He ran to the creek, but no sign of her. He tried to wade out into the water, but Miriam pulled him back. "I have to find her," he said, unable to break free from her grasp. With that red dress on, Annie would be easy to spot. He'd find her, he would. But Miriam held him back.

"Let me go," he commanded and begged, all in the same breath.

Miriam tilted her head, her expression serene and confused. "But Gideon, you've been free all along."

He looked down at his arm. Miriam was no longer holding him. He turned toward her, but she was standing yards away, Jamie stood behind her, half buried in her sodden skirts. Wet, but fine.

His family was safe. He could get Annie now. He could save her.

He ran toward the creek, stumbled—and fell.

Gideon jerked awake, drenched in sweat, breathing heavily.

His hands shook as he pushed his hair off his forehead and rubbed his eyes.

He glanced around. He was alone. There was no rain. No Miriam. No Jamie. *No Annie.*

With a steadying sigh, he pushed himself off the bed. His knees popped as he stood. He shuffled across the floor, out of the bedroom, and down the hall toward the kitchen.

He half-expected to see Annie curled up asleep on the couch, Louie at her feet. He drew in a breath and let it out slowly. She wasn't there. Then he stumbled into the kitchen and poured himself a glass of water.

With the amount of work he'd put in that day, he should have been in a deep, dreamless slumber, but his thoughts kept him awake with their churning.

He stared out the window over the sink, just able to make out the edge of the chicken coop and the north section of fence around the empty hog pen. He needed to buy some pigs, he told himself there in the dark. And a couple more chickens. Maybe a couple of goats. Anything to keep busy. At least until the day of his confession. After that, he could start living again. He would be free to forget about Annie, to let her go.

But until that day . . .

Gideon sat his glass down in the drainer and made his way back into the living room. Why did it seem as if his whole house was filled with Annie?

After the accident, he'd sold their farm, the *haus* and all the animals except for Molly, Kate, and Honey. He'd had to get away, the sharp edges of guilt slicing through him every time he looked out onto the fields, at their clothes, Jamie's toys—even at the meticulously-kept garden in the front of the little house.

So he'd gotten rid of it all only to move out here and now be constantly reminded of Annie. Everywhere he turned he found a piece of her. He eased down on the couch, positive he could still smell the scent of her shampoo and the dab of lavender she wore. Across from him sat the chair where he had dozed after pulling her in from the cold.

And the stack of books she'd brought in from the library. He turned on the oil lamp closest to him, then leaned down and traced the cover of the book on top—the one she'd borrowed about alpacas. The face that stared back at him was not unpleasant—dark, intelligent eyes and gentle-looking in nature. She'd said they were good creatures, though she had never seen one in real life. He'd seen them at the auction. He considered himself a good judge of people and animals, and the alpacas appeared to be everything Annie said they were and more.

A perfect alternative to sheep.

If a man decided he wanted to raise a creature like that.

And he hadn't.

Still, it wouldn't hurt to take a look.

Gideon picked up the book and sat back, propping it in his lap. He traced the cover one more time before opening it to the first page and starting to read.

He had to get off the farm. Gideon took one last tug at the harness rig on Molly and Kate, then swung up into the buggy.

He told himself it was because he needed to return her library books, and that he could use a few things from town. But really, he had to get away from her. At least in this open-air rig he wasn't confronted with her scent, her very presence, every time he rounded a corner.

He enjoyed the ambling trip into town, the sun on his face, and the smell of spring and horses all around. It was *gut*. *One day at a time*, he thought, pulling to the side so a car could move around him.

Tonight he was going over to his parents' *haus* to talk about his mother's treatments. Together they would make a plan that, with the Lord's help, would see them through. He knew Ruth Fisher's faith was strong, and he tried his best to steel his up too. But he . . .

*Nay. H*e pushed those thoughts away, tamped them down inside. He'd not go around doubtin'. He had to remain strong for his *mamm*, and that's exactly what he was goin' to do.

Gideon straightened his shoulders, and clicked Molly and Kate to a slower pace. They passed the sign welcoming them to Clover Ridge, *The Best Little Town in Oklahoma*. It was a *gut* town. The people there supported the Amish, let them set up shop right next door and sell their goods, Amish cheese, furniture, and even a restaurant that brought visitors in from all over the state.

Gideon pulled the buggy to a stop in front of Anderson's General Store. He'd pick up a few things for the *haus* before dropping off the books on the way back out of town.

"Mornin'," Coln greeted as Gideon stepped in from the sunlight. He tipped his hat in response and nodded once to Hester Stoltzfus's brother-in-law, then made his way over to the hardware section. He needed a few nails to brace up the fence posts around the hog pen. Wouldn't do any good to go get hogs and have them bustin' out and runnin' over the garden and crops. He might even need to get a couple of two-by-fours to brace it up as well. Which meant a stop at the lumberyard.

"Gideon Fisher."

He turned, not realizing how engrossed he was in his own thoughts until nearly startled out of them by the shopkeeper.

"Coln. *Gut* to see you."

"And you too, Gideon. But I don't see your lovely visitor with you today."

Gideon felt his heart twist inside his chest. "*Nay.*" His voice sounded a little rough. He cleared his throat, hoping no one noticed the cloud of emotion that settled over him.

"Well, I hope she'll be in soon. We have a new shipment of fabric. Just arrived. She was asking about something to make a new *frack*. I believe my wife said Katie Rose was planning to make her a dress."

Annie had said the same thing. The day he had brought her into town and had her father come and fetch her.

Gideon wagged his head. "She's gone home," he finally managed, thankful his voice sounded almost like himself.

Anderson's face fell. "Ah, well that's too bad. She was a lovely sight when she came in."

*That she was.* Gideon only nodded.

"You'll tell Katie Rose for me, in case she's still interested?"

Gideon nodded again. He wanted to pay for his nails and get back out into the sunshine. Away from even more memories.

He stepped around Anderson and walked toward the counter. "I'll just buy these now."

If Gideon was rude, Coln made no mention of it, not even a twitch of his expression to show that he felt slighted. *Gut.* Gideon wasn't trying to be rude. He just needed a breath of fresh air.

Finally he stepped out of the general store with his little bag of nails, everything else he'd thought to pick up while in town forgotten.

Perhaps he'd walk over to the library to return Annie's books. The air might do him some good, even though he'd gotten plenty of that on the trip into town.

He gathered the books and started off toward the library.

He'd not been inside the building since his *rumspringa*. Not that it wasn't allowed. More often than not, the Plain people passed knowledge down from one to another through word of mouth and teachings. He'd learned what he knew from his *dat* and his *gross-daadi*. Even Miriam's father had taught him much of what he knew about raising sheep.

The library was cool and well lit, but not too bright. The sky-lights from the ceiling added a natural effect to the indoors.

He stepped up to the counter and nodded to the woman seated there.

"*Guder mariye.*"

She smiled back at him. "What can I do for you today?"

"I need to return these books." He placed them on the counter and pushed them closer to her. "My guest borrowed them and . . ." he faltered. "I need to bring them back to you."

"All right. Were you able to get all that you needed from . . ." She looked up at him. "These were Annie's."

"*Jah,*" he said. "She's gone back . . . home." He couldn't help the slight hesitation before he said the word. In the time she was with him, he'd started to consider his farm her home as well. But that wasn't how it really was. She belonged in the big city. He did the right thing by making her leave.

"Aw, that's too bad. I so liked seeing her come in."

Unable to think of a proper response, Gideon just nodded. Then he shifted from one foot to the other as he waited for her to do whatever she had to do with the books. On his way home, he would stop by the lumber store. At least there he wouldn't have to listen to another person lament the fact that Annie had gone home.

"All set," the lady said, smiling up at him.

"*Danki.*" He tipped his hat as he turned toward the door.

"*Onkel!*" Mary Elizabeth stopped, her body half in and half out of the library. Something on her face made him wonder what part of the *Ordnung* she was breaking by being here.

"Mary Elizabeth." He tried to keep the surprise out of his voice.

"What are you doing here?" Her voice sounded unnaturally high pitched. Poor child, she all but wrung her hands.

"I came to return the books Annie borrowed from here." There, see, it was getting less and less painful to say her name. "What are you doin' here?"

Her face crumpled. "Please, please, please don't tell *Dat.*" She grasped his hand into her own, squeezing hard in her earnest. "*Please.*"

It wasn't in the Amish nature to say please. It was understood, a part of life. And that made Mary Elizabeth's anxiousness all the more curious. Still, she was a good child, and fast approaching her *rumspringa.*

Gideon looked around. "Is there something going on here that I should tell?" He nearly turned in a circle as he looked around. "I see nothing that deserves a tellin'."

A small, knowing light shone in his niece's eyes. "That's right. There is nothing to tell. I just came to read a few books."

"*Jah,*" he said, disentangling his fingers from hers. "And that you should do."

She almost wilted in relief. "*Danki, Onkel.*"

"There is no need to thank me."

Whatever secrets she harbored, his sweet niece could carry them with her another day.

## 15

Where are you headed so early on this fine Sunday morning?" Avery turned to face her father. She had hoped to get out of the house without anyone knowing she was gone. In the almost two weeks since her return, her father had been treating her as if she had some sort of twisted Stockholm syndrome and had fallen in love with her kidnapper—never mind that she hadn't been kidnapped. But every time she looked around, her father was right behind her. She turned a corner, he was there. She hadn't been alone more than five minutes since returning to Dallas.

Maybe this was for the best. Time alone would give her more time to think about Gideon. And that was one thing she wasn't going to do. Because thinking about Gideon led to tears and remorse and dwelling on past mistakes she didn't want to remember.

"Church," she said.

"Uh-hum." Her father scrutinized her with a critical eye, taking in every detail of her most conservative dress and her low-heeled designer shoes. "I see."

Which meant, *That's why you're dressed that way.*

Avery had not had the energy to pick up where she had left off. She had tried, but things she once considered to be of great importance, seemed trivial at best. She didn't look bad. For the most part, she looked like the "old" Avery. But she had yet to figure out where "Annie" fit into the English world. The girl she had been before was long gone, and her father knew it, even if he couldn't explain it.

"I called Ramon and got you an appointment to have your hair done before this weekend. We're lucky he could squeeze you in—especially after you missed your last appointment."

Avery raised a hand to her hair. She couldn't remember the last time it had been this long.

"And your nails. For heaven's sake, make sure you have something done to them—professionally—before the benefit." He tempered his words with a kiss on her cheek, as if the tiny token of affection could take away the sting of his criticism. Had he always been this shallow?

That wasn't fair. They came from a world where—sad, but true—appearance was everything.

"Yes, Daddy."

The children's hospital benefit was in less than a week, and Avery was expected to attend and play her part. That left six days to ready herself and maybe, somehow, find a little of the old Avery to carry her through.

He patted her on the cheek and continued toward his home office.

Avery watched him go, and then made her way to the garage. Her father had replaced her Mercedes with a brand new one, this one pearly white. She felt guilty driving the car. She would rather have had an ordinary Honda and send the rest of the money to Ruth and Abram—not that they would actually take it from her. Still, somehow she would find a way to help with the costly treatments.

Until then, all she could think about was Gideon. Since the Amish met every other Sunday, the day had finally come—his day of redemption. He'd be in the service right now, but she didn't know which family was hosting today's preaching. Though she couldn't say she understood the methods, she knew that today he would be forgiven and welcomed back into the community. Soon he would start courting another woman, and eventually he would marry her. A loveless marriage based on needs and finances and companionship.

Lizzie had told her during one of their many talks that the Amish didn't view love in the same way the English did. Love was a bonus, not the foundation of a relationship. Sometimes love came many years later—if at all—and didn't rule the emotions and decisions of the couple.

Avery could see the benefit in such thinking. Love had gotten her in too much trouble to count. In the past, she had given her heart away freely and had it handed back to her without remorse. This time was different. She'd left her heart with Gideon, and she knew it would never be hers again.

The parking lot of the Boston Avenue Methodist Church was packed when she pulled in. She liked the church because she could sneak into the balcony and listen without staring eyes. It wasn't as big as the First Methodist and other churches in the Dallas-Ft. Worth area, but it suited her just fine.

Today's message was love and forgiveness. As a man with dark, brown hair came forward to kneel and pray, Avery thought once again of Gideon. She bowed her head and prayed God would give her the strength to go on without him.

At the end of the church service, Bishop Beachy spoke. "I'd like to call a members meetin'."

Gideon twisted his hands together in his lap and waited. How fitting that he would repent at the service held at his parents' house.

The young people who hadn't yet joined the church, and the visiting members from other districts rose and glanced warily around, but filed out quietly all the same.

When the door had closed behind the last one, Gideon cleared his throat. "I want to confess that I have failed. I want to make peace and continue in patience with God and the church and in the future to take better care."

"Gideon Fisher, please come forward."

He caught his mother's eye, and steeled himself against the emotion he saw there. "Kneel before the church and tell us what is your sin?"

Gideon dropped to his knees on the hard, wooden floor surrounded by the members of the church and the walls that had protected him as a child. It served as just another reminder of all he stood to gain. "I didn't trust God. I went against the *Ordnung*. And I am truly sorry for the error of my ways."

"And now?"

"I'm ready to change."

The deacon stepped forward. "We know that many of you have heard the rumors. How Gideon Fisher shaved his beard and took up with an outsider. We all went out to talk with Gideon, and we are satisfied that he has repented from those ways. But as always, it is up to the church to decide."

"Gideon Fisher, you may leave," the bishop said.

He pulled himself to his feet and walked quietly to the door that led to the kitchen. From there he went out back and sat on the porch to await his fate.

He wasn't worried. The district was full of good people, and today's confession was just a formality. If no one had found out about his loss of faith, he wouldn't be here now. But since others had found out and started talking, the bishop had to do something public. Gideon understood. When he was called, he'd go back in, accept the discipline of the church, and would mostly likely be forgiven right away. His offense was not serious enough to warrant a six-week ban. Tomorrow he'd head over and state his intentions to Rachael Miller. And that would be that.

"*Bruder.*" Gabe stood at the door to the house, his brooding expression giving nothing away. "They're ready for you."

Gideon stood and followed his brother inside.

Crickets chirped and stars twinkled in the dusky purple sky. Gideon pushed aside the thought of a certain pair of eyes the exact same color and, instead, concentrated on the woman standing on the bishop's porch with him.

"*Danki* for supper, Rachael Miller. It was *gut* not to have to eat my own cookin' for a change." The bishop had arranged this evening meal prepared by his wife and Rachael, and Gideon had officially begun the courtin' of the young widow. He knew the others were watching from inside the *haus*.

Rachael smiled shyly and smoothed a hand over her apron. "You're welcome, Gideon Fisher."

He twisted his hat brim in his hands and walked the few steps to the ground, while she wrapped an arm around the support post and remained at a respectable distance.

He had to admit that she was a pretty little thing. The kind of woman that made a man feel strong and protective. She had silky brown hair tucked under her prayer *kapp* and big brown eyes, sweet and honest. She could cook like the dickens and had two of the sweetest girls he had ever had the pleasure of being around. She would make a fine wife.

"There's been some talk about the district," she said into the still night.

"So I've been told."

"It's been said that you fell in love with the *Englischer* who stayed with you this spring."

He didn't know how to respond. He had fallen in love with Annie Hamilton—Avery Hamilton—but the feelings had no place in his life.

"I know where this is going, Gideon. Why you came to supper tonight. You don't have to confirm or deny those feelings. I think it's only fair that you know what's being said. It makes no difference to me either way."

"*Danki*, Rachael."

"So." She raised her shoulder in a half shrug. "I guess I'll see you in town and such."

"I think your uncle would like that." He held out a hand, and she placed hers inside. It was warm and calloused like a workin' girl's should be. But he didn't feel even a glimmer of the spark he'd felt with Annie. No matter. He ran a thumb over the back of her hand and squeezed her fingers gently before letting her go. "*Gut nacht*, Rachael Miller." He released her and made his way to his buggy, aware the whole time she watched him from the porch.

Early Wednesday morning, Gideon took a sip of his coffee and made a face. How he'd managed to survive for nearly a year drinking his own coffee was a mystery of the ages. He sat down on the porch and watched the sun peek above the tree line as the day dawned. He'd milked the cows, fed the horses and the mule. Soon Gabriel would be by to ride with him to the auction over in Tulsa. He'd decided that he would go get some hogs, and maybe even another milk cow. With two little girls running on the farm, there'd be plenty need for milk.

He'd been to supper a couple of times at the Miller *haus*. He'd decided to go a couple of more before he took her out for a Sunday drive. It was so different courtin' as an adult than it had been when he was a teenager. Then, everything had been done in secret. Even the parents of the intendeds didn't know the couple was courtin' until they announced their desires to get married after harvest time.

He smiled, remembering how he and Miriam had decided they'd court. They had left the barn dance and singing held by a friend in another neighboring district. They had danced around the barn, enjoying their time to run around and appreciate the world before settling down and joining the church. Gideon had taken her hand and led her over to the refreshment table. There he had handed her a plastic cup full of red punch and asked her if she wanted to get some fresh air.

She'd fanned herself and nodded yes, her eyes sparkling with heated delight. They had waited until no one was looking, then they each slipped out a separate door and met in the shadows behind the old barn.

"Miriam King," he said, his voice a little wobbly on the end. He told himself it was because he was out of breath from all that dancing, but now he could admit how nervous he had been. Miriam would make a fine Amish wife. She was easy on the eyes, knew how to sew and put up jellies, and she made the best *snitz* pie in three districts. But what if she told him no?

"*Jah*, Gideon Fisher?"

"I was hopin' that we could begin courtin'."

"And what is this we've been doin'?"

"That's not what I mean." The words sounded like they'd been spoken by a bear, all gravely and rough.

"Then what do you mean?"

*Ach*, he wished he could see her face, had just a hint of what she was thinking.

"I mean a true courtin'. We'll spend the summer gettin' to know each other better. Then in September we'll tell our parents that we're gettin' married and that will be that."

And just like that, on a cool April night, he had asked her to marry him in the fall.

He could see the white edge of her prayer *kapp* as she tilted her head to one side and thought over his request. He should have asked her in a better light. Or at least let what little light there was stay behind him. As it was, he couldn't see enough of her face to know what was going on inside her head.

"Miriam King . . ." Again that voice of a bear spoke for him.

He thought she was playing with him, using some of the tricks she had seen the *Englisch* girls use in the motion pictures they had watched in town. Then she turned her head again, and he saw the sparkle of a tear on her cheek.

"Miriam, what's wrong?" His voice had turned quiet and gentle, the bear now gone. He stepped closer to her, running the pad of his thumb over the smooth skin of her cheek, whisking the moisture away with one gentle swipe. It was the first time he'd ever touched her save the clasping of hands during their swingy dances in the barn.

"Oh, Gideon," she cried. "You've made me so happy!"

"I have?" She certainly didn't look happy, so he had to take her word for it.

"*Jah.*"

He had kissed her then, with no one watching out behind the barn. He had known from the start that they were supposed to be together. God had put them that way and no man would tear them apart. There was no way he could know that years later it would be a decision he made that brought about their separation.

*Jah*, courtin' was done a lot different when it had to begin all over due to a death. It wasn't all secret. There were a lot of dinners and vistin'. Well, he guessed it was a lot the same, but it was all known about. And since his fall from grace and redemption, everyone in the district was watching to see what he'd do next.

He'd make it through this too. If he could lose Miriam and Jamie and then Annie, there wasn't anything the district could do that he couldn't survive.

He propped his feet on the rail and tried not to miss Annie so much. He missed her rat of a dog too. Truth was, he was downright miserable without her. She had brought sunshine and hope, love and forgiveness, back into his life. And try as he might, he missed her something terrible. But he was glad she had been a part of it at all. He'd hate to think of where he'd be now had it not been for her. He had been so close to the brink, but she had dragged him back to safety. Now he owed her—he owed himself—the chance to move on. Yet he still felt the drag on his heart.

He caught movement out of the corner of his eye and turned. He had expected to see Gabe coming down the lane, but instead the buggy rolling his way belonged to Miriam's parents.

He stood as they pulled to a stop. John King got down first, then he helped his wife to the ground. Abigail smiled kindly as she lifted her skirts and came toward him. Gideon had no choice but to meet them at the bottom of the stairs. He was completely unprepared as Abigail wrapped him in a warm hug.

"Gideon Fisher," she said, laying a hand against his cheek. "It's good to see you."

He could only nod through the clog of emotion blocking his throat. He hadn't talked to them since the funeral, had been avoiding them. He couldn't face them. Or the fact that their *dochder* and grandchild would be alive had it not been for his hasty instructions that stormy day a year ago.

"We know it's early, son, but . . ." John clasped his hands behind his back as if he didn't know what else to do with them. He rocked back on his heels, then straightened his hat. "Well, we're movin' to Ohio. Today. Abigail's got some kin there, and we thought it was time we got to know them better."

"I see." Somehow he'd missed that bit of news. Or maybe his hiding had been more successful than he'd realized.

"We couldn't leave though. Not without talkin' to you first."

He didn't know what to say. So he waited for Abigail to continue.

"John and I know this has been hard on you."

"It's been hard on all of us," John added.

"*Jah.*"

"Miriam was so special to us," Abigail continued. "Though the good Lord saw fit to take her before we were ready to let her go. And little Jamie . . ."

John wrapped his arm around her and pulled her to his side. "Does no good to leave a job like this to a woman," he said with a small shake of his head. "We heard your confession at church and, son, you need to know that you can't go through life blamin' yourself. The Good Lord has a plan for us all, and it's revealed to us through Him. You can't take these burdens onto yourself."

Gideon couldn't stop the hitch in his breath. Of all the things he expected them to say, this was the last. "And you . . . forgive me

. . . for what happened?" Of course they did. It was the Amish way, but to know it and to hear it were two different things.

"There's nothin' to forgive."

"It was a terrible, terrible accident," Abigail said. "But it *was* an accident. The only forgiveness needed is for you to forgive yourself."

Emotion washed over him—relief, sadness, grief, and love for this couple who had treated him like a son. He took one step forward, then another, until he had his arms wrapped around both of them.

How long they stood like that was anyone's guess. When Abigail pulled away, tears streamed down her face. John wiped his eyes, and Gideon pretended not to notice while he did the same.

He looked from one of them to the other. "Why don't you come in?"

"We've got to go. The driver will be to our house soon," Abigail explained.

"And we've got to get the buggy back to the deacon."

Gideon looked over to the familiar horses and rig. "Isn't this your buggy?"

"We sold it to the deacon for his grandson to have."

"It would be too hard to move it all the way up north. And Clara—that's my cousin—she said they drive gray-colored buggies up there. Just like they do in Lancaster County."

"You don't say?" Gideon couldn't keep the smile from his voice. Abigail King's excitement was infectious. He was happy to see her so thrilled about moving.

He smiled as the Kings got into the buggy. They waved as they ambled down the lane, off to discover whatever was waiting for them in Ohio.

A new buggy . . . a new state . . . a new beginning.

He watched until they disappeared out of sight.

A new beginning. He was goin' to get one of those for himself too.

Starting today.

"You're mighty quiet over there, *bruder.*"

They'd gotten an early start for the auction, and the horses marched along at an easy pace. Once they got into town they would meet up with the driver who would take them on to Tulsa and the livestock auction. The sky was a beautiful blue, the sun shining like a blessing from above.

"*Jah.*" Gideon's mind was still on his early morning visitors.

"You have somethin' heavy in your thoughts?"

"*Nay.*" He hated telling his brother anything but the truth, but he wasn't ready to expose all the details. They had been close their entire lives. Having birthdays barely a year apart could do that. Most of the time Gideon loved the camaraderie and fellowship he shared with Gabe. Just not today.

They rode in silence for a few minutes, the creak of the tack gear and the jingle of the harness practically the only sounds for miles.

"Do you love her?"

"What?" Gideon faced his brother.

"I asked if you love her."

"Does it make any difference?"

"It could."

Gideon knew that Gabe had the soul of a romantic buried somewhere beneath his grim exterior. He had been one of the exceptions. Gabriel had loved his wife dearly and had since the first day he'd laid eyes on her. They'd had something special and everyone around them could see it. But romantic love was a plus.

Companionship and compatibility were much more important for the years to come.

"Are you goin' to keep on courtin' Rachael Miller?" Gabe asked after awhile.

"*Jah*. Rachael is a fine woman." With more and more to do around the farm, he needed someone to help.

"Just remember this"—Gabriel glanced at his brother—"true love is hard to come by."

"And what did true love do for Katie Rose?"

"Samuel Beachy was a fool."

Gideon raised an eyebrow at his brother's tone. "I hope you're glad *Mamm* can't hear you say that."

"You ought to listen to me on this one," Gabe continued, not looking at Gideon as he spoke. "Love is special. You shouldn't throw it aside so carelessly."

❧ ❧

Gideon managed to push Gabriel's words to the back of his mind for the remainder of the day. It wasn't hard to do as they soon arrived in town and met with the driver. After discussing the fee they would pay him—which included money for gas, lunch, and three jars of their mother's homemade pickles—they started for Tulsa.

It had been a long time since Gideon had been in a car, and he had to admit that it wasn't his favorite way to travel. Things passed by in a blur of light and color. It was hard to see out the windows and enjoy the sights. Once he started to concentrate on one thing, the car passed right by it before he could truly enjoy it.

Thankfully they weren't hours away from their destination, and they pulled into the fairgrounds a short time later. Their driver parked, and they agreed to meet back at dinnertime. They would get a bite to eat, and he would take them back to Clover Ridge.

Gideon and Gabe weren't the only Plain people in attendance, but they were far outnumbered by the *Englischers*. They received a few stares as they passed the pens of creatures up for bid.

"I want to go have a look at the hogs," Gideon told his brother as they passed stalls of mares.

"*Ach*, but you could use a dray or two for your farmin'."

He was right, of course. Molly and Kate couldn't continue to be the only farm horses and pull the wagon every time he needed to go to town. Still, Gideon hadn't turned his entire land over to growing crops, and he had the mule. He had plenty of pasture that would most likely remain grazing land. It was too hilly for much else. Buying horses to farm just seemed like too much of a commitment to Gideon. If he bought more work horses, then there was no turning back. He'd be a farmer, wholeheartedly. Or at least it would seem that way. Gideon wasn't sure if he was ready to turn into a farmer.

*That's what you wanted.* The voice inside him whispered, but it wasn't true. He'd just wanted to die, but then Annie came along and pulled him away from that ledge. He had made his peace and was ready to move on, but as much as he wasn't ready to invest in livestock, he surely wasn't ready to turn his entire farm into neatly-planted rows of corn and soybeans. He had agreed to buy pigs, and he bought a mule. What more could a man do?

Gabriel stopped. "Go on with you, then." He waved Gideon toward the large door that led outside to the pens that held the swine. "Get your pigs. I'll be here."

Gideon heard the disappointment in his brother's voice, but didn't say anything to correct it as he made his way outside. He would never be able to explain to Gabe how he felt, how he needed to take the healing process at his own pace. There would come a time when it didn't hurt so bad, the loss of his family and of Annie. Jumping in and buying draft horses wouldn't make it go away now.

He walked among the *Englischers* and the pens, studying the pigs as he moved along. He wouldn't need many, maybe three or four to start. A boar and a couple of sows. His goal wasn't to breed pigs, but raise them for meat. He looked around the pens, taking note of a particular swine or two. A saddleback with a white belly. The most popular American Yorkshire with its straight up ears. All good lookin' creatures. Well-cared for and healthy. He'd take his chances when they got to the auction block.

"Gideon Fisher?"

He turned at the sound of his name.

A familiar-looking man stood behind him. Gideon didn't recognize him right away, then it dawned. "You breed alpacas." The man was the breeder Gideon had talked to at the last auction when he had bought Buster the mule.

"That's right. I didn't expect to see you here today."

Gideon shrugged. "*Jah*," he said, pointing toward the pigs. "Thinkin' about raising some swine. You sellin' today?"

"That's right." He turned and pointed down the row. "Got a pen right back there. Some of the prettiest creatures you'll ever want to see."

"Have you now?"

"Would you like to come take a look?"

Gideon tried not to appear too interested. After all, he'd come for pigs. If he couldn't be talked into a dray nag or two, he surely couldn't be convinced to invest in alpacas. "Sounds fine," he said. "Mighty fine."

*True love is hard to come by.*

Even as he fed the dogs and poured chicken feed around the barnyard for the hens and the strutting rooster to enjoy, the words came back to haunt Gideon.

His *bruder* was right. Foolishly romantic, but right. Love didn't come along every day, and he loved the dark-haired Miss Hamilton from Dallas, Texas. But was it true love? And what difference would it make if it were? They were too different. From opposite worlds. She seemed to fit into his easily enough, but for how long? How long could she go without the creature comforts she was accustomed to before the strain of Plain living became too much to shoulder? He knew one thing without a doubt—he could never survive in hers.

So the only thing he could do was to go on. Live. Court. Farm. They were the only options he had. So that's what he would do. Live. Court. Farm.

He grabbed up the pitchfork and headed into the barn. Now was as good a time as any to start. Honey needed milking. Buster needed some oats. Molly and Kate needed to be brushed down.

There was something poignant in the air inside the barn, the sweet scent of hay and better times. His childhood spent running barefoot through the barnyard, chasing kittens, and milking the cows. There were times when he missed those days, the ones before he knew what could be snatched away.

He wanted that again, that peace and joy, that lightness of spirit. That faith. And the comforting voice that whispered long into the night assuring him that all was well.

From John and Abigail he had received his forgiveness. Now he needed it from God, and more important, from himself. Maybe then he could move ahead. Go forward toward the life he should be living and not the one he'd been trapped in all these months.

Without thinking, Gideon dropped to his knees.

"Dear Lord in heaven above. Father, God of all things, please forgive me. I have been so long without You, without Your guidance I—" Gideon faltered. "I don't know what to do. I need Your help, Lord, Your wisdom and kindness to shine down on me. Even though I am not worthy, Lord, please make me so to accept the blessings of Your gifts, the gift of life. And help me, Lord, start living again."

As he prayed, tears streamed down his face. The world stopped moving around him. There were no sounds in the barn, no rustle of leaves from outside. Just him and God. And Gideon felt the spirit of the Lord move within him as a peace like he had never known settled into his heart.

A week passed and then another, and once again Avery's father had countless things for her to do. Library dedications, children's hospital fund-raisers, ribbon cuttings. The list went on and on. She had never felt more useless in her life.

The city was big. Too big. Even bigger than she remembered. Faster, louder. She couldn't hear God there. There was too much noise, too much distraction after the quiet of Clover Ridge. Not just country life, but *Amish* country life. With Gideon, her life had taken on purpose and meaning. She hadn't floated from one party to another, to a press meeting and then to dinner and another party. She'd had chores and responsibilities. She had loved working in the garden and trying to cook and setting the table while she waited for Gideon to come in from the fields. With Gideon, she'd been different. She'd been better.

She sent a letter to Lizzie explaining as best she could what had happened between her and Gideon. She left out the part that she hadn't wanted to leave and that her father had practically ripped her from Gideon's side. She omitted the part where she had cried and begged him to let her stay, and how he hadn't even looked her in the eyes as he told her it was for the best.

Avery knew Gideon felt that what he had done was in the best interest of everyone involved—even if it wasn't.

Lizzie sent her a letter back, saying how much she missed her and how she had hoped she would've stayed. Avery cried when she read it. Cried when Lizzie told her that her *onkel* had started courtin' the sweetly Amish widow, Rachael Miller. It was what was expected and demanded of him by the church.

Then she packed up the freshly laundered *frack* with its matching cape and white apron and sent it back to the Fishers. She'd included a note that said simply, *Thank you*. There were not enough words to say how much her time with Gideon—her time with *all* of them—had meant to her. And how very glad she was to have met them and been a part of their family, even for a short time.

Avery glanced around the ballroom at all of the politely bored faces and tried to remember how she felt before her time in Oklahoma. She couldn't. Before she went to Amish country, she had wondered if there was something more. Now she knew there was.

"Avery, sweetie. So good to have you back." Natalie Esteban sauntered up beside her and kissed the air at each cheek. Once upon a time Avery had considered Natalie to be among her best friends. That was before she truly knew what friendship meant.

"Heather Daniels said the after party is at her place tonight. You up for it?"

Avery opened her mouth to tell Natalie no, then closed it again. Maybe her father was right. Maybe she wasn't making enough of an effort to her return. It wasn't like Gideon had tried to stop her from leaving. He practically dumped her at her father's feet. There was no going back to Amish country. There was only going forward in Texas.

"Absolutely," she said with more enthusiasm than she felt.

With any luck, if she pretended that this was where she wanted to be, eventually she would come to believe it was true.

"That's my girl." Natalie blew her another kiss then glided away, bracelets jangling.

Avery straightened her shoulders. It was time to start living again. This was the life she had been given, and she had to do the best with what she had. She was going to have fun tonight—if it killed her.

This party was going to be the death of her. Avery watched her once upon a time best friend jump into the swimming pool fully clothed in a dress that cost enough to feed a small country. The partygoers at poolside all laughed and cheered as she resurfaced, sputtering and trying to keep her head above water, her sequined dress saturated and dragging her down. Someone handed her another drink as they hauled her out of the pool dripping wet. Natalie downed it in one eye-watering gulp, then pulled her dress over her head. Avery thought the man who pulled Natalie from the pool was Carson Henry, heir to the Henry Electronics billions. It was hard to tell. He leaned in and passionately kissed Nat while she stood in her strapless black bra and lacy thong underwear. Natalie wrenched away and with a laugh, pushed her savior into the pool, and then jumped in behind him.

Avery sighed. Same party, different day. Had this really been how she passed her time? She had never been one to drink to excess, but she had gone along with the crowd for appearances, showing up at parties and hanging out because there was nothing better to do.

Or maybe because she hadn't realized there *was* something better to do.

With a barely audible sigh, she took her virgin cranberry juice into the house where the party was still thriving, but a little less rambunctious. At least, there were no pools to jump into.

She collapsed on the sofa and sipped her drink.

"You can't change them, you know."

Startled, Avery looked over to see Natalie's younger sister, Meredith, sitting next to her. She had been so wrapped up in her own thoughts she hadn't noticed the young girl seated on the expansive white leather couch. Meredith with her long, dark, board-straight hair was all of seventeen, but it was more than her age that set her apart from the other guests.

"Pardon?"

"I said you can't change them."

Avery glanced around at the chaos called a party, and at the moneyed drifters who were supposed to be her friends. "I guess not."

"All you can do is hope for the best."

"I don't know what you mean."

The somber dark-haired girl flicked a wrist vaguely. "Hope that one day, they'll grow up into productive citizens."

"I grew up once." Avery didn't mean to say the words aloud.

"Sorry?"

"Nothing."

"I heard you and Jack Welch broke up."

"True."

"I never liked him. He was just so . . . smarmy."

*Out of the mouths of babes.* As true as the statement was, it still stung. Avery felt the well of unwanted tears in her eyes.

"Oh, don't cry. I'm sure you'll find someone much better. Mother is always telling me that I don't think before I speak, and—"

"No, no. You're right. I will find someone better. I already have."

Meredith looked around trying to spot someone new in the familiar crowd. "Is he here?"

"No."

"Then where is he?"

"In Oklahoma."

"If you love him, why are you here while he's in another state?" *Why indeed?* "I'm not sure if he loves me back."

"You know how to tell though."

Avery shook her head.

"That song, silly. From the movie *Mermaid*. His kiss." She sang the words just a little off key and brought a smile to Avery's lips. "You know."

She did, and those simple words brought back a wealth of memories—she and Gideon on their last picnic, the way his lips clung to hers as if he couldn't help himself. She initiated the kiss, but he kissed her back. She had accused him of still being in love with Miriam, but now he was courting another woman. An Amish woman. When he should be with her.

"I also heard that you spent some time with the Amish." Meredith said this as if it were some kind of state secret.

"I did."

Her brown eyes grew wide. "Really? What was that like?"

"It was . . ." Avery hesitated. Not once since she had gotten back from Oklahoma had anyone asked her how it felt to be among the Amish. Never had she tried to sum up the experience with mere words. "It was slow. But in a good way," she added. "Quiet, but that was good too."

Meredith made a face. "Sounds boring."

Avery shook her head. "It was wonderful, actually."

"And they really live without electricity?"

"Yes."

"Bet you missed that, huh?"

"No." *I miss Gideon*.

"Who's Gideon?"

Had she said his name aloud? "He was the man I stayed with while I was there. A farmer." Those words sounded too mundane to describe Gideon, but none other seemed to fit either.

"He's Amish?"

"*Jah*. I mean, yes."

"And you miss him."

"Yes," she said quietly. And she missed Lizzie and Samuel, Ruth and Abram—even Gabriel and his scowl. She missed having the coffee she had made each morning and trying to get the dough right to make chicken pot pie. She missed the stories and the peaceful solitude. And Gideon, she so very much missed Gideon.

A cheesy old quote came to mind, *If you love something set it free*. He had set her free. What if she proved her love by returning?

Avery's heart gave a sudden lurch, then pounded in her chest.

"Avery?"

"Huh?" She twisted in her seat to stare at Meredith, while a plan turned over and over in her mind.

"I asked if you wanted another drink."

"No. I . . . I need a cab."

"You haven't had that much."

"I know. I need a cab."

"I haven't seen you drink all night."

"Your sister has, and she's my ride."

"You're leaving? I thought the fun was just beginning." She looked around at the couples dancing, her sister outside still kissing the half-clothed Carson Henry in the shallow end of the pool.

"I've got to go," Avery said quietly. She had to get back to Gideon, to show him how much she cared. She might get there and he might turn her away, but she had to try. She loved him too much to just let everything they had go.

Meredith got a knowing light in her brown eyes. "You're going back."

Avery nodded.

Meredith plucked her cell phone from her tiny, sequined evening purse. "Baxter, please bring the car around. And hurry. I have a friend who needs to get home as soon as possible."

A truer statement she had never heard.

Meredith walked her down to the front of the building and saw her safely to the Esteban's limousine. Secretly Avery thought Meredith had fancied herself to be some sort of undercover matchmaker by helping her get back to Amish country. Avery supposed she kind of was. In fact, Meredith rode with Avery all the way out to her house where Maris was waiting with a small overnight bag and Louie all ready to go.

"Thank you, both," Avery addressed the women, worlds apart yet they had united for her.

Maris smiled and pressed her keys into her hand. "I'll tell your father you'll call him in a day or two."

Avery nodded. Her father was smart. He'd understand why she had to go. Okay, maybe understand was too strong of a word. But one day he'd realize that she did it all for love. She just hoped Gideon understood too.

She couldn't let herself consider the fact that he could send her away a second time. She had faith, hope, and love. Wasn't the greatest love? Surely that would carry more weight than the life differences they faced.

Avery kissed Maris on the cheek, hugged Meredith, and loaded Louie V. into the pearly-white Mercedes. She started the car and waved good-bye before heading down the driveway and through the gates that led out into the city.

"All right, Lou. Let's go home."

# 16

The sound of an engine roared from the road, but Gideon didn't look up from the fence gate. He had done so much this spring, but the fences were still in bad need of work as May was coming to an end. It had to be done soon. His alpacas should be arriving today. Excitement buzzed around him. He never thought he'd feel this way about hairy animals that could spit thirty yards, but this was a new day. His new beginning.

He and Rachael had begun their courtin', but were taking it slow. *Jah*, she needed a few things done around the house, and he could do those odd jobs for her. Until they actually got married, Gabriel's oldest boys had signed on to help her. They would bring in this year's crops, and Mary Elizabeth was helping her can relish and chowchow to sell in the market.

He wouldn't let himself think about Annie and what she might be doin' now. He couldn't start over by lookin' back. But at night, when everything was quiet, she snuck into this thoughts.

Gideon pushed and pulled at the fence post, testing its stability. Satisfied with the results, he hooked the latch and peeled off his gloves. It would do for now. Hopefully soon, he would be able to upgrade the fencing. The orange tabby that had come up a couple of days before wound her scrawny body in between his legs, then rubbed her face against the new post.

The property looked so different than when he first bought it. At the time, he had wanted to escape, but now he enjoyed the seclusion. Not many traveled this far from town without a purpose.

He heard a truck door slam. He'd finished just in time. His alpacas were here. Wouldn't Annie be surprised to learn he had followed her advice? Mary Elizabeth had written Annie at least one letter, but he refused to let himself ask what it said and whether his niece had heard back from their *Englisch* friend. Asking one question would only lead to more—and he couldn't afford to keep dwelling on what could never be.

As much as he told himself it was for the best, he could never forget the wounded look in her eyes when she knew he was sending her home. He hadn't wanted to. He missed her something terrible. But it was better to lose her now than when she owned even more of his heart.

A familiar voice called out behind him. "Thank you!"

It was worse than he thought. Now he was hearing her voice.

He shaded his eyes and searched the line of trees next to the road, hoping to spot the delivery truck full of alpacas. But instead he saw . . .

"Annie?" The word came out as a whisper. He feared that if he spoke any louder she might disappear. Surely he had imagined her. He closed his eyes. Counted to three, couldn't stand it any longer, and opened them again.

Annie!

She waved to the driver of the car that had dropped her off, her too-short black dress flashing in the sunlight. Then she bent, took off her shoes, and started toward the house.

He held his breath. He couldn't afford to be prideful, but what reason would she have for coming back now, if not for him? He watched her walk slowly up the lane toward him. Well, it *seemed* like she walked slowly. She didn't run, and she didn't hurry to his side.

Louie made it to him first, then Annie. His sweet, sweet Annie.

She stopped a little more than an arm's length away. "Hi."

"*Guder mariye.*"

The Oklahoma wind feathered through her hair. He would have brushed it back had she been even a few inches closer. Instead, he scratched the pooch behind the ears.

"I came back." Her words were breathless as if she'd run the whole way from Dallas.

"I can see that."

She looked at him, her violet eyes steady, but uncertain. "I have three things I need to ask you."

He nodded. "*Jah?*"

She took a deep, shaky breath. "You told me once that you still loved your wife."

"*Jah.*"

"Do you love me?"

"*Jah,*" he said without hesitation. "I do."

Her lips trembled, then she pressed them together, the only sign that what he'd said had affected her at all.

"And are you still planning on courting another woman?"

"It was what the bishop wanted."

"And now?"

He shrugged, unable to say the words, hesitant to be too hopeful. Rachael was a fine Amish woman and would make any man a *gut* wife. But nothing he would ever feel for her could compare to how Avery set his heart to soarin'. Plain livin' could be difficult for those born into it. It was next to impossible for those wantin' to join up.

She took another deep breath, this one steadying, and her eyes darkened. "How does the bishop feel about outsiders living in his district?"

Gideon swallowed hard. His heart hammered in his chest. "That'd probably depend on who wanted to come live here."

"Me," she said. "What about me?"

He cleared his throat, pushing down the hope rising within him. He was as nervous as she, and he wanted to take her hands into his own and tell her everything would work out just fine. But that wasn't something he knew for sure and for certain. "I think he'd be *allrecht* with that. Once he gets to know you."

"And what about you?"

"That's more'n three questions." Then he took the first step that brought them closer together and pulled her into his arms.

She was warm, melting into his embrace. Gideon buried his face in the curve of her neck and breathed in the lavender scent that was all Annie.

"Why'd you make me go?" Her voice came out raw and scratchy, but she kept her arms locked firmly around his neck in a tight, loving grip.

"I thought it best."

"You were wrong."

"I was wrong."

She pulled away just enough to look into his eyes. "All my life I've been searching for something. I found it right here."

"God?" he asked.

Annie smiled through her tears. "God. Love. *You.*" She paused. "Please don't make me leave again."

Those words brought it all home. Reluctantly, he set her away from him and kept her at an arm's distance. "It's not goin' to be easy."

He was stone-cold serious, but still she smiled. "The things worth having usually aren't."

"You'll be givin' up a lot."

"Nothing worth having."

"There's a lot more than cars and clothes that'd have to be left behind."

She flashed him her dimples even as the tears continued to spill from her amazing violet-colored eyes. "I love you more than electricity."

"That's good to know." His heart pounded once again. She loved him! He wanted to dip his head right there on the spot and kiss her breathless. Kiss her like he had wanted to that day down by the creek. But the rumble of a truck followed by the blare of a horn kept him in line.

"They're here."

"Who's here?" She turned, and he pulled her back against him and wrapped his arms around her middle as a truck rolled to a stop at the end of the lane.

He was sure they made quite a pair, a Plain man and a beautiful *Englischer* in a shining *frack*. But he didn't care. Annie was back. His Annie had come home.

A man hopped out of the truck and approached them. "You G. Fisher?"

"I am."

"I've got sixteen alpacas here for you."

He heard the intake of her breath. "Alpacas?"

"That's right," the driver said.

Gideon smiled into her hair. "Let's get 'em in this pasture." He released Annie. For now. He moved away from her toward the back of the truck and its waiting animals.

Now that he had her, he hated to let her go. It was probably for the best. Otherwise he'd go on holding her, maybe even kissing her until he got his fill. They'd shock the whole district and that would never do.

Avery gathered Louie into her arms and without a care for the cost of her dress, climbed onto the top rung of the fence as Gideon and the truck driver unloaded the alpacas. The first one out of the trailer was a soft, beige female with thick, wooly fur. They were everything she had read about and more: Long eyelashes like a camel, velvety soft noses. They were indeed docile in nature for they ambled out of the trailer without so much as a fuss, then gladly moseyed into the pasture, poking around at the unfamiliar ground and nudging at each other.

She tamped down her worry and tried just to enjoy the sight of all these beautiful creatures. Gideon's fresh start on life. She hoped she could be a part of it. He hadn't asked her to leave, but he hadn't said she could stay either. He'd seemed so happy when she had arrived. That had to be a good sign.

She just hoped she hadn't been too hasty in leaving her car at the General Store with a big For Sale sign on it.

If only he'd kissed her, like Meredith said, like the song, then maybe she would know that he loved her enough to let her stay. And that he was willing to take the chance that they could make it together. As it was, she could only watch as he unloaded alpacas. A rusty-colored male that would make the prettiest raw yarn, another small female as close to snow white as she had ever seen, and a larger male so dark brown he almost looked black.

Avery could hardly wait to see them up close, touch them, watch them graze and frolic on the tall grass. She just hoped she got the chance.

Finally, all sixteen were in the pasture, and the driver paid.

The man climbed into his truck and headed off back down the country drive.

Avery's heart gave a hard pound as Gideon secured the fence and headed her way.

He stopped mere feet in front of her, his hands on his narrow hips, his wide-brimmed straw hat tipped a little to the side by the Oklahoma winds.

"*Ach*, then, let's *geh*, Annie Hamilton."

"*Geh?*" What did that mean?

"Let's go."

"Go?" She hadn't wanted to say the word, but it slipped through her lips.

"*Jah. Geh.*"

He reached for her waist and pulled her down from the fence, setting her gently on her feet.

Avery soaked in the warmth of his hands on her, wondering if it would be the last time she'd be this close to him. He loved her, of that she was certain, but it didn't seem like he thought they could overcome their differences and make a life together work.

"Gideon, I . . ." She had to give it one last chance, make him see how good it could be between them. What kind of woman would she be to just let it all slip through her fingers without giving a fight?

"You talk more'n any woman I've seen."

"But—"

He dipped his head and covered her mouth with his, effectively cutting short anything she would have said. Not that Avery minded. His kiss said it all, was more than she could have hoped. It was sweet, promising, and filled with love.

When he lifted his head, his green eyes shone with emotion, his voice thick with the same. "Your dresses are in the bedroom closet. I suggest you put one on before we go to my elders' *haus*. I don't think my *dat* will be glad to see you wearin' this little *frack*."

"*My* dresses?"

Gideon smiled. "Go on, now, we have a lot to decide tonight. Where you're goin' to stay. And then we'll have to talk to the bishop."

Avery clapped her hands together. "You mean it?"

"*Jah*." His expression turned serious once more. "It's not goin' to be easy."

"But I'll be with you," Avery said.

"*Jah*."

She raised up on her tiptoes and planted a kiss at the corner of his mouth. "As long as we're together, it'll all be worth it."

"*Jah*." He kissed her on the mouth one last time, then gently nudged her toward the house. "Change your dress."

And with a laugh, Annie headed toward the house. Her new life—her new adventure—had begun.

# Glossary

*Ach*—Oh
*Aemen*—Amen
*Aenti*—Aunt
*Appeditilch*—Delicious
*Allrecht*—All right
*Bensel*—Silly child
*Brechdich*—Magnificent
*Bruder*—Brother
*Bu*—Boy
*Danki*—Thank you
*Dat*—Dad
*Deutsch*—Pennsylvania Dutch
*Dippy eggs*—eggs cooked over-easy
*Dochder*—Daughter
*Elder*—parents
*Englisch, Englischer*—non-Amish person
*Frack*—Dress
*Geb acht*—Be careful

*Geh*—Go

*Grossdaadi*—Grandfather

*Grossmammi*—Grandmother

*Guck datt hie*—Look there

*Gut*—Good

*Guder mariye*—Good morning

*Gut nacht*—Good night

*Halt*—stop

*Haus*—House

*Jah*—Yes

*Kaffi*—Coffee

*Kapp*—Prayer covering, cap

*Mamm*—Mom

*Meidung*—Shunning

*Mudder*—Mother

*Naerfich*—Nervous

*Natchess*—Supper

*Nay*—No

*Onkel*—Uncle

*Ordnung*—Amish rules written and understood

*Rumspringa*—Running around time (at 16)

*Snitz pie*—Dried apple pie

*Sohn*—Son

*Unser Satt Leit*—Our sort of people

*Wunderbaar*—Wonderful

# Katie Rose's Oven-Fried Chicken

8–9 pieces of chicken—breasts, thighs, and legs

1 tsp. paprika
1 tbsp. salt
1 tbsp. onion powder
1 tbsp. garlic salt
1 tbsp. dried marjoram
1 tbsp. pepper
1 cup flour

1/3 cup butter, melted
1/3 cup vegetable oil

3/4 cup buttermilk
2 drops Tabasco

Preheat oven to 375 degrees. Place oil and butter in a shallow baking dish and melt together in heated oven. In a large sack, mix together flour and dried spices.

In a medium-sized bowl, add Tabasco to buttermilk and stir. Coat chicken pieces in buttermilk, then shake them in the sack. When evenly coated, roll the pieces in the melted butter and oil mixture. Place the chicken in the pan, skin side down, and bake for 45 minutes. Turn over and bake for another 5 to 10 minutes until skin starts to bubble and juices run clear.

Best served with creamed potatoes and fresh green beans.

# Ruth Fisher's Shoofly Pie

1 tsp. baking soda
3/4 cup molasses
1 cup hot water
1 pinch salt
1 pinch ginger
1 1/2 cups all-purpose flour
1 cup dark brown sugar
1/2 cup lard
1/4 cup butter
1/2 tsp. cinnamon
unbaked pie shell

Stir soda into molasses until frothy. Add water, salt, and ginger, then set aside.

Mix flour, brown sugar, and cinnamon, cut in lard and butter. Stir until crumbly.

Line a 9-inch pie plate with pie shell and pour in 1/3 of the molasses mixture. Sprinkle 1/3 of the crumb mixture over and continue alternating layers with crumbs as top layer.

Bake at 375 degrees for 35 to 40 minutes, or until golden brown on top.

# Annie Hamilton's Chicken Pot Pie

1 small chicken
4 medium-sized potatoes, peeled and cut into cubes
1 onion, diced
2 stalks of celery, diced
1/2 bell pepper, diced
1 carrot, peeled and thinly sliced
Salt and pepper to taste

Boil chicken over the stove until partly tender. Then add onion, bell pepper, carrot, potatoes, and celery. Continue to cook until chicken is completely done. Remove meat from the pan and allow to cool. Remove meat from the bones and skin.

**Pot Pie Dough**
2 eggs
2 cups of flour
2 to 3 tbsp. of milk or cream

Mix together eggs and flour, adding the milk to make a soft dough. Roll the dough as thin as possible. Cut into 1 x 2 inch strips with a knife.

Heat broth to a boil. Add pastry strips and allow to cook 20 minutes or until tender. Add chicken and serve piping hot.

Dear Reader,

Name's Abram Fisher, and I live in the Amish community of Clover Ridge. It's in the greenest part of Oklahoma, mighty close to Arkansas. Close enough to share some of the rolling hills, green pastures, and towering trees.

Sometimes I don't understand why God works the way He does. I never thought I'd say that. I've always been taught to accept the Lord's will and make the most of all I've been given. This is the best way. And it's the Amish way.

Yet, the Lord does see fit to throw us into situations that test our faith. Or maybe He's just giving us an opportunity to strengthen it. After my son's wife and son died in a tragic accident, I noticed that Gideon had more and more trouble dealing with his pain and grief. So much, he sold their family farm and moved to the outskirts of the district. He quit going to church services and shaved his beard. I was mighty worried about Gideon those days, as was his *mamm*.

And then a miraculous thing happened. This purty young Englisher crashed her fancy car, and the only soul around to help was my Gideon. He pulled her in from the cold and tended to her injuries. He even cared for her tiny whelp of a dog.

Annie (that's what we call her) comes from a very wealthy family in Texas, but as time went on, she seemed to adapt more and more to our ways. But the best part is, she seemed to bring Gideon out of himself and find that piece of him that was lost and buried along with his family.

Now, I don't know for a fact, but it seems to me Gideon and his Annie are *wunderbaar* together. Somehow, she helped him get back right with the Lord. And he helped her slow down and learn to enjoy life, to see God in places she might not have ever known. *Jah*, they're *gut* for each other, my Gideon and his Annie, but there are so many obstacles standing between them and true happiness.

We're all questioning if Annie can for sure and for certain let go of her worldly life and embrace the practices of the Plain folks here in Clover Ridge. After all, it's much more common for Plain folk to jump the fence than it is for Englishers to convert. And what about Gideon? I can't help but wonder if he'll be able to put the past behind him and learn to believe again. To live again. And maybe even with God's help, learn to love again.

# Discussion Questions

1. An Amish man's beard is the mark of his faith and family, yet Gideon shaves his beard after the accident. How does this show the level of his grief? How is his decision viewed by the other members of the district?

2. How does Gideon's farm offer Avery refuge from her broken engagement and the mantle of responsibility of her life in Dallas? Have you ever wanted to get away like Avery? How did you accomplish this or handle feeling overwhelmed with your day-to-day life?

3. Though most people would consider Avery's life in Dallas to be perfect, Avery enjoys her time on Gideon's farm. Is she hiding from reality or embracing a new way of life?

4. Avery comes from great wealth and privilege, yet she embraces the rural chores and lifestyle. Have you ever wished for a slower lifestyle? What changes have you made to achieve it?

5. Gideon refuses to sleep in the house with Avery—not even in a different room. How does this reflect the Amish respect for each other, their community, and God? Is chivalry dead? Can it be found again in secular society? If you could bring back an old-fashioned notion such as this, which one would you revive and why?

6. In the house garden, Avery tells Mary Elizabeth about coercing Gideon into promising to attend the work frolic. Mary Elizabeth in turn tells Avery that the voice of God played a hand. How do you feel about the Lord speaking through us? Do you feel you've heard the voice of God? Did you obey what was said or no? Were you sorry or grateful for that decision?

7. After Avery's arrival, Gideon goes into town, plants crops, and begins to restock his animals. How does her arrival spurn him to action without her direct encouragement? Do you think this is an example of how God works in our lives without us even realizing it?

8. Ex-fiancé Jack is the reason Avery came to Oklahoma Amish country. How does his appearance solidify her views of her friends and her time with the Amish? Is Jack an accurate representation of the secular world? Or is he merely the personification of the intrusions we all face when walking in faith? How do you deal with these intrusions into your life?

9. Avery encourages Gideon to invest in alpacas and make his farm self-sustaining again. How could raising different livestock help Gideon? Have you ever had to start over from scratch? How did starting over affect your family and friends?

10. Ruth's cancer diagnosis is the breaking point for Gideon. How does this news end up renewing his faith and bringing him closer to his family? How has such news in your life affected your family? What could you do to bring family closer together in the face of tragedy?

11. Avery believes that Gideon is reluctant to kiss her because of his love for his late wife. Most Amish marriages are based off need and compatibility, but not romantic love. How does Gideon use Avery's misconception to temper their attraction? Have you ever allowed someone to misunderstand in order to protect your heart?

12. The underlying theme of *Saving Gideon* is "love heals all wounds." How does God's love heal us? Have you ever been in a situation where the love of God or the love of another person healed/saved you from grief (or worse)?

13. Does Avery save Gideon? Or does Gideon save Avery? How is this reflected in what Jesus sacrificed for mankind?